T0355017

UNGODLY
INTRUSIONS

UNGODLY INTRUSIONS

Harvey Marks

ARCHWAY
PUBLISHING

Archway Publishing books may be ordered through booksellers or by contacting:

Archway Publishing
1663 Liberty Drive
Bloomington, IN 47403
www.archwaypublishing.com
844-669-3957

ISBN: 978-1-6657-6139-0 (sc)
ISBN: 978-1-6657-6141-3 (hc)
ISBN: 978-1-6657-6140-6 (e)

Library of Congress Control Number: 2024918633

Print information available on the last page.

Archway Publishing rev. date: 10/28/2024

To Lynn, with love and gratitude

PART I

Spring 2018

Inch by inch I conquered the inner terrain I was born
with. Bit by bit I reclaimed the swamp on which I
languished. I gave birth to my infinite being, but
I had to wrench me out of me with forceps.

—FERNANDO PESSOA, *THE BOOK OF DISQUIET*

CHAPTER 1

Mrs. Lambert's charity ball was underway. Through the crush, waiters circulated, lofting trays laden with white wine, champagne, and cunning little delectables—each new item expertly color-balanced, layered, or sliced—not so much food as its rarified essence.

Covering the event for the *Goldmont Sun*, Oregon's fourth-oldest newspaper, Nora Stanfell edged through the crowd trailed by her photographer, Jack Spitzer. Every time Nora stopped, Jack scarfed, grabbing quick bites and gulping champagne.

Summoned forward, he'd wipe his hands on his thighs and aim his camera at a smiling couple or grouping of strangers willing to come together for a picture for the lifestyle section. Before moving on, Nora always checked to make sure she had the names right and maybe get a comment to weave into the story.

Working their way through the party, Nora detected muted emanations of interest from some of the men, but she pretended not to notice. As usual, she'd worn her dark-green cocktail dress, purchased from a local resale shop. A red enamel bracelet trimmed in gold adorned her right wrist. The only good piece she possessed, the bracelet had been borrowed from a friend a long time ago and never returned.

A twentysomething blonde came into view. About the same age as Nora, she was dressed in a red gown, strapless, plunging, and slit high on her thigh. She didn't have a name tag; there was no place to stick it. "A weekend in dullsville, how wonderful." The blonde pouted as she swiped a peekaboo lock of hair from her eye. "I can't believe Brad dragged me here."

"It's business," her companion replied in a matter-of-fact voice. He was wearing a tux but without the tie, and his name tag was upside down. "The Lamberts have money, and we need it. Museums don't build themselves."

"Oh that," the blonde said. "It's an ego trip. One more thing you guys can slap your name on. When we get back, Brad promised me a new car. I'm thinking a Porsche."

"Get a white one." Her companion perked up slightly. "Blondes in white cars look amazing."

Not on my list, Nora decided. *Probably part of the Portland contingent.* Busy with her notebook, she'd gone a half-dozen steps before she realized she'd lost her photographer. She backtracked and found Jack gazing at the spot the blonde and her companion had vacated.

"Sorry, Jack," Nora said drily, lightly touching his upper arm, "she's taken."

"Yeah, Nor, I know, but can't a guy dream?"

"All he wants. Just hang in there." She smiled encouragingly. "We're almost done."

By ten thirty, they were. Nora stood in the entryway, double-checking to make sure she'd gotten everyone on her list while Jack fiddled with his camera.

"Well, that was fun," he said, looking up. His face was very round, and when he smiled his eyes crinkled into tiny slits buried in his chubby cheeks. Recently he'd begun shaving his head to compensate for a severely receding hairline, which solved one problem while accentuating the others.

"Was it that bad?" Nora asked, looking to make sure no one was in earshot. "They're just people."

"People with money and all the shit money can buy," Jack corrected her. "They've got it. We want it. It's not complicated."

Nora sensed the yearning in his voice. *He's still thinking about that blonde*, she thought, letting her attention drift through the archway toward the party. She needed to go back and say good night to the Lamberts. *It might be a good idea to bring Jack with her. Mrs. Lambert might want more photos. No, better skip it*, she decided, remembering Mrs. Lambert's look of suppressed astonishment when Nora had introduced Jack.

She turned in time to see him pointing his camera in her direction. "Hey," she called out, shielding her face.

"Just checking." He lowered the camera with a jokey grin, adding, "You're in luck. It looks like some of the pictures are in focus and hardly anyone's head is cut off."

"And am I in any of them, with or without my head?" Nora asked, not trying to hide her annoyance.

"No, of course not."

"Are you sure?"

"Yes, Nor, I'm sure," he replied, a touch of exasperation in his voice. "Why would I take your picture? I know you don't like it."

"All right." Nora allowed herself to be mollified. "But remember, I need all your in-focus, heads-intact photos by nine tomorrow morning." Tomorrow was Saturday, but the party was important, and the paper wanted to feature it in the Sunday edition.

"I don't know, Nor. Nine's pretty early," Jack teased.

She wasn't worried. He wouldn't let her down. They'd worked together before, and he'd never blown an assignment or missed a deadline. "Well, at least you got a free meal out of it," she bantered back.

"Free meal? Is that what you're calling it? I'm not even sure it was food." Patting his stomach, he added, "I have a big investment here."

And getting bigger all the time, Nora thought but didn't say it. Jack was the only one she knew who wouldn't need to stuff a pillow in his shirt to play Santa at the *Sun's* Christmas party, not that anyone would ask him, not after last year's party. "Well, that's it for now," she said instead. "Remember: nine a.m. tomorrow."

"Right." He bent down to tuck his camera in his bag then

hoisted the bag to his shoulder. "Okay, kiddo, I'm out of here." He sauntered to the door. His hand on the doorknob, he hesitated and turned toward her. Light from a ceiling fixture slanted across his face, leaving the rest of him in shadow, making it almost seem as if his head were floating.

"Yes?" Nora asked, disconcerted by the illusion.

"Don't take it the wrong way, but do you ever regret coming to Goldmont? I'm glad you did, but this place is dead. It's my hometown, so I can talk."

"No regrets. I like it here."

"Dullsville" the blonde had called it. Fifty thousand souls in the middle of nowhere. An hour and a half from Portland, almost four hours from Seattle. But it suited her. Nora needed a job that wouldn't force her to moonlight as a waitress or run too rapidly through the rest of the money from her father's insurance policy. It also helped that the *Sun* didn't check references.

"Good night, Jack. Take it easy," she said.

"Right." A thought appeared to strike him. "And if you can't take it easy ..." His face contorted into a grin. "... well then ..." The grin grew broader. "... you'd better take it any way you can."

The wit and wisdom of Jack Spitzer. "Oh, Jack, you're full of it," Nora blurted out, more amused than critical, but he was already halfway out the door, so he might not have heard.

Back in the great room, Nora lifted a champagne flute from a passing tray and set out in search of her hosts.

She found Frank and Bunny Lambert holding court in front of an enormous picture window. On the other side, a fountain with stone lions gushed amid a profusion of rosebushes, receding into landscaped darkness.

Nora positioned herself on the periphery and waited her turn, dividing her attention between the Lamberts and their lions.

From what she'd read in the newspaper morgue file, Frank Lambert had made it big in the waste management business in

Portland, sold the company, and had come back to Goldmont with a wife seventeen years his junior.

Bunny Lambert's entry had been rocky—a classic case of too much splash, not enough pond. But eventually she'd managed to calm the waters, establishing herself as a generous backer of local causes and the parties that supported them.

Tonight's fundraiser was for a regional museum, but in Portland, not Goldmont. Mrs. Lambert was branching out. Various naming rights were available if the Lamberts wanted to pony up. It didn't look like anything was going to be announced tonight. Too bad; it would have made a nice scoop.

Nora spotted an opening and advanced. "Thank you again for inviting us into your lovely home," she began, projecting her voice above the background cacophony. "It's a wonderful occasion, and we're pleased you've allowed the *Sun* to help publicize it."

"Not at all, my dear, not at all. I trust you got everything you needed," Mrs. Lambert replied.

She was a slender woman in her sixties with strawberry-blonde hair. Judging from her eyelids and tucked cheeks, she'd gotten some work done, but all very tasteful. Beside his wife, Frank Lambert smiled affably. He was plump with a rosy complexion and wispy white hair. His tuxedo was slightly rumpled, and his bowtie was askew.

"Oh, yes. Everyone was very helpful," Nora answered. "You can expect a full page in Sunday's lifestyle section. Mr. Harkness, our editor, will be glad to arrange extra copies if you like."

"That would be very nice, but only if it's no trouble," Mrs. Lambert murmured.

"Of course. We're glad to do it." For the *Sun*, catering to the rich and powerful was a civic necessity, a lifeline in an increasingly fraught business climate.

As Nora was getting ready to say good night, a figure emerged from the crowd. Tall and powerfully built with an athletic gait constrained by evening clothes, he swaggered toward them, holding his champagne flute aloft. His black hair was combed straight back, breaking over his collar in curls, and he had green-gray eyes, framed and intensified by his wire-rimmed glasses. Those eyes took in Nora, read her name tag, and lingered a moment before alighting on Mrs. Lambert.

"Congratulations, Bunny. What a brilliant occasion," the newcomer greeted her. "How clever of you to make all these people come here. You're putting our little city on the map."

He leaned forward, clasped her hand, and let his lips lightly graze her cheek. Still holding her hand, he turned toward her husband and with mock severity said, "Frank, I hope you realize what a treasure you have here."

"She's got the gift, all right," Frank Lambert replied. "When Bunny wants something to happen, watch out. It's a done deal."

So, you were able to come after all," Bunny said, reclaiming her hand, not looking overly impressed. Glancing in Nora's direction, she added, "This outrageous liar is Alexander Wyman. He heads up the oceanfront renewal project. Alex, this is the girl from the newspaper."

"I know, Nora Stanfell. You're in good hands. I read her stuff all the time. Pleased to finally meet you, Nora."

"Thanks, it's always gratifying to meet a fan," Nora replied, working to keep her surprise from showing. Until recently, most of her stories had been unsigned, and she couldn't have many male readers. Her last piece had brewed up great advice for herbal tea lovers. In a couple weeks, she would be attending the home show to report on what's cooking in the world of major appliances.

By now, Mrs. Lambert was looking restless. With a magisterial sweep of her hand, she excused herself and started across the marble floor. Caught off guard, her husband hastily shuffled after her.

"Now, there goes a happily married man," Wyman said, his voice quietly mocking.

"He probably is," Nora replied. "I don't think he likes parties very much. By the way, thanks for the vote of confidence. Just out of curiosity, have you read anything I've written?"

"I'm sure I will," Wyman said with a gallant but not necessarily sincere smile.

There was a moment of silence while Nora tried to decide whether to go or stay. "The oceanfront renovation project, how's it coming?" she asked. She didn't know much about the project, only that it had kicked off with great fanfare sometime before she'd come to Goldmont. The *Sun* continued to support the project but no longer actively promoted it.

"It's coming. We're moving ahead slowly and deliberately, consulting with and working to get buy-in from our stakeholders. There are a lot of stakeholders, the Lamberts included. If she'd rather support a project in Portland, that's her business." He smiled sourly. "I hope you're not going to quote me."

"Not unless you have something nice to say about our hosts. Are you in real estate then?"

"Hardly." The idea seemed to amuse him. "In my day job, I deal in antiquities: art and sculpture, old books and coins, occasional houseware items—especially if the house was a palace or a temple. But it could be almost anything that's stood the test of time."

"Sort of anthropology with a dollar sign."

"No, not really. Money doesn't much interest me unless it's old and no longer in circulation. There are lessons to be learned. The past isn't dead if you know where to look and how. Sorry." He interrupted himself with a smile. "I'm afraid you got me started."

"That's all right. As a journalist, I mostly focus on the here and now." It was time to wind up their conversation.

"Well then, to the here and now. I'm looking forward to reading your story," he said, and raised his champagne flute.

They clinked glasses, and Nora took a small sip. "I'm afraid you'll have to excuse me. It's late, and I'm on deadline."

"Of course. A pleasure meeting you, Nora. Good luck."

He extended his hand. She reached for it. To her surprise, he grasped her wrist instead. His fingers splayed across her bracelet, and she felt his thumb insinuate itself, violating the tender underneath of her wrist with its groping presence.

As Nora struggled to break his grip without attracting attention, her champagne flute slipped from her grasp and shattered on the marble floor. Champagne fizzed at her feet, spiked with broken glass.

Wyman relinquished his hold. No longer clutching her wrist, he stood across from her with his hand pressed against his thigh. Two servers were approaching with a bucket, a mop, and a stack of cloth napkins. As far as the world was concerned, it was a minor domestic mess, nothing more.

"Don't go," Wyman said, on his face a fierce mixture of pain and exhilaration.

Nora started across the floor, not running but fleeing nonetheless. She thought he might be pursuing her, but when she glanced back, he was where she'd left him, holding up his hand, examining it with something akin to wonderment.

Home again, Nora impatiently climbed three flights of stairs to her apartment and unlocked the door, stepping into a time capsule from four hours ago. The clothes she'd scattered as she dressed lay where she'd dropped them.

On her kitchen table, which doubled as a desk, her laptop sat surrounded by file folders, some open with their contents spilling out. On the sink counter, a half-empty mug of peach tea remained where she'd set it after taking a last swallow and heading out the door.

In the bathroom, Nora anxiously tugged off her bracelet and examined her wrist. To her relief, it was unscathed. The tattoo, concealed beneath her bracelet, was as pristine as ever. After all these years, it continued to captivate her, and she paused a moment to admire the tattoo's curves, whorls, and subtle shadings.

Best not to take chances, she decided and reached into the medicine chest for a bottle of hydrogen peroxide, her disinfectant of choice.

Pouring it on her wrist, she watched the peroxide fizz, momentarily obscuring her tattoo under a sea of foam.

Damn him, she thought with an anxious feeling in the pit of her stomach. *He knows. Now. After all this time. Why?*

CHAPTER 2

In the middle of the night, Nora's wrist began to throb. If she'd been sleeping, it would have awakened her, and for the longest time she tossed and turned, trying to ignore it. Finally, not sure what else to do, she got out of bed and anointed her wrist with more peroxide. It didn't help. Restless and increasingly anxious, she knelt in front of her nightstand and opened the bottom drawer.

Rummaging, Nora found what she was seeking lodged in a back corner—a cheap silver bracelet much the worse for wear. Holding it in her hand, she let her thoughts travel back to when she'd first bought it almost four years ago, how pleased she'd been with her purchase.

She'd worn it every day for at least two months, even showered with it, until one day she noticed the bracelet had lost its shine. The silver had worn thin, revealing reddish-orange metal underneath. Her silver bracelet was mostly copper.

Not sure why she'd thought of the bracelet after all this time, she slipped it on. The metal felt cool and soothing on her skin, almost caressing. Mollified, her wrist slowly began to hush. Nora drifted off to sleep.

When the alarm rang, it took her a long time to find her way back and silence it. Throwing on a cotton robe, she ventured into the kitchen to fix a vivifying mug of green tea infused with cayenne and a pinch of ginger.

Seated on the couch, her legs crossed under her, Nora sipped the potion cautiously and waited for it to kick in. When she couldn't delay any longer, she put the half-drunk mug down, threw on a pair of jeans and a work shirt, fastened a hairband, and headed out the door. She was still wearing the copper-silver bracelet.

The *Sun* sat in a dead zone. Located on the edge of Goldmont's small downtown, the paper occupied one floor of the Funeral Corp Building, a seven-story steel-and-glass box owned and primarily occupied by the company of the same name.

Across the street, the old municipal cemetery slumbered behind an iron fence, and in the building itself there was a funeral museum. A dark-glass partition with the museum's logo etched in the glass in a repeating pattern bisected the lobby, offering the only hint of what lay on the other side.

Most of what Nora knew about the museum came from a pamphlet she'd found in the women's room and taken back to her desk. From it she learned the museum housed an impressive collection of caskets, coffins, and other tools of the trade. Permanent displays highlighted mourning customs around the world and offered insights into how various cultures say goodbye, and there were special exhibits. Often when someone eminent died, the museum paid its respects by staging a tribute to a life well lived.

What the brochure left unanswered was why the museum was taking up valuable space in Goldmont's tallest building. That answer had been supplied by the *Sun's* business writer. Nora had been finishing up her first week at the paper and was standing in the lobby, steeling herself before proceeding past the museum's valley-of-the-shadow expanse of glass. He'd come up from behind and introduced himself.

"Have you visited it yet? It's interesting," he said, following her gaze. He was in his thirties, tall and decently built, with dark-brown hair combed into a painstaking pompadour. A pair of reading glasses dangled from a cord around his neck.

"No, just wondering why it's here," Nora replied. "There must have been better places to put it."

The business writer had recently done a story about Funeral Corp and didn't mind showing off. "That's the genius of it. The company's CEO needed a place to display his collection. It took a while. He had to grease the skids, but city council finally decided the museum was an important cultural resource and granted him an abatement. The museum pretty much pays for itself."

"In other words, a sweetheart deal," Nora said, wondering if it could be an exposé: *Shady Dealings in City Hall.*

The business writer headed her off. "A tax break, and perfectly legal. The paper has ten months left on its lease. Rumor has it they're going to kick us out and move the museum upstairs." They were walking now, heading for the elevator, and his glasses bobbed against his chest.

Nora was concerned. She'd moved to Goldmont at her own expense and didn't want to think her new employer was failing. On the other hand, if the paper was simply relocating, she wouldn't need to walk past a funeral museum every day.

"It's a blessing in disguise," he added. "The paper needs to downsize. In this day and age, there's no reason for reporters to come into the office at all. They can work from home. As for photographers, they're a dying breed. Who needs them? We can take our own pictures. If Harry wasn't so old-school, we could be a helluva lot more efficient."

"I see," Nora said, careful to keep her voice neutral. Harry Harkness, the paper's editor, was her boss.

By the elevators now, he summoned the car. "If you'd like to check out the museum, I could show you around sometime," he said while they waited.

Nora's thanatophobia, that old fear of death, self-diagnosed from a psych textbook, was kicking in. "Thanks," she forced herself to say, working to keep the anxiety at bay, "but I'll have to pass."

He opened his mouth, thought better of it, and closed it again. The elevator took its time. There hadn't been a follow-up conversation, and a few weeks later he was gone, but only to another job.

As expected, Nora found Jack's photos in the shared drive under "Lambert Party Pix," and every single one was in focus and appropriately framed. Now all she had to do was write the damn thing. And truthfully, it wasn't that big a deal. Today's story might be more significant than usual because of the people involved, but it was pretty straightforward and kind of a dead end. It didn't lead anywhere.

Nora finished with time to spare. After that, it was a simple matter of going down the list and making sure that everyone important—socially, politically, or because they were advertisers—had gotten their picture in the paper with their names spelled correctly. Just to be sure, she skimmed the article one last time before she hit send.

On the right corner of her desk, a small stack of pending projects waited. She pulled one out of the middle of the stack, decided she didn't want to do it right now, and reached for another: a press release extolling a local retailer's new high-end flooring options.

Good enough. As a contract employee, Nora got paid based on what she published. If the paper ever wanted to get rid of her, they wouldn't have to fire her. They could simply cut off her supply of new projects and let the pile on her desk dwindle to nothing.

Despite this impermanence, other staff members, at least some of whom were also contract, tended to colonize their space with photos, posters, knickknacks, and other items from their personal lives. Not Nora. If something happened, she could toss her office supplies and laptop into a box—the newspaper didn't supply any of the tools of the trade—grab her purse, and depart.

The *Sun* was her third stop since college, and it had fallen into her lap at an especially bleak period in her life. She'd been running late. Her shift at the restaurant started in a half hour, and she'd almost ignored the ringing in her purse.

She quickly locked her apartment door behind her, answering the phone as she paced down the hallway. Someone named Joyce was calling from the *Goldmont Sun*. She had Nora's résumé in front of

13

her and was wondering if Nora might be interested in interviewing for a job as a reporter.

Stunned, Nora had stopped walking. "Yes, I'm interested," she said, acutely aware of the excited thudding of her heart.

"Great. It looks like you're down the road in Portland. If you're coming up to Goldmont anytime soon, our editor would love to talk to you."

Nora got the drift. They had a job, and they wanted to fill it as cheaply as possible. No travel expenses.

"I think I can arrange to be in town sometime next week if that works for you," she said, striving to keep her voice level. She was standing in the middle of the hallway. She should either go back to her apartment or duck into the stairwell. *The stairwell*, she decided, and sat down on the landing with her back against the wall.

"Actually, we were hoping you could come tomorrow. We want to fill the position as soon as possible," Joyce replied.

"Of course. What time should we say?" If proximity and speed were the deciders, Nora was practically there.

Elated, Nora hung up the phone and in her excitement bounded down four flights to the lobby. Anxiety and apprehension came behind and accompanied her on the drive north to Goldmont. People exaggerated; a résumé is an aspirational document, but Nora had walked up to the line and stepped across—all the way across. She'd faked a degree in journalism, made up references, and fabricated her work history.

Brazen? Beyond a doubt. And given her past, perverse. She'd dropped out of school in the middle of her senior year, and she'd majored in psychology, not journalism or even English. But in a way, it was pragmatic. Nora didn't have many marketable skills, and she could write.

She was still pecking away on the high-end flooring article, one hand on the keyboard, the other supporting her head, when her computer pinged.

On the screen, a message from Harry asked her to stop by when she had a moment—which, of course, meant right now. A summons to his office wasn't that unusual. It could mean any number of things, most of them routine, but given Nora's counterfeit credentials, she always worried it meant one thing in particular.

Harry was in his mid-fifties with a physique that was growing increasingly pear-shaped, and he had a bad back that made walking look like an uphill struggle into a stiff headwind. As a result, he hardly ever left his office and never appeared unexpectedly to peer over her shoulder. There was no way Harry could sneak up on anyone—a trait Nora appreciated in a boss.

That didn't make him a pushover. Far from it. Harry was hard as in hard-bitten, hardheaded, and hard-nosed, but also hard to like and hard to work for.

When she'd first started, she'd responded to some directive with a humorously intended "Okay, Chief, I'll get right on it." That had obviously been a mistake, and his response had put Nora in her place.

"I'm not your chief. I'm your editor, and the answer isn't 'okay.' I'm not asking you to agree. I'm telling you what I'd like you to do." Sensing that he'd gone too far, he added, "Of course, I'm always interested in your ideas."

After that, in search of insight, Nora had set out to find what made Harry tick. Sleuthing around the office, she'd learned that he'd been married twice, had no children, was a cat fancier but didn't have one, and apparently had played football for Ohio State. That last conclusion turned out to be dead wrong and was based on an item she'd seen in his office—a framed photo of Harry in a football uniform, crouched in a three-point stance.

Nora had puzzled over it. The person in the uniform, while unmistakably a younger version of Harry, was pudgy, not at all athletic, and he was wearing a very retro-looking leather helmet. Unless Harry was a lot older than he seemed, the photo was a joke, although an obscure one. The point was further reinforced when she discovered he hadn't gone to Ohio State.

If that wasn't perplexing enough, there was his novel, *Dead Certain*, written about three years ago and featuring one Max Rage, private eye.

"Hardboiled fiction at its finest," the blurb on the back cover said. "Max Rage is on the prowl, dodging bullets and leading with his fists in a town full of hot women, hot tempers, and hotter-than-hell action. With death lurking around every corner, one thing is dead certain—Max isn't taking crap from anyone."

The book was out of print, but used copies were readily available. When Harry first joined the paper, they'd cautiously circulated since no one knew how Harry felt about his creation.

Jack was a Max Rage fan, and he'd lent his copy to Nora. In Max's world, every blow shattered jaws, broke ribs, ruptured spleens. Occasionally, when reason failed, as reason always did, Max blew his enemies away with his trusty .38 Special, and on one occasion, he used his car to mow down an annoyingly resilient villain.

That was where Nora checked out, closing the book for good while Max cursed the dent justice had left in his front fender.

As Nora approached, the author of all this mayhem sat at his desk, staring intently at his computer screen. Looking up, he beckoned her in. The office was small with a glass front, but at least it had a door and walls that reached the ceiling. Reference books, workaday files, and clippings filled most of the space. The football picture was on the bookshelf behind Harry, and Nora glanced at it, struck as usual by the difference between the prankish Harry in the picture and the irascible one behind the desk.

"You've worked here, what, about five months?" he began once she'd sat down across from him.

"Something like that," she agreed. It was a little over three. Maybe he was going to increase her pay rate, although he could just as easily be getting ready to cut her loose.

"Well, I think it's time we tried you on something besides House and Home," he said, hastily adding, "Not that House and Home

16

isn't important." He reclined in his chair. "What do you say? Are you up for it?"

"Yes," Nora promptly said.

Harry lifted a folder from his desk and handed it to her. "This might be a good place to start. It's a paid profile for Business, so you'll need to strike the right balance. The CEO expects a call. He wants to be interviewed. Go through his assistant."

With a nod, Nora flipped open the folder and read:

Wyman & Associates
Alexander Wyman
Managing Director

"He's spearheading the waterfront project," Harry continued, possibly not noticing Nora's bleak expression. "We've already covered it out the wazoo, but so what? Maybe you can find something new to say or recycle something we haven't said recently. Your story should mostly focus on the man, but use the project as your hook. Everything you need to get started should be there. Any questions?"

"No," Nora said, and shut the folder, working to keep her emotions under control. Her heart was pounding.

"Good. Wait until Monday to call. We don't want to seem overeager. And be sure to keep me in the loop."

"Right." She stood. "Is that everything?"

"Yes. Close the door on your way out." Not waiting, Harry went back to his computer and scowled at the screen.

In her cubicle, Nora skimmed the material in the high-end flooring file, comforted by its banality. Slowly the dazed feeling receded. *Wyman is stalking me*, she thought, anxiously glancing at her patchy silver-and-copper bracelet. But she had all weekend to decide on a plan of action.

In the meantime, it was getting late, and she had a meeting at *Motherlode* magazine, "Your in-the-know guide to everything Goldmont," according to the slogan on the magazine's masthead.

About six weeks ago, Nora had pitched an idea to the magazine and been given the go-ahead to write twenty-five hundred words on a subject of local historical interest. The fee was modest, $200 payable on publication, but that didn't matter; it was a labor of love.

Flush with enthusiasm, Nora had devoted her evenings and weekends to research and writing. The finished story was not quite as definitive as she'd hoped. There were places where the trail petered out and she had to speculate, but overall, Nora was pleased.

She submitted her story and waited a week … two weeks. Finally, toward the end of the third week, her hacked-up story came pinging back, interspersed with sniping comments.

Today's meeting was to review her rewrite and move toward publication—at least that's what Nora wanted to believe. She was due at *Motherlode* at one o'clock—fifteen minutes from now. There was no way around it; she was going to be late.

As Nora waited for the elevator, she realized she'd left the Wyman file on her desk. Exasperated with herself, she went back. *You could have picked it up after your meeting*, it occurred to her, but by then she was at the elevator again.

It was already ten after one when she pulled into the municipal parking garage. But instead of rushing, she reached for the file resting on the seat beside her and started to open it. *No, focus, get on with it*, she reproached herself, and set it down, slamming the car door behind her.

༄

Oddly enough, the *Motherlode* story had been sparked by Harry. During Nora's second week on the job, he'd asked her to put together a short article on the Goldmont Historical Society.

The article could have easily been composed from information gleaned over the phone. To Nora's surprise, Harry had suggested visiting. Possibly he was being thoughtful, making her first out-of-the-office assignment an easy one. That Harry could be thoughtful was a revelation, something to think about later.

"I'll get right on it," she said, remembering not to call him "Chief."

"Good," he said, standing in the doorway to her cubicle, as far in as he was willing to venture. "Don't forget you can't bill your travel time, just your mileage. See you Monday."

What happens Monday? Nora had wondered. She decided she was being paranoid—that all Harry meant was "It's Friday afternoon; you don't need to come back today."

As it turned out, the mileage was negligible. The newspaper faced the back of the municipal cemetery. The historical society was on the front side in a converted bungalow near the entrance. Its president, a septuagenarian named Paul Tsitak, greeted her.

"The last name's Greek. It's pronounced 'Seat-ache,' but please call me Paul" he said, offering his hand.

"Hi, Paul, I'm Nora," she replied, struck by his mischievous blue eyes above a bushy white moustache and his bright-red suspenders. If Nora had a grandfather, she'd want him to look like Paul Tsitak.

"I've never been interviewed before," he shyly admitted. "Why don't I start by showing you around the place?"

"That would be great," Nora said, discreetly picking up a handout of upcoming events from a stack on the counter as they passed. "Just so there's no misunderstanding, it's going to be a short article."

That was putting it mildly. It was going to be two hundred words at most, followed by a listing of the society's upcoming events, and she'd mostly composed the two hundred words on the way over—subject to reconsideration, of course.

"Well, you're the expert. Whatever you think's best," he replied, beckoning for her to follow him. It wasn't much of a tour. They stopped briefly in the doorway to his very cluttered office, passed a meeting room with dark wood paneling covered with photos and maps, and ended up in the library.

A heavy oak table occupied the center. Floor-to-ceiling bookcases covered all four walls and were stuffed with books, scrolls, notebooks, and barely contained sheaves of paper. Around them, stacked in front of the shelves, boxes and crates formed makeshift walls with gaps for passageways.

"Donations. We're drowning in them," Paul said, seating himself across from her. "Every time granny dies and they clean house, we get the books and papers. We do our best, but our resources are limited."

He threw up his hands. "Hopefully your story will help." Still smiling—his blue eyes had a definite twinkle—he leaned toward her. "So, where do we start, Nora?" With old-fashioned gallantry, he added, "It's a lovely name. Hebrew, isn't it? I believe it means 'shining light.' In Greek, you'd be Eleanora. It suits you."

With a start, she realized he was flirting with her. "Thanks." She smiled. "You could begin by telling me about the historical society's mission."

Paul's knowledge was vast and disorderly. Their interview quickly became a ramble as meandering as a Goldmont city street, which tended to go up, down, and around but hardly ever straight ahead.

At first Nora's notetaking was cursory, but after a while, almost despite herself, she began to get interested. For a place that was only forty square miles, Goldmont was surprisingly complex. According to Paul, even the ground beneath their feet wasn't nearly as solid as it seemed.

"It's a slurry," he explained, "a watery mixture of sand, gravel, and clay, highly unstable and prone to sudden shifts."

"So watch where you step," Nora said, lifting her left hand from her notepad and flexing her fingers—writer's cramp. Paul had been talking for almost an hour.

"Always a good idea regardless of the terrain," he agreed. "Did any of that help?"

"Yes, thanks. It was great. I got what I needed." *And more,* Nora silently added. But she wasn't complaining. On her way out, a thought occurred to her, and she asked if he could recommend a book on the area's history.

"No, sorry." Paul shook his head ruefully. "The outside world hasn't paid much attention to us, and no one local has ever taken it on. I've thought about it, but I'm not much of a writer. Don't have the patience for it. Is that something you need for your story?" He sounded concerned, as though a critical lack of reference material might doom their project.

"No, just curious," Nora reassured him. It seemed odd that amid all the historical society's moldering paper and decaying bindings no single book chronicled the town's history. She had an inkling of an idea, but it was a passing whim, and she wasn't going to act on it.

A week later, Paul called to tell her how much he liked the historical society story. As they talked, Nora finally came out with it.

"I'm still thinking about Goldmont and would like to know more," she said, trying to make it sound like mere curiosity. Curiosity was certainly part of it, but it was more than that—an anticipatory eagerness she couldn't explain.

"Of course. Come by anytime, Eleanora. You don't need an invitation," Paul said in a pleasantly reproachful voice. "Tomorrow if you'd like. I'll be around."

Back the next day, Nora was pleased to see her newspaper story laminated, framed, and hanging next to a topological map of Oregon. The story's prominence seemed like a good omen, a kiss on the forehead from a favorite elder. As before, he ushered her into the library, and while she waited, he brought out a tray holding two ceramic mugs and a plate of chocolate chip cookies.

"Something you might like to try," he said, unloading the tray and placing a mug in front of her. "But be careful. It's a wee bit alcoholic."

Cautiously, Nora lifted the goblet, watched him take a swallow, then took a sip. She didn't exactly dislike it. She took another sip. It was alcoholic but kind of sweet and chewy, too.

"What is it?" she asked, setting the goblet down.

"It's an old recipe. I've re-created it, barley water and wine—preferably Greek, but that's not important. Then I stir in honey and top it with a sprinkling of grated goat cheese. Odysseus and his crew drank it on their voyage home from Troy, and with certain pharmacological additions it can be used in religious rituals. Nothing to do with Goldmont, of course, but as an antiquarian, I dote on stuff like that. What do you think of my little concoction?"

"It's interesting," Nora said, taking another perfunctory sip and setting it down, this time for good. She was tempted to ask him what it was called, but she had other things to discuss, and Paul did tend to go on.

"Thanks for agreeing to see me," she said. She reached into her purse, pulled out a small pad, and flipped it open, nervously glancing down at her notes—not the ones from their first meeting, but a distillation with some additional information she'd dug up on her own. Reassured, she went on.

"When I thought about our conversation, I was struck by all the conmen and criminals who have come to Goldmont and the oversize role they've played in the town's history. It's a real rogue's gallery, a hundred seventy years of malfeasance, and it looks like no one has properly documented it. So there it is. This is what I'd like your opinion about."

She paused for a moment to study Paul. He was still drinking his concoction and waiting for her to continue. He didn't seem perturbed by her unflattering characterization of his town.

"When I reviewed my notes, one figure stood out—elusive, mysterious, cloaked in shadow," she continued. "A founder who named this town after himself, then vanished in the middle of the night under suspicious circumstances. You're the subject-matter expert. What can you tell me about Tony Goldmont? Is he worth pursuing?"

Nora looked at him, uncomfortable and concerned with what he might say. His reaction surprised her.

"Have you been next door yet?" he asked. "There's something you should see." Paul's blue eyes gleamed with excitement.

Mystified, Nora shook her head. Next door was the cemetery. "Why? What's there?" she asked, alarmed at the thought. It couldn't be Goldmont's grave. No one knew where he was buried or even when he'd died. It was part of the mystery.

"You'll have to wait and see. We can go now if you have time," he said with an enthusiast's eagerness. "If you want to find him, it's the place to start."

"All right," Nora said, overruling herself. Traipsing through a cemetery was the last thing she wanted to do, even further down on her list than visiting the funeral museum, but she could do it. Of course she could.

"Are you sure it's important?" she asked, trailing behind as he stopped in his office and donned a brown bomber jacket and a pair of aviator shades with mirror lenses. He held the front door open for her, and she stepped out and waited while he bolted the lock and hung the *Be Back Soon* sign from the knob.

The cemetery entrance was down the street at the end of a long block. Paul had to be almost three times Nora's age, but he set a quick pace.

A metal sign on the cemetery fence listed visiting hours and instructed guests to register at the visitor center, a one-room structure to the left of the gate. Waiting just inside the doorway, Nora watched as Paul approached a uniformed figure seated behind a metal desk.

Beanpole thin with buzzed hair, he looked young even by Nora's standards, but apparently not too young. His badge said "Goldmont PD," so he was moonlighting. A textbook was open in front of him, and he was holding a yellow marker.

Turning her back, Nora let her attention wander through the open doorway toward the street. "Thanks, Artie, I appreciate it. We won't be too long," she heard Paul say as he came toward her holding a key attached to a small block of wood.

"Let the adventure commence," he proclaimed, his high spirits showing. Nora took a deep breath and followed him through the doorway to the back of the hut where two golf carts were chained to a post.

"After you, Eleanora. The steed on the right is ours," he said with elaborate courtesy, extending his arm in a sweeping motion.

Reluctantly, she got in, dismayed not only by where they were going but also how they were getting there. She didn't like golf carts. They brought back memories. *Not now*, she chided herself. *Stay focused*. "Where to?" she asked

"All the way back. Better hang on," Paul said with an exaggerated gesture, gripping the steering wheel in the three-and-nine position. With a sedate lurch, they set off; the golf cart putt-putted into motion down a winding gravel path.

As they meandered along, Nora glanced left and right, distracting herself by trying to pick out names on the crumbling tombstones dotting the landscape. She told herself there was no reason to be agitated. The cemetery was peaceful. Nothing was stirring, no bagpipes wailing "Amazing Grace," no coffins being lowered into the ground while families looked on with mournful expressions.

"It's quiet," Nora said with constrained displeasure.

"A combination of bad planning and bad luck," Paul replied with a chuckle, apparently missing the note of discomfort in Nora's voice.

"The cemetery suddenly ran out of room in 1903. A thunderstorm rolled in from the southeast, bringing torrential rain and hail. Goldmont Creek flooded. A wall of water rushed through town—fifteen feet high according to some accounts, up to fifty feet according to others, but I'm skeptical. One hundred forty-seven people drowned, and dozens of buildings were destroyed.

"After that, a typhoid epidemic ripped through the town and took another twenty-eight lives. All those bodies at once filled the place up." Paul removed a hand from the steering wheel long enough to gesture at their surroundings. "I have more details back at the office if you're interested."

Nora paused long enough to make it seem as if she were tempted. "No, thanks," she said.

The golf cart whirred to a stop at the bottom of a small rise. About a hundred yards to her right, Nora could see the cemetery's back fence. The Funeral Corp building was somewhere on the other side.

"Up there," Paul said, pointing. "Behold."

On top of the rise, a bronze figure stood, dressed in a nineteenth-century statesman's frock coat and cravat. In his right hand, he clasped a rolled document. His other hand, lifted in welcome, seemed to urge them onward toward the clustered gravesites carpeting the space around him.

"The old scoundrel himself, Tony Goldmont. The only known image. Moved here from its original location," Paul said.

Beneath her bracelet, Nora's pulse was throbbing. *No*, she thought, looking away. *It's just a statue. I'm fine.*

"It's quite a story," Paul was saying.

"I'm sure it is," Nora replied. "Why don't you tell it to me on the way back."

CHAPTER 3

Robin Zandy, the managing editor and founder of *Motherlode Magazine*, tore into a slice of pizza left over from yesterday and eyed the young woman seated across from her in the conference room. With the dimmed lighting and no windows, it felt like twilight although it was only about 1:20.

"Thanks for coming in, Nora. Obviously, punctuality isn't one of your strong points," she said between bites. If Robin's parents had named her with hopes of getting a songbird, they must have been disappointed. This Robin was short and wide, and her expression suggested an aroused bulldog except with more teeth.

"I'm sorry. I was delayed," Nora said, and eased back in her chair, feet planted, hands in her lap. Beside Robin, near the open pizza box, the original version of the Tony Goldmont story waited. Although handy for shaming purposes, the document was no longer relevant since the meeting wasn't about the story's original deficiencies, but the revisions Nora had made to address them. The new version wasn't on the table, which struck Nora as odd.

Apprehensively, she watched the editor take another bite of pizza, then flip the crust into the box.

"How are you and Harry getting along? He's quite a character, isn't he?" Robin surprised her by asking.

"Harry's great. Working for him has been a terrific experience," Nora replied, sensing a trap. "I've learned a lot."

That she worked for Harry was no secret. As a contract employee, she could do that and freelance, but it was a gray area. You were supposed to be discreet. The story wasn't a good fit for the *Sun*. It was historical, and it had the wrong slant. Otherwise, she should have offered it to Harry first.

But that was only part of it. He might reject it, and then where would she be? If somebody else published her story, it would have a stamp of approval. Who knows? Harry might even be impressed.

"Good. I'm pleased it's working out." Robin's expression seemed both skeptical and sympathetic. If Nora wanted to complain, it appeared Robin would gladly listen.

"Oh yes, it's great," Nora said, not taking the bait.

With a vague nod, Robin glanced at the manuscript on the table.

"When you first pitched your project, I thought you might be onto something," she continued, her face disconcertingly somber. "I liked your passion and enthusiasm. A new slant on an old subject, you said, and I thought, 'Well, that could be interesting.'"

Placing her hand on the manuscript, she shoved it across the table.

"But not this. It's opinionated and wildly speculative. It's obvious to me …" She shook her head, wise and implacable. "It's obvious to me you're not a writer."

"It's the wrong version. There's a newer one. I sent it," Nora said quickly, the words tumbling out.

"I know exactly what this is," Robin replied. "I spent the better part of a Sunday morning editing it. So imagine my surprise when I got your second draft and discovered it was more of the same.

"Really, Nora, there's no such thing as writing; there's just rewriting and more rewriting, taking direction, honing your craft, learning from experience until you finally get it right. That's what real writers do. I didn't print out your revision because there was no point. I can't use it. You didn't follow my instructions."

"I thought I had."

But even as Nora said it, she knew that wasn't quite true. She had moved a few paragraphs around, added some qualifiers, and tossed in some additional details in hopes of placating Robin without ruining her story. When she pitched it, she'd promised revelations, and that's what she'd delivered—whether Robin liked them or not.

"I'm sorry, but I'm going to have to kill it. It leaves a hole in my editorial calendar, but that's my problem, not yours. I'll figure something out. I always do."

"Oh," Nora said, her anger and humiliation honed to a single syllable.

"I'm doing you a favor. Someday, when you look back, you may thank me. Not everyone is willing to tell you the truth."

My cue, Nora thought. *I'm supposed to slink away. Years later, lesson learned, I'll come crawling back, sadder and wiser.* Submersed in her thoughts, she barely heard Robin say "Good luck. It's great to be young." Placing her hands on the armrest, she started to rise.

"Should I send you an invoice for the work I've already done?" Nora said, not budging, her face and throat flushed. The story was spec work, payable on publication. Robin didn't owe her a thing.

Robin leaned forward in her chair. "Tell me, I'm curious," she replied with narrowed eyes. "What do you think your little effort's worth?"

"I could settle for half," Nora said, not sure what had gotten into her but pleased to see Robin turning red.

"You have a high opinion of yourself. Have you done anything to earn it?"

"Half seems about right," Nora repeated.

"One-quarter. Just to humor you."

Nora did the math: fifty dollars. It was hardly worth fighting about. She was beginning to cool off.

"And I own it," Robin added. "With a significant amount of rewriting, I might be able to make something of it. Not under your name, of course." She raised her hands as if to say, "More work for me, but oh well."

"I've changed my mind. It's not for sale." Nora stood, reached across the table, and rescued her hacked-up story. A calculated half-step behind Robin, she followed her out.

"Well, goodbye and good luck," Robin said at the door in a tone of voice that sounded more like good riddance. "Tell Harry I said hello."

Nora emerged into hazy afternoon sunlight, The emotional spike she'd been riding was ebbing, and she was beginning to slump. After pausing to get her bearings, she strode down the street in the opposite direction from the municipal garage, walking to clear her head. *It's a good story*, she reassured herself as she strolled, wondering if she believed it. What if the story was as bad as Robin claimed?

Up ahead, the light turned red. Beset by doubts, Nora stopped and waited. By now, the parking garage was a good two blocks behind her. She should turn around. If she went back to work, she could finish the high-end flooring article and get a start on another project. *Easy money. Take it while you can*, she told herself, echoing Jack.

Or she could go home. And do what? Sulk and brood, relive her meeting with Robin. *No thanks.* The Wyman file was still in the backseat where she'd tossed it. But there was no rush. She had all weekend.

The light changed, and Nora crossed the street. Up ahead, she saw an ice-cream parlor, and it occurred to her that she was hungry, that it was after two, and that she hadn't eaten today. Even better, the place was empty, and the double scoop of pistachio she ordered was cool and soothing, perfect to spoon while staring into space.

Finished, temporarily at ease, Nora started back. As she approached *Motherlode*, her good mood started to dissipate, and she hurried past the doorway, slowing down as she entered the parking garage. In its concrete gloom, she saw her little hatchback. It appeared she'd left the dome light on. Just her luck if the car wouldn't start. But it did; the engine turned right over.

I don't care what Robin says. I'm onto something. I know it, Nora thought as she descended the parking garage ramp. At the exit, waiting for a break in the traffic, Nora sneaked a quick peek at the dashboard clock. Not home or back to work. There was a third alternative. *One last visit, and that's it. After that, I'm through.*

It was a couple of miles from *Motherlode* back to the *Sun's* parking lot. Leaving her car there, Nora zagged across the four-lane road. Gates and locks were no deterrent. She grasped the chain-link fence, waited for the anxiety to level off, then clambered up and over, landing in a crouch inside the cemetery. While her actions were clandestine, they were also pragmatic. Over the fence was the shortest route to the Goldmont statue.

After their first visit to the cemetery, Nora had waffled, not sure she wanted to do the story after all. *It's going to be a lot of work, and maybe it's not the best use of my time,* she told herself, aware she was rationalizing.

"It's entirely up to you, Eleanora," Paul had replied when she shared her doubts with him. "Perhaps we should take another look at the statue. It might help you make up your mind."

Nora's expression turned grave. "Okay, but just a quick jaunt," she had replied. She hated to disappoint him.

The trip was uncomfortable but not quite as bad as the first time. Paul parked the golf cart at the bottom of the rise, and together they walked up the hillside to the statue.

As they stood in front of it, Nora's thoughts spiraled. *It's only a statue, and this is just a cemetery. It's only a statue, a statue in a cemetery. Just a statue ...*

"So what's the verdict?" Paul had intervened.

A statue in a cemetery, just a statue ... "I want to do it," Nora had said, shaky but resolute. "With your assistance, of course. Let's give the old scoundrel his due."

Since then, she had been back—Nora had lost count—*three or four times, something like that. Today's definitely the last time.*

Wending through a stand of fir trees, Nora came to what she thought of as her spot: a moldering concrete bench situated near the statue. The manuscript was in her back pocket. Telling herself it was a mistake, that she should forget the whole stupid affair and move on, she pulled it out and sat down.

"Tony Goldmont's Fatal Gamble," she read, the story's title. In an opening that had gone through numerous drafts—*so take that, Robin, I do too revise*—Nora had chronicled the town's founding:

> On an improbable spit of land where glacier-carved cliffs plunge to the water's edge and the ground is an unstable slurry of sand, gravel, and clay, Tony Goldmont planted a town and founded a newspaper to help promote it.
>
> Nor was that his real name. He was Count Anthony Montagna d'Oro, the last surviving member of an old Sicilian family with a pedigree as great as the pile of debts it rested on.
>
> Fleeing his increasingly clamorous creditors, the count had surreptitiously set sail for New York City. Seventeen days later in September 1890, he disembarked a new man, or at least a man with a brand-new identity. Count Anthony Montagna d'Oro—the last name is Italian for "mountain of gold"—was now Tony Goldmont.

Inserted in the text, Robin had written, "This opening is too self-consciously rhetorical. You're showing off. Consider rewriting this paragraph to make it less highfalutin, and let's banish the negativity. A story or any extended piece of writing is a voyage of discovery, and your snide tone discourages readers from accompanying you."

The story continued:

> Heading west, with a gentleman's disdain for getting his hands dirty, the former count supported himself as a gambler. In Chicago, his luck was suspiciously good, and he had to hightail it out of

town. In Omaha, he went bust. And in Cheyenne, he emerged from an all-night poker game flush with cash.

Finally, Goldmont reached his destination. In northwestern Oregon, with a continent at his back and an ocean in front of him, he placed his biggest wager yet. He purchased ten square miles of wilderness and peddled it to settlers, promising them "gladsome prospects in a temperate setting where all things conspire to cheer the spirit and where nature offers up an abundance of its blessings." He was lying, of course.

"What's your source for all this information?" Robin wanted to know. "I did a quick online search and turned up next to nothing. I hope you're not making this stuff up."

Paul. Her source was Paul, bolstered by documents from his chaotic library. That and some guesswork. Nora had offered to acknowledge him in the text.

"Thank you, Eleanora, but I prefer to stay out of the limelight," he'd replied. "I'm delighted to be of service, but this is your project."

Nora sighed. She wasn't looking forward to telling Paul her story had been shot down.

"But scholarship aside ..." Robin again. "I'm increasingly concerned about your negative attitude. A more balanced account would bolster our confidence in you as a chronicler. This is beginning to feel like a hit job."

Not fair. I'm reporting the facts, Nora defended herself. By sheer coincidence, her path and Goldmont's had overlapped. He had passed through Indianapolis, Nora's hometown; and his route west would have taken him through Camicus, back then a small village, today the site of the state university where Nora had wasted three years of her life. And now she was in the town Goldmont had founded.

Turning the page, Nora skipped ahead:

It would have been just another real estate swindle if silver and traces of gold hadn't been discovered in Goldmont Creek and in the foothills northeast of town. Gripped by greed, people poured in, and the town hustled to accommodate them. Hills were leveled to create more usable ground. Piles of crushed stone left by the operation were dumped into the harbor, at first to dispose of the rubble but eventually to form boggier, subsidence-prone soil on which the town could expand.

Within a few years, the gold and silver petered out, but not before enriching a few individuals, shrewder and luckier than their peers. Sadly, Tony Goldmont wasn't among them. Six months after founding his town, before the boom, he disappeared. The report in the *Sun* was a masterpiece of obfuscation: "Mr. Goldmont is known to be a man of an active and energetic disposition. Undoubtedly, he has chosen to exercise himself in some enterprise of note, of which we look forward to hearing about as details emerge."

"Once more, your flippant tone detracts from the story you're trying to tell," Robin griped. "The rise of a significant American city could be depicted in a far more positive light if you weren't committed to cynicism and disparagement."

No details emerged. Most likely he was murdered and his body tossed from a cliff, never to rise again. Meanwhile, the town he founded, created from crushed hills and get-rich-quick fever dreams, endures—his legacy in a place where he has been largely forgotten. Perhaps that's good enough.

"Whoa, slow down. What you're suggesting is sheer conjecture and way too melodramatic. You're forcing the facts to fit your preconceived notions, and the strain shows. You need to …"

Nora looked up. It was a reasonable surmise. Fleece investors by selling them worthless, flood-prone land in a place where only a mountain goat could feel at home, and an angry mob might come after you, too. Some of the people he swindled were no doubt buried in this cemetery, possibly right here around him.

Nora stood, folded her manuscript, and tucked it into the back pocket of her jeans. Lifting her head, she took a last look at the statue. According to Paul, it had showed up at the old city building around the time Goldmont disappeared. He must have commissioned it. How he'd paid for it remained a mystery, perhaps with funds diverted from the town treasury. Not knowing what else to do, the town had eventually hauled it here, its final resting place.

Retracing her steps, Nora hopped the fence and crossed the road to her car, one of the few remaining in the parking lot. Halfway home, she happened to glance down. A small object lay on the passenger-side floor. Startled, Nora pulled off the road. It was a matchbook. She picked it up. On the cover in an Old English typeface, she read,

Junior's Old Fart Club
1010 Westwind Road
Stop in and shoot the BREEZE

Taking out her phone, she googled the address. Junior's was in a run-down neighborhood not far from the old waterfront. Putting the car in gear, not sure what she expected to find, Nora headed there.

CHAPTER 4

It was only four-thirty, but Junior's rutted parking lot was already half full. On the right as Nora faced the building, the lot dropped away, running down to Goldmont Creek, where a grocery shopping cart lay partially submerged along with something that might be a rolled-up carpet.

Over the years, a few cars had also ended up in the water, possibly because their drivers were too drunk to remember how their transmissions worked.

Currently, two of the bar's regulars stood at the edge, flinging dry cat food into the creek. A third member of the crew peered through binoculars, seeking signs of aquatic activity. According to their T-shirts, they were Old Farts.

Standing by her car, Nora hesitated, not sure how to proceed. A familiar-looking brown pickup, parked at the end of the row, caught her eye. Walking halfway toward it, she saw with dismay a half-scraped-off bumper sticker advising passersby to

**KEEP CALM
AND
KISS MY
ASS**

Jack's truck. She found its owner seated by himself at a corner table on the patio, a raised wooden platform elevated from the parking lot by a short flight of steps. Head propped in his hand, he stared into space, looking lost in thought. His other hand was wrapped around a bottle of beer. An empty bottle sat by his elbow alongside a pack of cigarettes, one of which was smoldering in the ashtray. If she left now, he'd never know.

"Hi, Jack, interesting place. I didn't know you were an Old Fart," Nora said when she was standing across from him. She'd meant to keep it light, but it came out sounding like an accusation.

It took a moment for Jack's expression to catch up. "Oh, that. It's not my deal. Some of the guys put it together," he replied with a disdainful gesture in the direction of the parking lot crew feeding the fish. "What are you doing here?" he asked, nodding toward the black metal chair across from him.

"Looking for answers," Nora said, sitting down, working to keep her voice even. The umbrella shielding the table from the late afternoon sun listed to the right, and the light shone in her eyes. Nora dug in her pocket, pulled out the Old Fart matchbook, and slid it toward him, her copper-silver bracelet scraping the table.

"When I went back to my car this afternoon, the dome light was on, and I found this on the floor," Nora said, moving her hand away like a magician exposing a card. "Any idea how it got there?"

For a moment, Jack stared at the matchbook; then he picked it up. The butt in the ashtray had burned itself out. He tapped the pack, looking at Nora questioningly. She nodded, waiting as he took out a fresh cigarette, plucked a match from the book, and lit it. Taking a drag, he conscientiously turned his head away from her before exhaling then let his hand rest on the table. Wisps of smoke curlicued upward and hung over them in a tobacco cloud.

"I must've dropped it. While you were meeting with Robin, I bugged your car," Jack finally said.

"What? Why on earth would you do that?" she asked loudly enough for the people at the next table to glance in their direction.

"It's complicated." Jack sighed and took another drag from his cigarette, exhaling slowly.

Nora forced herself to lean back, reminding herself they were in a public place. The last thing she wanted was to make a scene. "How is it complicated?" she asked quietly, her hands under the table, folded tightly together.

"It just is."

Nora waited for him to continue.

With another cigarette-smoke sigh, Jack said, "A while back, I got a call out of the blue. It was some guy telling me he has a job if I'm interested.

"'It depends. What is it?' I say. Turns out it's surveillance work. He says he wants me to keep an eye on someone." Jack glanced down at his cigarette smoldering in his hand. Looking up, he smiled ruefully and said, "That someone is you."

"Me? Why me?" Nora protested, forgetting to keep her voice down.

"I have no idea. It surprised me."

"Did you ask?"

"Yeah. He said I didn't need to know. 'That's the job. Take it or leave it, but if I were you, I'd take it.'

"'Why's that?' I asked, although I'm pretty sure I shouldn't have. He didn't sound like the sort of person who likes answering questions.

"'Just one reason,' he says. 'It makes me unhappy when people tell me no, and it's easy money.'"

"That's two reasons," Nora said.

Jack shrugged.

"The money—is it that good?"

"It's good. Envelopes stuffed with cash. Well, not stuffed, but damn full. Someone must think you're important," he added, a note of wonderment in his voice.

"I'm not. I'm no one."

Jack's cigarette had burned down, and she watched as he carefully lifted it, flicked the ash, then snuffed it out. When Nora looked up again, a waitress was standing at their table. How long had she been there?

"Hey, Michelle," he greeted her, looking pleased.

"Hi, Jack. Ready for another?"

"Always, and see what my friend's having."

Michelle appeared to be in her late twenties. She was wearing skinny jeans and a formfitting T-shirt with "Junior's" stenciled across the front. Dark-brown hair flowed to beneath her shoulder blades and swung as she turned toward Nora. Her expression seemed to suggest that a woman at Jack Spitzer's table might not be an everyday occurrence.

"Red wine," Nora said. It was probably the wrong thing to order in a shot-and-beer bar, but she didn't expect to stay long enough to drink it.

With another hair-swaying nod, Michelle acknowledged Nora's order and turned to leave. Jack watched her all the way across the patio until she disappeared through the double doors at the far end.

"So, you don't know who he is or why he's interested in me?" Nora asked when she had Jack's attention again.

"No, and that's how I want to keep it."

Wyman, Nora thought. *His doing.* Except on reflection, she wasn't so sure. Wyman was devious, but Jack's mystery employer sounded like a thug.

"Can you at least un-bug my car?" she asked.

"No, sorry. I wish." Jack shook his head.

"Hey, folks, here you go," a voice intruded.

Michelle had returned bearing beverages. With a smile, she set down Jack's beer and a full-to-the-brim glass of wine for Nora, some of which sloshed on the table. It was the wrong color—white, not red.

"Thanks, Michelle," Jack said, and lifted his beer. "You're a lifesaver."

Again he followed her with his eyes.

"You should come by more often," he joked when Michelle was out of sight. "The service is a lot better when you're here."

Nora let it pass. *If Jack wants to moon over their waitress like a lovesick basset hound, let him.* She carefully raised her overfull glass and took a sip. The wine was cloyingly sweet, and she set it down.

For a while, neither spoke. It was getting late. The sun was setting behind the office park across the street. The Old Fart crew on the hillside had packed it in, and cars were piling into the parking lot. From inside the bar, old-time rock 'n' roll bled onto the patio, where the crowd was mostly women. They had accompanied their menfolk this far but no further.

"Did you see me go into *Motherlode*? Nora asked, ending the impasse.

"And watched you come out. Were you job hunting?"

"No, working on a story. She didn't like it."

"Well, it wouldn't be the first time," Jack said, visibly relaxing, possibly because they weren't talking about that other thing anymore. "She's notorious. Did you know Harry used to work for her?"

"Did he?" Nora asked with a touch of dismay. It was a little too close to home, but it might explain some things.

"Yeah, right before he started at the *Sun*."

"And would it be safe to say they don't like each other?"

"Yes, quite safe."

"I hope they never talk." She didn't trust Robin, and she certainly didn't want Harry to hear about her freelance fiasco. There was no telling how Robin might twist it.

"They probably do. It's a small town. Paths cross."

Of course they do, Nora thought. *I ought to tell Harry herself. Monday morning, first thing. If he fires me, so be it. At least I won't have to deal with Wyman.*

"So, to recap, you've been shadowing me, you bugged my car today, and you took my picture at the party," Nora said from the midst of her funk.

Jack was lighting another cigarette. "I'm sorry," he breezily replied, waving the match to put it out. "But if I hadn't done it, someone else would have."

"Yeah," Nora agreed. As apologies went, it was accurate.

Michelle's voice rang out. "Hey, folks. Just checking. Do you need anything?" She was standing between them.

Jack lofted his beer and chugged.

"Another," he said, wiping his hand across his lips.

"And for you, ma'am?" Michelle dutifully asked, noticing Nora's abandoned wine glass. By now, it had migrated to the middle of the table and was resting alongside the umbrella pole.

"Nothing. I'm leaving," Nora said with half-suppressed anger. It was beginning to feel as if Michelle were the third person at their table. And she shouldn't encourage Jack. He was drinking way too much.

Michelle finally departed, and Nora started to get up.

"The Empire Theater," Jack blurted out, looking surprised to hear himself say it.

Puzzled, Nora settled back.

"What about it?" she asked.

"It's the old burlesque house in the Roman Empire District. It's been closed forever. They want me to stake it out. His voice dropped to a conspiratorial whisper. "I don't know why. It might be worth a look. But not tonight," he added. "It's dangerous after dark."

"Right, not tonight," Nora agreed. Part of the original city, the empire district had been laid out by Tony Goldmont himself with street names drawn from roman mythology. These days it was a desolate place. Hardly anyone lived or worked there.

Nora was getting ready to leave, this time for real when the patio doors swung open; the music from inside went from loud to blaring, and a ragtag chorus of Old Farts trooped out to serenade the patio, with rowdy enthusiasm singing along to Credence Clearwater's "Bad Moon Rising."

In the center, an Old Fart with a Mohawk swayed, eyes scrunched shut as the music moved through him. While the others sang, he turned his back. His hands went to his waist, and his pants tumbled to his ankles, showing off what seemed to Nora a remarkably hairy behind. The other farts enjoined him to pull up his pants. Instead he bent over and waggled his haunches.

"His nickname's Sasquatch. I think you can see why," Jack said over the din of the music.

Nora watched as two farts grabbed Sasquatch by the arms and lift-marched him inside. His still-mooning posterior slowly disappeared from sight as the song raced to the end:

> I hear hurricanes a-blowin'
> I know the end is comin' soon
> I fear rivers overflowin'
> I hear the voice of rage and ruin

"Yeah, well, I guess you're not an Old Fart after all," Nora said, the song's gleeful nihilism still ringing in her ears. Reaching across the table, she lightly tapped the matchbook. "But you're close."

Jack sighed and started to reach for his beer, remembered the bottle was empty, and scanned the patio for Michelle.

"What's next? Where does Nora go from here?" he asked when he was focused on her again.

"It depends," Nora said. Her anger at Jack, submerged for a while, was percolating up again. She had a lead: the Empire Theater, for whatever it was worth—probably not much. But as for where she went from here, she didn't know, and it was none of Jack's business anyway.

"Depends on what?" he asked.

"Nothing," she replied. "Nora goes home; she brews a nice pot of chamomile tea and curls up with a good book—something uplifting, I imagine."

"Do you even own an uplifting book?" Jack asked, looking pleased to have his old sparring partner back.

"No, and only old ladies drink chamomile tea." Nora stood and pushed in her chair, careful not to bump the table. "Good night, Jack. If I were you, I'd take it easy or at least slow down."

"'Night, Nor," Jack replied with a grin and cocked his head. Michelle had reappeared on the patio and was coming toward him with another beer.

CHAPTER 5

Nora wasn't planning to visit the theater, but it was only about three miles from Junior's. How dangerous could it be to swing by on her way home? She wouldn't even have to get out of the car. Pulling out of the parking lot, she headed down Westwind Road, picked up speed as she approached Venus, zoomed past Mars, and got all the way to Saturn Avenue, where she came to a dead stop, stymied by a collegiate-looking crowd that had spilled into the roadway, blocking her path.

Her reporter instincts piqued, Nora decided to investigate. It took a while, but she found a parking place on an unmarked side street and hoofed it back, making sure to pay attention to where she was going. Her car might be bugged, but that wouldn't help her find it when she was ready to leave.

It was a laid-back crowd. From the periphery, Nora saw kids hanging out, drinking beer, smoking dope, even playing a little hacky sack. She was still getting her bearings when a guy emerged from the crowd and sauntered toward her.

He looked young with frizzy brown hair and a scruffy haven't-shaved-in-a-week beard. He was wearing cargo shorts and a T-shirt featuring a cockroach and the name of a pest control company in Louisiana. It looked to Nora like a garment you'd find on a resell shop's ten-cent T-shirt table.

"You're just in time," her new acquaintance announced with a smirk.

"For what?" Nora asked, eyeing the insect on his chest. It was large and standing on its hind legs, which gave it a Godzilla-esque quality.

"Maybe nothing," he said with the air of someone enjoying a private joke.

Nora waited for him to go on.

"It's a pop-up concert," he finally continued. "Rumor has it Curse the Dark's coming, but then again maybe he isn't. You never know," he added, punctuating the remark with a shrug.

"So this is cursing," Nora said. She had heard of Curse but only because she occasionally helped write the newspaper's entertainment capsules. A shadowy figure, he had shown up in Goldmont around the same time she had. Cursers, as his fans were called, came to concerts and brandished candles they made a point of not lighting.

"I prefer to think of it as existential loitering," he said, savoring the phrase as though it was pure seminar gold. "You get the word, you show up, and you wait around in the dark. Curse may come or"—he paused and his voice dipped—"he may not. But that's the way it goes. It's all good."

An undergraduate, Nora decided, taking another look at the crowd. If this was existentialism, it had a definite party vibe. There was no story here, certainly not one she could submit to Harry.

What to do? The people around her might be exercising their free will through their paradoxical decision to turn nothing's happening into a happening, but if she was going to the Empire Theater, they were in the way.

Quite possibly the police had already been summoned to disperse the crowd, which would make it even more difficult if—big if—she still intended to check the theater out tonight.

Nora cast an appraising glance at the boy standing across from her.

"Planning to bail?" he asked.

"Thinking about it."

"Stay and I'll let you hold my candle," he said, smirking again. Reaching into his pocket, he pulled it out and extended it to her.

Nora shook her head.

"Not into candles?" he teased.

"Not into yours," she said and started walking.

Like most crowds, this one had seams you could slip through. Soon Nora was all alone, trekking past crumbling warehouses and abandoned storefronts, slumbering behind burglar bars. A salt breeze coming off the water chilled her, and a crescent moon shone dimly through broken clouds. Up ahead, a plywood sign weighted with sandbags informed her she was entering the Waterfront Redevelopment Project Area, Alexander Wyman, chairman.

As Nora rounded the corner, turning from Saturn onto Jupiter, the Empire Theater loomed into view, a glowing neon-lit hulk on an otherwise deserted boulevard. Only when she got closer could she see the reality behind the glow: concrete walls covered with aerosol explosions of graffiti, shot-out windows, and a smashed ticket booth. The marquee, suspended over the sidewalk, sagged precariously. One side proclaimed,

Girls Galore

The other side had originally said "See a Show Tonite." Some joker had vandalized it to read

See how To

with rusted cavities where letters had been pried out.

By the theater door, an enormous figure stood dressed in roman soldier garb. Astonished, Nora stopped and regarded him warily.

A metal helmet decorated with an ornamental brush covered his head. Draped across his shoulders and flowing down past his knees was a sumptuous white toga with a purple border. His right hand was crossed over his heart, and in his left hand, pointed straight up, he held a wicked-looking metal pike. It was at least as tall as Nora and punctuated with a tri-pronged tip.

"Hello," she called out, cautiously edging closer.

The sentinel, if that's what he was, remained impassive. His eyes, dark stones in a great boulder of a head, impassively registered her presence.

"Hello," she tried again, and reluctantly took another step toward him. It felt as though she were hollering up a mountain, straining to be heard.

"Hello," he finally responded in a gravelly rumble of a voice that managed to suggest tremendous power while being so low as to be almost inaudible.

"Were you expecting me?" Nora managed, for a moment wondering if Jack had set her up. *Not likely*, she decided, and it didn't matter. Whatever this was, it went way beyond Jack.

"No, not yet," the sentinel replied, taking his time. He didn't appear to be at a loss for words, just not in any rush to use them. "You might as well go in," he added after a long moment. "He'll want to see you." With impressive agility for someone so large, he turned, gripped the door handle and opened the door. A growing slice of interior revealed itself, red and flickering with a pulsing bass undertone.

Nora hesitated. The sentinel patiently waited. Perhaps she was imagining it, but his expression seemed friendly. She entered. Behind her, the door quietly shut, and she found herself in a musty hallway about a dozen feet long and three feet wide. Shimmering scarlet fabric draped the walls, illuminated by flickering ceiling lights. The tom-tomming was more urgent now and seemed to be coming from just past the entryway.

Eyes adjusting, Nora inched ahead. The corridor opened into a cavernous space stripped to beams and posts. At the far end, a raised platform remained. Under a bank of colored spotlights with gaps where bulbs had burned out, a solitary figure stood.

It was Alexander Wyman, and he was dancing. Not ballroom, it was more muscular and surprisingly graceful.

As it unfolded, Nora imagined a phantom partner dancing alongside him. She was elegant and supple. Sometimes she followed Wyman's lead; other times she counterpointed it with gestures and movements of her own. To Nora's astonishment, she realized she was imagining herself in that role, and she forced herself to look away.

The performance ended, the music stopped, and Wyman stepped down from the platform and strode toward her. His sleeves were rolled to his elbows, and the top buttons of his shirt were undone to reveal an expanse of throat and chest. A light sheen of sweat glistened on his skin, and one damp lock of hair had fallen across his forehead, just asking to be stroked into place.

"Miss Stanfell, what a pleasant surprise," he said when he was standing across from her. Reaching into his pocket for a handkerchief, he lightly dabbed his face. "You caught me in the middle of a workout. It's quaint, I know, but there was a time when people thought being a skillful dancer was a warrior's attribute, that it correlated with prowess in battle."

"Well, I hope I'm not intruding," Nora said, not sure what to make of that. "The person out front suggested I come in."

"Yes, Hector. I'm glad you did. The other night you left much too soon."

"I was on deadline and it was late," Nora replied, following his lead. They were dancing after all.

"I suppose you want to discuss the profile."

"Yes," Nora played along. The file Harry had given her was still in the backseat, where she'd tossed it, but she could bluff her way through.

"I was thinking a historical approach might be interesting," Wyman continued. "What if we tied the revitalization plan to the town's past? It's the next chapter in an unfolding saga. I'm sure you can say it better than I can. We might even throw in a few tidbits about the notorious Empire Theater to spice things up. What do you think?" he asked with an expectant smile.

"It's possible," Nora grudgingly conceded. History, especially Goldmont's, was the last thing she wanted to think about right now.

"Well, it's just an idea. We don't have to decide tonight. As long as you're here, how about a tour?" he added, his voice deceptively casual. "You might find it interesting."

"You mean right now?"

"Why not?"

"But is it safe?" Nora asked, curious despite herself. Something old and buried was beginning to stir.

"Safe enough. And we can turn back any time. It's up to you. Whatever you want."

"Is it that interesting?"

Wyman didn't respond, and it wasn't a real question anyway.

"All right," Nora said. "Show me."

Together they started across the auditorium. At the far end, they came to a hallway haphazardly lit by wall sconces, and they turned into it. Decay hung in the air, and Nora could hear scrabbling sounds coming from the walls. *Rats.* The very thought creeped her out.

Midway down the hall, they turned again and entered a large dressing area illuminated by florescent tubes running the length of the ceiling. About half of them were burnt out, and the remaining lights hummed faintly. A tarnished, badly pitted mirror ran the length of one wall with a long vanity counter underneath. Across from the mirror, two wooden rods extended across the room intended for costume changes.

"It's only a mirror," Wyman said, looking at the one directly in front of them. "But wouldn't it be interesting if you could gaze into it and see what's yet to come, anything but the current moment? My question is purely conjectural of course."

Nora grimaced. Peering into it, all she saw was their dim distorted reflection. She was standing too close to him.

"I'd rather not," she said, and stepped to the side.

"And why is that, if you don't mind my asking?" Wyman said and took a step toward her so she could see him out of the corner of her eye and reflected in front of her.

"I don't trust mirrors."

"You think they lie?"

"No, not exactly." Nora groped for words to explain it. "I think they deceive. They distort things, play tricks, and lead you astray. It's dangerous to believe anything you see in a mirror."

"Then we should move on. There's more if you're game."

"All right," Nora said, her voice grim. "Go ahead."

With a nod of acknowledgment, Wyman led the way out of the dressing area. The theater was honeycombed with passageways dimly illuminated by naked bulbs casting a faint purplish light. As they penetrated deeper, the smell of dust and decay grew. The scrabbling sounds in the walls got louder, and cobwebs brushed Nora's face.

Her wrist was starting to throb, an angry pounding rising in intensity the further in they went. Turning, they entered another hallway, smaller than any that had preceded it. There was just enough light to tell it was a dead end. Alarmed, Nora stopped. Wyman continued all the way down it, beckoning to her. Reluctantly, she came forward.

"If you were going to choose, which one would you pick?" he asked, startling her. Along the right side of the hall in the purple darkness, Nora could make out three doors. The doors were narrow with tarnished brass knobs. Each door was painted a different color: green, yellow, and red—traffic light colors.

"I'd like to go back," she said. Her throat was tight and dry. The pounding in her wrist had become even more frantic, and her head ached.

"Of course," Wyman said immediately, no disappointment evident in his voice. Crossing behind, careful not to brush against her, he backtracked with Nora trailing behind.

Their return trip seemed to take no time at all. Reentering the auditorium, they crossed in front of the platform where Wyman had performed for her. His jacket was draped across the back of a metal folding chair.

As they passed it, he reached for the jacket and in a swirl donned it without breaking stride. *More dancing,* Nora thought as she followed him to the front of the building and waited while he opened the door. Stepping out, Nora took a deep breath. They were alone. The sentinel—*Hector,* she remembered his name—was nowhere in sight.

"What's your verdict? Did you find anything you can use?" Wyman asked as they faced each other, careful not to stand under the sagging marquee. The neon glow, reflecting off his lenses, blurred his eyes and gave his skin a pinkish cotton-candy hue.

"No," Nora said. "I'm afraid not." The night air was helping. Her headache was fading, and her pulse felt almost normal.

"Well, you're the expert," he said, appearing to dismiss the matter. "Do you remember, the other night you said people who care too much about the past risk getting trapped by it?"

"Kind of. It sounds like something I'd say."

"But turning your back on the past, running from it, that's also a trap. I'm speaking hypothetically of course."

"Well, we all have one. A past, that is," Nora said, thinking, *Mine's a mess. All the time you've spent blundering around in the dark, chasing shadows. And where has it gotten you? Nowhere. The shadows kept shifting.*

"Right, and why be bound by that past when you can always move on and start over? Am I twisting your words?" Wyman asked with a sweeping gesture, giving the back of his hand to the theater, the neighborhood, and everything beyond.

"It's more complicated than that."

"Of course it is," Wyman said with a chuckle. "I'm going to enjoy working with you, Nora."

"Likewise," she replied, not meaning it. She turned her head and looked down the boulevard. Somewhere on an unmarked, unlit side street, her car was parked. She had a long walk ahead of her, and she wasn't sure she remembered the way. Just then, a pair of headlights turned the corner and blazed toward them.

The car, her car, whizzed past accompanied by a long horn blast, made an abrupt U-turn, and squealed to a stop in front of the theater. The door sprang open, and a pair of extremely large sandal-clad feet extricated themselves, followed by legs, a torso, and finally a head. Hector was back.

How did he find it? But then she remembered—her car was bugged. *Thanks, Jack.* Struck by a sudden thought, Nora gave Wyman a quizzical look.

"No, not our doing. Your friend's not nearly as clever as he thinks he is," he said with unexpected candor.

Right, Nora thought. *Jack's in over his head. But at least I won't have a long walk in the dark or another run-in with the Curse crowd.*

Hector had remained beside the car with a hand on the doorframe. Nora passed by him without a glance, sat down, and braced for a door slam. There wasn't one. The door closed slowly and softly. The window was rolled down, and Hector's face filled the frame, regarding her with friendly interest. She'd been wrong about his eyes. They were light brown, not dark, and flecked with yellow. It might be a mistake to spend much time gazing into them.

"Good night, Nora," he said in that deep, rumbling voice. Nora blinked and waited for him to continue, but all he said was "Be careful."

CHAPTER 6

Once Nora left Junior's, Michelle stopped hovering. She quit bringing Jack refills almost before he could ask and hardly glanced in his direction as she made her way across the patio. *Was it possible Nora had been the prime attraction? That Michelle liked girls?* Jack had to wonder.

Or did she swing both ways? She had a boyfriend. His motorcycle was parked by the patio. When her shift ended, she would hop on and wrap her arms around his chest and ride away, her dark brown hair whipping in the wind.

Jack sighed. He could fantasize all he wanted. He stood no chance with Michelle or any of the other barmaids, and it was all because of an innocent blunder. For the *Sun's* last Christmas party, he'd invited a waitress named Mary. Mary was in her mid-thirties with a bit of a beer belly and bottle-blonde hair, and she called everyone "sugar."

But it was her breasts, hyperinflated and confined in a tight dress, that caused the commotion. Mary's breasts were the gorilla in the room. You couldn't acknowledge them or ignore them. Not that the guys necessarily objected to a woman who dressed like a porn star, swore, and drank too much, but not at Christmas, and not in front of their wives and girlfriends.

Mary sulked; Jack hid behind a sickly smile, and Harry, who hadn't expected to enjoy himself, didn't, but at least he now had a reason not to schedule any more office parties. Mary had since moved on, but not before telling everyone at Junior's about her experience.

For Jack the irony stung. He'd invited Mary because he didn't have anyone else to ask and didn't want to seem like a total loser. Instead he'd become the antisocial jerk who sabotaged Christmas, which made him that much more of a loser, especially at Junior's, a place that practically defined the category.

Looking down, Jack realized he was holding the Old Fart matchbook. *I am not*, he thought with a scowl, and defiantly plucked out a match. He struck it, placed the matchbook in the ashtray, and watched the fire consume the cardboard.

Flames flared as the remaining matches caught. Tendrils of smoke and a whiff of sulfur drifted upward and tickled his nostrils. Just as quickly, the flames died down, leaving only ashes, not evidence. A few people turned to look but went back to minding their own business when they realized he was just playing with fire, not setting the place on fire.

Restless, slouching in his chair, Jack surveyed his surroundings. No Michelle. Nora's practically untouched wine glass remained on the table, but he wasn't that desperate. *Had Nora gone home?* He was almost willing to bet she hadn't, that she'd gone to check out the lead he'd given her. It was probably a waste of time, and she shouldn't go wandering around in the dark. *Whatever happens, it's not my fault. I confessed*, he defended himself. *We're even.*

Jack was still refusing to feel guilty when Michelle finally returned. "Hey there," he said, sitting up, watching through drink-blurred eyes as she placed her tray on the table.

"Drink up, Jack," Michelle said, handing him a beer. "You look like you could use it. Where's your friend?"

"She left," he said, enunciating carefully, aware of how thick and clumsy his tongue had become.

"She seemed upset."

"Do you think so?"

"A little. Sounds like you were trying to help her."

"We do what we can." Was that admiration he heard in Michelle's voice? Had the Mary curse finally lifted?

"Well, drink up. It's on the house." Michelle picked up her tray. "But don't tell Roy," she added with a conspiratorial smile. "He wants you to pay your tab. Don't worry; I told him you'd already left."

Taking her warning to heart, Jack chugged his beer. Swaying to his feet, he got his bearings and edged toward the stairs. With both hands, he gripped the wobbly railing and began his descent, giving the matter his undivided attention: left foot, right foot, pause, repeat.

In the parking lot, he stopped and fumbled for his cigarettes. *Not here. I must have left them on the table. Damn, I need to go back. Wait. What's this? In my shirt pocket the entire time.*

Jack held up the pack, peered in and found his last cigarette, stuck it between his lips, then crumpled the pack, and let it drop. *Matches?* He slapped at his pockets. *Not in my pants. My shirt? Oh, right, I burnt them.*

A voice came out of the dark to greet him. "Here you go, pal."

Jack saw a lighter spark, and a flickering blue flame rushed toward him, stopping just shy of his nose. "Much obliged," he mumbled, aiming for the flame, waiting for his cigarette to catch. *My lucky day. First Michelle—there's hope—now this.* He took a puff.

"No problem," his benefactor said. "Hope you didn't drink the place dry. The rest of us are thirsty, too," he added with a friendly swipe across Jack's shoulder as he passed by.

Caught by surprise, Jack staggered but didn't fall. *You can do this,* he reassured himself, surveying through a veil of tobacco smoke the perilous terrain before him. The spot next to the building, reserved for Roy's Dodge Charger, a former police car bought at auction, was empty. *Odd. Michelle must have been mistaken. I didn't need to rush after all. Oh well, no turning back now.*

The boyfriend's Harley was in its customary spot. Jack turned his head to glare at it and almost missed the pothole looming in front of him. *Left or right? Too late.* He stepped in, stumbled, but kept going. *It can't be far now. Or have I already passed it? No, wait. Right there, front wheels on the grass, nose facing the hill, my truck.*

A black Chevy Tahoe was parked next to it. Focusing on the narrow space between the two vehicles, Jack maneuvered himself into position and sidestepped through. *No danger of falling here. You're almost home. Keys. I need them.* With his free hand, he patted his front pockets. *I should have taken them out sooner. This is a very tight spot.*

A harsh voice shattered the silence. "Good evening, Jack. I've been waiting for you."

Startled, Jack looked around, squinting to see. His cigarette had burned down, and he let it drop from his lips.

"Hello?" he called out.

Silence.

"Hello," he tried again.

A hand shot out of the darkness, seized him by the wrist, and propelled him toward the edge of the hill, at the last moment bringing him to a gut-wrenching, shoulder-jarring stop. Jack cautiously reopened his eyes. He was perched on the brink, his anonymous assailant beside him with an arm draped across Jack's shoulders.

"Who are you? What do you want?" Jack asked in a terrified whisper.

"If I told you, I'd have to kill you," the voice chuckled in his ear. "I'm kidding. I can tell you. Who am I? I'm bad news. We're not happy with you, Jack. You're careless, your work is sloppy, and you talk way too much."

"I'm sorry," Jack said, not sure what he was apologizing for. "Give me another chance. I'll do better."

"I'm sure you will. You just need some time to reflect."

The arm across his shoulder withdrew, and for a moment, Jack teetered, then managed to regain his footing. Balanced on the brink, he listened in vain for the sound of retreating footsteps. A faint breeze had begun to stir. He could feel it on his face. *Concentrate,* he told himself. *Don't get distracted. Step back. Slowly. One foot, then the other. Keep doing it and you'll be fine.*

A hand planted itself on his back. "No, please," Jack called out and felt the hand press lightly, just a slight nudge. Arms windmilling, he fell. As he tumbled down the slope, rocks jumped out of the dark to pummel him and shrubs slashed at him until finally he crashed to a halt facedown in the stream.

Struggling, Jack managed to roll onto his back and inch out of the water. It hurt to breathe, and his mouth was full of blood. Above, a car engine started, followed by the sound of tires scattering gravel. Music, laughter, and raucous voices drifted down from Junior's and mingled with the sounds of sluggishly lapping water and buzzing insects.

Oh, God, please. Don't let me die.

CHAPTER 7

Harry Harkness liked his whiskey neat, but the rest of his life was a mess: two ex-wives; no children, thank God; a back so gimpy it belonged in a medical journal; and job prospects that were becoming increasingly problematic. Harry used to brag that he had only applied for four jobs in his entire life and had gotten three of them, but lately his track record had taken a hit, and the *Sun* was beginning to seem like his last stand.

Now, wandering through his townhouse, he found nothing to interest him. The big tomcat that occasionally squeezed through the kitchen window hadn't appeared in almost two weeks. That wasn't surprising; he came when it suited him, and he never stayed long.

The cat had first shown up three months ago. Harry had responded by cracking the window just enough and courting him with dinner scraps and milk. No dice, but Harry was persistent, and eventually his determination paid off.

One night he heard a thump coming from the kitchen and went to investigate. As he stood in the doorway, glowing yellow eyes scrutinized him from across the room, eventually resolving into a cat with a notched ear, a truncated tail, and a large lumpy body—no one's idea of a pet, not even Harry's. Nonetheless, their courtship had progressed from bristling suspicion on the cat's part to something like tolerance as long as Harry kept a respectful distance.

But not tonight. *Good luck out there*, Harry thought, resisting the urge to look. *Hope you never run into more trouble than you can handle.* Moving on, he left the window open just in case.

In the study, on his laptop, a second Max Rage novel, working title *Dead End*, was slowly, very slowly, taking shape. After a long hiatus, Max was coming back, still dodging bullets, throwing punches, and stalking villains in a landscape filled with violence and deceit.

Why Harry was bothering, he couldn't say. It certainly wasn't for money or fame. The first Max Rage had sold about three thousand copies and garnered a depressing three-star rating on Amazon—the $65,013^{th}$ most popular book in the crime fiction category.

Apparently a novel where all the women are seductive and scheming and all the men are violent and dumb except for the hero, who's violent but not dumb, didn't appeal to any segment of the reading public. Perhaps you really can go broke underestimating people's intelligence—or, even more dismaying, overestimating your own.

No writing tonight, Harry decided as he stood by his desk, hands on the chair, scowling at the words on the screen. On the shelf above his desk, another copy of Harry's football photo looked out, flanked by a small library of books: some Mickey Spillanes followed by James Cain followed by Raymond Chandler next to a worn copy of *Flash Gordon and The Lion Men of Mongo*. Purchased at an elementary school book fair, it was the first book Harry had ever bought. He'd read it twice, once avidly, the second time mostly out of curiosity. Yes, it was a good read. No, it hadn't reminded him of what it felt like to be nine years old.

The row ended with *The Unadulterated Cat* by Terry Pratchett, a present from his first wife with an inscription that read "For someone who likes cats more than people. Hope you're happy." Harry had opened the book exactly once, and its survival on the shelf remained something of a mystery. It certainly wasn't nostalgia.

Restless, Harry headed to the closet for his trench coat and a battered fedora, putting them on as he walked down the hall. From habit, right before he exited, he adjusted his hat in the hall mirror, then slammed the door behind him.

The sign on the window simply identified it as a bar. Harry had discovered it early on and stopped in two or three times a month. It was his kind of place: dimly lit, small but impersonal, and the drinks were strong. Tonight, as he entered and made his way to the front, he saw a few solitary drinkers scattered through the room's wood-paneled interior. Taking a seat, Harry placed his fedora on the counter and waited. The bartender slowly made his way over and asked Harry what he wanted.

"Double Jack, no ice or water." He always ordered the same thing, but the bartender never presumed, or possibly he didn't remember. Either way, that was fine with Harry. On the way out, he'd leave a good tip. He might be unfriendly, but he wasn't a cheapskate.

As Harry worked on his drink, a man at the far end of the bar hoisted his beer in Harry's direction. Dismayed, Harry raised his glass with a smile that could be mistaken for the onset of rigor mortis.

The stranger promptly stood up and came toward him. He appeared to be in his late thirties with a swarthy complexion and dark brown hair that hung down in a rattail. A formfitting black T-shirt showed off a muscular torso. Over the T-shirt he wore a shiny black-leather jacket.

"Hello, friend, looks like you could use some company," the stranger said as he planted himself in the seat next to Harry. "There are times when you don't want to be alone with your thoughts."

"Thanks for saving me from myself. I appreciate it," Harry replied, resorting to weak sarcasm.

"Glad to help." The stranger thrust his hand in Harry's direction. "The name's Emil Ratskeller, but most people call me Ratdaddy."

"Hello." Harry reluctantly allowed his hand to be grasped. It was an odd nickname. *Don't comment*, he cautioned himself. *You'll only encourage him.*

"I guess you're wondering what brings me here." Apparently,

Ratdaddy didn't need encouragement, but at least he'd released Harry's hand.

"I'm sure you have your reasons," Harry sensed menace in Ratdaddy's beady eyes and clenched smile. Throw in that weird nickname, and Ratdaddy could have been a character in a Max Rage novel. If events followed their usual course, the scene would end with a pool of blood and someone lying in it.

"We have some things to discuss. It's in your best interest," Ratdaddy said.

Harry's heart sank. Stalling, he glanced in the bartender's direction. The bartender had stationed himself at the other end of the bar and was making a point of not looking in their direction. No doubt he was working on an alibi that would explain how he could have been present the entire time and have seen nothing.

"What things?" Harry reluctantly asked.

Ratdaddy reached into his jacket, pulled out a photo, and handed it to Harry. "Recognize her?" he asked.

"Yes," Harry said, taken aback. It was a photo of Nora. Her right hand was raised, half obscuring her face, making her look vaguely guilty, possibly of nothing more than trying to protect her privacy.

"Good. Let's start with why you hired her."

"Why I hired her?" Harry said with unfeigned astonishment. It was none of Ratdaddy's business, but now wasn't the right time to say so. *Nora, what have you done?* he thought as he put the photo down on the bar.

"Right. Why you hired her," Ratdaddy repeated, his expression perceptibly more clenched.

"Because she's one helluva journalist. We were fortunate to get her," Harry heard himself say, leaving out the part about constrained budgets and how useful it was to have a woman on staff to cover the stuff guys didn't want to do. If Nora hadn't come along, someone else would have, and someone after that. Writers at the *Sun* were like Kleenex: use them, discard them; another one always popped up.

"I see," Ratdaddy said. "You checked her résumé, of course, made sure everything was legit."

"I looked at it," Harry answered, thinking he probably had. "She was an obvious hire." Despite himself, he was beginning to find Nora interesting. She had secrets. Good for her. Harry had some of his own. He didn't have to like her to take her side.

To his relief, Ratdaddy didn't ask the obvious question. Given her obvious talent, why was Harry's ace reporter spending her time covering charity events and writing about kitchen appliances and household decor? Even the Wyman story was a puff piece, and assigning it to her hadn't even been Harry's idea.

Have I been too hard on her? Harry wondered. Memories of Dan, Nora's predecessor, flashed unbidden into his thoughts. Dan had seemed like a real pro. He could handle anything and never break a sweat. Then his stories started landing on Harry's desk. It was possible Dan never read anything he wrote, perhaps on the assumption no one else would either. After two weeks of haste-and-waste journalism, Harry had axed him.

On his way out, Dan had swaggered over to Harry's office to shake Harry's hand and wish him well. "The job's beneath me," his manner said. "Never mind that I can't do it." Compared to Dan, Nora was a jewel.

"What about her?" Ratdaddy asked. He reached into his pocket, pulled out another photo, and handed it to Harry.

Harry reluctantly accepted it, not trying to hide his surprise. The woman in the picture was dressed in a red thong and nothing else. Ash-blonde hair tumbled to her shoulders in calculated disarray, framing a doll-pretty face. Her eyes were cornflower blue, she had cherry-red lips, and her breasts were large and firm. Across the bottom right corner in a diagonal scrawl, Harry read:

Give it to me!!!
Felony Foster!

"Recognize her?" Ratdaddy asked.

'No," Harry said sharply, putting the photo on the bar counter next to Nora's.

"It's a publicity shot. She's also been Gianna Global, and for a while she was Fiera Foxx. But she's really Jillian Wexler from Evansville, Indiana."

"Well, whoever she is, she seems to like alliteration." Harry's name alliterated, too, but he hadn't picked it.

"Ironic, don't you think?" Ratdaddy continued, looking at the two photos side by side on the bar.

"How so?" Harry unwillingly asked, not sure Ratdaddy knew what the word meant.

"On the one hand, we have a porn star named Felony Foster," Ratdaddy held his right fist out to represent that side of the proposition. Harry couldn't help but notice how large and scarred his knuckles were.

"And on the other"—Ratdaddy brought his left fist into the conversation—"we have a newspaper reporter named Nora Stanfell. Different women. They don't look like they could have much in common, but when you get right down to it"—he brought his fists together hard enough to make his point—"they do. They have a lot in common. A lot."

Ratdaddy paused.

I'm supposed to ask, Harry thought. Admittedly, he was curious, but he didn't need to know. It was none of his business. "All right, what's the link?" he forced himself to say.

"Did you ever hear the expression 'If I told you, I'd have to kill you?'" Ratdaddy exercised his face into another one of his smiles. His hand went to Harry's shoulder, and he squeezed hard enough to hurt.

"Relax; I'm just messing with you." he continued, relinquishing his grip. "Nora and Felony Foster were college roommates, and they're best friends. Could be a scandal. You might want to get in front of it. You know, nip it in the bud."

"I see." *Guilt by association. Do I care? No. It's interesting Nora has one—a friend, that is.*

He watched as Ratdaddy picked up the two photos, his eyes lingering on Felony Foster.

"Hell of a name," he muttered, which was odd criticism from someone who went by Ratdaddy. "You're wondering how I got my nickname," he added, tucking both pictures into his jacket pocket.

"I'm sure there's a good reason." Harry allowed himself a quick glance toward the door. Once he made it out, he was never coming back.

"I started out in the pest-control business," Ratdaddy began with the air of someone who's told a story numerous times and still enjoys hearing it.

"Right away I figured if you want to succeed, you need to know as much as possible about your adversary—especially how they think. So, I paid attention, studied them until I instinctively knew how they'd behave in any situation. The rodent mind is complicated, and they have impressive survival skills. After a while, people recognized my gift and started calling me Ratdaddy."

"I see," Harry said. It sounded like pure bullshit.

"It's a lot better than my old nickname."

"What was that?" Harry asked because he was supposed to.

"They used to call me Emil the Eliminator. Can't say I ever cared for it." With a scowl, Ratdaddy stood, pulled some bills out of his wallet to pay their tab, and tossed them on the bar along with a business card.

"Call me when you've looked into the matter," he said. "I think you'll agree it's in your best interest." And without waiting for a response, he got up and left.

Perturbed, not watching him depart, Harry picked up his drink and sipped, finding solace in the barrel-aged burn of the whiskey. *What was that about? What's his deal?* He put down his empty glass. *By now the coast should be clear.* Donning his fedora, Harry stepped out. Ratdaddy's card was still on the counter.

CHAPTER 8

In a restaurant a thousand miles down the coast, Felony Foster unwound over a late dinner of champagne and escargot. On-screen sex was always a challenge, but today's scene had included one very large mud puddle and three guys. At the last moment, she'd been tempted to cancel, but Felony was a professional. She'd signed a contract, and after three weeks of enforced idleness, she needed the money.

With a scowl—she was thinking about all that mud—Felony stabbed a snail, dipped it in garlic butter and slowly chewed, savoring the sweet, dense, slightly earthy flavor. She'd done well for herself. The big Audi, her twelfth-floor apartment, and the seventy-dollar bottle of champagne cooling in a wine bucket beside her table all attested to her success and helped explain the perilous state of her finances.

It was a paradox. As long as she worked, she could afford almost anything she wanted to help her feel better about working.

She'd first realized it a month ago during a session with her analyst, Dr. Silverblatt. At the time, it had seemed like an important insight, but now Felony was mostly surprised at how long it had taken her to figure it out. And knowing didn't change anything. She was still in a rut, still going around and around and getting nowhere.

"And where would you like to go? What would be a good outcome?" Dr. Silverblatt had asked, seated across from Felony in her big leather armchair. The doctor was short and stout, and she didn't resemble Felony's mother at all. Felony had never hugged Dr. Silverblatt, but she imagined it would feel very comforting to be immersed in all that flesh.

In the three weeks since that session, Felony hadn't come any closer to answering Dr. Silverblatt's question. She still had no idea what she wanted. Looking down at her plate, she lightly tapped the empty escargot shells with her fork, arranging them into a question mark. Out of the corner of her eye, she saw the waiter returning and scattered them.

"Looks like someone didn't like her meal," he joked, pulling up beside her and flashing a smile. He was young and skinny with thinning reddish-blond hair combed forward. As he lifted the champagne bottle from its bucket and bent to pour out the last trickle, she could see pinkish scalp peeking through.

"Would you care to see the dessert menu?" he asked. He paused a beat with a knowing smile before adding, "Miss Foster."

Busted, Felony thought with a mixture of pride and dismay. It was good to have fans, but tonight she'd wanted to go unnoticed, had deliberately dressed down in a simple flower-print blouse, jeans, and scuffed-up sneakers—no jewelry and hardly any makeup. A ball cap with an Indianapolis Colts logo rested in her lap.

"Thanks, but not tonight," Felony said with a trace of hesitation, for a moment flashing back to this afternoon's mud scene. A vigorous scrub followed by a long soak in the jacuzzi, and she still didn't feel clean.

"Are you sure I can't tempt you?" the waiter asked, exaggerating his disappointment with a pouty face.

"Well, I guess it can't hurt to look," she relented. She wasn't ready to go home, and she could afford to indulge herself.

"Excellent. I'll be right back," the waiter said, no doubt heading to the kitchen to spread the word: "It's her; I told you so."

That session with Dr. Silverblatt had produced one other memorable moment. Everyone in the industry got tested regularly for STDs. Felony's latest test had come back positive. She was on vacation, unpaid of course, until she got it taken care of.

"How long has it been?" Dr. Silverblatt had asked, leaning slightly forward.

"About a week."

"And are you taking care of it?"

"Yes," Felony answered, not looking at her. "Or no, but I'm going to," she reversed herself, still not making eye contact. "Right after I leave here."

"Good," Dr. Silverblatt's tone was carefully nonjudgmental. "And this delay in taking care of it, what do you suppose that's about?"

"I don't know. But it's nice to step off the carousel for a while."

"So being sick is a good thing?"

"No, I'm going to take care of it, but it's a lot easier to say no when no one's pressuring you to say yes."

On her way home, Felony had stopped at the drugstore. While she waited for the pharmacist to fill her doxycycline prescription, she drifted over to the school-and-office-supply aisle and scanned its selection of notebooks, for the hell of it choosing one with a chartreuse cover.

She was going to start a journal. It was one of Dr. Silverblatt's ideas. Get your thoughts down on paper, the better to examine them, the doctor had suggested. At the time, Felony had been evasive, and Dr. Silverblatt hadn't pushed it. But if you want to change your life, you have to do things you wouldn't normally do.

Home again, Felony left the notebook on the kitchen table and didn't return to it until later that evening. Sitting down with a glass of wine, she opened the notebook and, on the top of the first page, wrote, "Where I Go From Here." Right below that she added, "Route 1," and then nothing. She couldn't think of a single thing.

Two days later, Felony took another stab at it. With more wine and some Bikini Kill, a favorite band, playing in the background—the old stuff was still the best—she opened her notebook and under "Route 1" wrote,

> Don't change. Adapt. Felony Foster is a character, and she still has fans who will pay to see her. Milk it. Play strip clubs. Do trade shows. Sell merchandise and photos. Create digital content.

Taking a moment to reread what she'd written, Felony inscribed a big fishhook of a question mark through it, skipped a couple lines, and continued:

> Or how about this? Instead of sleazy, go legit. Build on your notoriety as Felony Foster and go into show business. How about a music career or a slot on a reality TV show? No talent required. So what if you can't sing or act.

The waiter was coming back, and none too soon. Thinking about her notebook exercise was depressing the hell out of her.

"Here you go, Miss Foster." He handed her the dessert menu, reverently waiting, hands clasped in front of him, as Felony opened it and scanned its frenchified names, searching for her perfect dessert.

"Chocolate mousse," she finally decided. "And this," pointing at a liqueur whose name she couldn't begin to pronounce.

"An excellent choice. One of my favorites," the waiter said. "Are we perhaps celebrating something this evening?"

"No," she replied sharply. It was an odd question. Did it look like a celebration? And how was it any of his business? She snapped the menu shut and held it out, not bothering to watch him go.

Under Route 2," Felony had written,

> Start over as someone else.

1. Choose a new name, something inconspicuous.
2. Change your appearance. Get a new haircut and some plastic surgery, gain 40 pounds.
3. Find a real job.
4. Hope people forget Felony Foster ever existed.

Except they wouldn't. They would lose interest, maybe, but not forget. Her past lay scattered across the internet, never more than a couple clicks away. There was even an official Felony Foster website she didn't control, not to mention a Facebook and Instagram account and a Twitter feed she occasionally checked to see what she was up to now.

Whatever she did, wherever she went, the past would always be out there waiting to find her, even if it was mostly made up and ridiculous.

Felony sighed and glanced at the picked-clean shells on her plate. Maybe she should look on the bright side. She was going to grow old and die, but Felony Foster would always be in her twenties and smoking hot.

Finally, under "Route 3," Felony had wondered what it would be like to come clean. Currently, only Dr. Silverblatt was allowed to call her "Jillian," but what if she reclaimed her name and all the baggage that went with it?

She'd head home, seek out friends and family, and attempt to make amends or at least apologize. Old wounds would get reopened; raw nerves would be exposed. Not everyone would understand, at least not right away, but ultimately there would be tears and hugs, forgiveness and closure.

A fantasy. It's pure soap opera. The reality was a domineering bully of a father and a hypochondriac invalid mother. *Reconcile yourself to that. Go ahead, I dare you. And what about Nora? After the way you treated her, all the lies you told her, how could you possibly atone? Why should she even listen?*

"Here you go, Miss Forster. Enjoy!" The waiter surprised her, beaming as he set down the mousse and a glass of mystery liqueur.

"Thanks, you're a lifesaver." Felony raised the glass to her lips, pleased to discover she was drinking cognac. She meant to only sample the mousse, but the first spoonful was pure perfection, light and airy with a dusting of cinnamon, and the second spoonful was just as good. She ended up eating the whole thing and ordering another cognac.

When the waiter presented the bill, Felony had a pleasant surprise. He'd comped dessert and only charged her for the first cognac. With woozy pleasure, she signed the credit card slip and added a tip: 30, 40 percent—something like that.

"Thank you for dining with us tonight, Miss Foster. It was truly a pleasure serving you." The waiter was hovering again, but Felony no longer cared. "Could I get your autograph?" he asked.

"Of course. What's your name, darling?"

On the back of her napkin, she wrote,

Roger!

Thanks for a great time!!
You really know how to make a girl feel special!!!

Forever,
Felony

CHAPTER 9

Nora was fibbing when she told Jack she didn't have any chamomile. She had nearly a full tin left over from her herbal tea article. Seated at the kitchen table, hair wet from her second therapeutic shower of the night, she gave the tea bag a last swirl, added enough milk to cloud the surface, then stirred in a teaspoon of honey.

Taking a sip, she savored the tea's suffusing warmth. In front of her, a late supper of sorts was laid out: some crackers thinly spread with goat cheese, a bunch of grapes, a jar of olives. Not exactly a feast, but it was what she had on hand, and it would suffice.

Reaching for a cracker, Nora took another look at the file Harry had given her. It wasn't much: An article from the *Sun* extolling phase one of the waterfront project; a few puff pieces from other sources, including one from *Motherlode* (rather indifferently written, Nora thought); and miscellaneous paragraphs mindlessly aggregating the same thin strands of information.

About fourteen months ago, the city had unveiled its plans for a mixed-use commercial/retail/residential complex. The *Sun* had done its part. It had splashed the story across the front page and proclaimed it "a bold blueprint for the future built on a sound, solid, and sustainable foundation."

And then nothing. The favorable publicity hadn't helped, or it hadn't helped enough. The project had stalled, dragged down by financing issues and infighting among stakeholders. Wyman had said as much. Those issues might get resolved, or then again, they might not. Nothing Nora wrote would make a difference. But, of course, that wasn't the point. With a pained expression, she polished off another cracker and washed it down with the rest of the tea.

She'd put aside a screenshot of the Wyman & Associates homepage, and she returned to it now. No photos, no buttons, not even contact information—just text, and not much of that. "Dawn-of-time relics, lost treasures, whatever you seek, no matter how difficult, we can help you acquire it," the page asserted.

Jumping to the bottom, Nora lingered on the last paragraph:

> Every quest is conducted under the auspices of Alexander Wyman, supported by a band of uniquely talented operatives. Together we possess the knowledge and guile to guide you past traps and tricks, sudden reversals and treacherous surprises. We can't guarantee your success, but if it were easy, you wouldn't need us.

I don't need you, Nora thought. *I just need to be left alone.* Scowling, she put down the printout. *Harry … is he part of this? How much does he know? He gave you the file, but it was a handoff. Most likely, he barely glanced at it. Good. Whatever's going on here, he's not implicated. At least I hope not.*

Getting up from the table, Nora ventured into the bedroom and sat on the corner of the unmade bed, ignoring the rumpled sheets. The alarm clock read 11:36 p.m.

Is Wyman right? she asked herself, remembering their encounter at the Empire. *Is turning your back on the past and running from it a trap? An appropriate sentiment for a dealer in antiquities, but obviously he's much more than that. I don't want to think about it.* Closing her eyes, Nora drifted, letting the current take her where it would.

☙

She's nearly six and standing beside her father, Mitch, looking on as he chuffs steam into a steel pitcher brimming with milk.

"Almost ready. This is going to be good," he says, adjusting a dial. The espresso machine emits three short puffs, then shuts down. There are two mugs on the counter. One's white with a large blue *N*—for "Nora," of course. The other's red with "Top-Notch Novelties," his company, in funky white letters, and underneath that:

If it's one of ours, it's Top Notch.™

Carefully handling the pitcher, he fills their mugs with foamed milk. Just for Nora, he adds a triple dash of sprinkles, and in his mug he pours a shot of bourbon. "Be careful; it's hot," he says as he hands Nora her mug and reaches for his. "To us, you and me. We're a team."

He raises his mug. They clink just the way he's taught her, and he watches as Nora cautiously sips. "Well, what's the verdict? Is it any good?" he asks. He sounds a little anxious.

To tease him, Nora pretends to think about it for all of five seconds. "It's delicious. Your best concoction yet," she replies, smiling through foam-coated lips.

"Concoction"—that's one of his words. As the owner and sole employee of Top-Notch Novelties, contraptions and concoctions are her father's stock in trade, and Nora loves them all: potions and elixirs marketed with suspended disbelief, a candle that spews confetti, a machine that burns diamonds (industrial, not her mother's) to power a small fan. Admittedly, it's pointless, but it's supposed to be; that's somehow the point.

The scene fades. *Whatever happened to that espresso machine?* Nora wonders. It was big and impractical, a counter hog, and eventually it disappeared. Her mother's doing, she supposes. She died before Nora's sixth birthday—cancer, one of those rare aggressive kinds— and Nora hardly remembers her.

After her death, she needed bedtime stories to help her sleep, ones her father made up just for her. There were different kinds of stories. Color stories could be about anything but had to feature a color. Otherwise, the choices were adventure, far and away Nora's favorite, or funny, which she sometimes chose. Sad wasn't an option. Her father only knew stories with happy endings. The stories stopped around the time Nora turned eight. She was getting too old, but they were the bedrock her childhood was built on.

"Tell me a bedtime story, Daddy." Nora closed her eyes again, and tried to conjure up her childhood bedroom and place her father in the chair beside her bed. An image slowly forms. She's seeing him but through adult eyes. He's in his thirties and handsome although he's putting on weight, and his reddish-brown hair is showing some gray. She'd forgotten about the moustache. It didn't last long.

"A young girl, let's call her Nina, goes to sea in a gleaming copper-colored boat," she hears him say. "She's had a full day of adventures, and now she's sailing home with a nice breeze at her back.

"All of a sudden, without warning, her beautiful copper-colored boat slams into the Invisible Island, so called because you can't see it, and once you're there, no one can see you.

"Nina is thrown clear of the wreckage and lands on her feet on what is most likely a beach, because when she wriggles her toes, they feel sandy. Her beautiful boat is nowhere in sight, so maybe it's sunk, or it could be hiding in plain sight along with everything else on the island.

"After giving the matter great thought, she decides to explore. But how do you explore something you can't see? It's not dark; it's empty, whatever color empty is."

"Gray like the middle of a cloud," Nora's younger self says.

"And then she makes a discovery," her father continues with a nod. "She figures out that the best way to travel across the island is to jump across it, because when you have both feet off the ground, the island becomes visible—but only until you land again.

73

"Nina sets out. She jumps, and she jumps some more, and while she's jumping, she notices a large hole. It's there right beneath her feet, so she decides to explore it. The hole turns out to be enormously deep. At first she's surprised, but after a while she gets used to floating downward, and when she lands, it's with a gentle bounce, not a big bump.

"Nina picks herself up and dusts herself off. She glances up, but all she can see is a big patch of gray emptiness at the top like the inside of a cloud. But down here it's different. She's in a tunnel, and before her there's an underground road that twists and turns and winds off into the distance.

"'Hmmm,' she thinks. 'With a good deal of effort, I could possibly climb back up, but since I'm down here and since there's a road, I might as well take it. Roads generally go somewhere.'"

A good decision. Nora can't fault Nina's logic.

"So she starts down the road," her father continues with a quick peek at his watch. "She walks for a very long time, and in the end, after numerous untold adventures which we're saving for another day, she comes out right here in her own bedroom.

"Her mother and father are overjoyed to see her, and they aren't the least bit upset about the copper-colored boat. If islands are going to be invisible, well, what can anyone do? Of course, when she goes to school everyone wants to know where she's been."

"And did she tell them?"

"Not at first, but they wouldn't stop bugging her, so she finally gave in. Some people thought, 'What a wonderful adventure. I wish I'd discovered an invisible island and traveled umpteen miles underground to find my way home.'

"But the people in charge, the adults, they just shook their heads and said, 'There she goes again, making things up. Obviously, this girl has far too much free time. She needs a lot more homework and plenty of after-school activities to keep her focused.'"

"She shouldn't have told them."

"Well, the next time and all the times after that, she didn't."

Her father stands and moves toward the head of the bed. "Better get some sleep, sweetheart." Leaning forward, he kisses her forehead and starts toward the door, turning the light off behind him.

With nothing more to see, Nora opened her eyes. It was 11:58. Getting up, she went to the dresser and pulled out the bottom drawer.

From under a nest of clothes, she found a book—a copy of *The Little Prince* with its cover illustration of a small boy on a tiny planet gazing into an infinite sky. Sitting down again—it always made her smile—she flipped to the inscription on the flyleaf and read,

> *Nora Darling,*
> *Trust yourself. You're Top Notch.*
>
> *Love forever,*
> *Dad*

CHAPTER 10

Harry lay in bed and stared at the ceiling, waiting for the Vicodin to kick in and dull the ache in his back. In the theater of his mind, shifting images, more shadow than substance, flickered: Ratdaddy, Max Rage, Nora, an ex-wife with a permanent scowl. And to banish them all, one special story:

It's a chilly fall morning around daybreak. Harry nervously blows into his hands and glances around. The coast is clear. Beside him, his buddy removes bolt cutters from his backpack and sets to work, grunting with each snip as he cuts a hole in the stadium's wire fence. Done at last, he returns the cutters to his backpack and, with a sweep of his arm, invites Harry to go first, which Harry does, crawling on his hands and knees, avoiding the snipped fence's bristling prongs.

Side by side, they cross the open concrete moat where yesterday they were part of a crowd of three thousand cheering the Prairie State Bulldogs to victory against the archrival Tigers. But this time instead of going through the main gate, they veer off toward a side door marked "Employees Only."

Standing behind his crouching buddy, Harry slants a flashlight beam toward the lock while his buddy attempts to pick it using burglary tools won in a poker game.

"Come on, you son of a bitch, open," his buddy curses softly as he probes, feeling for the tumblers. "Damn it, Harry, hold the light still."

All of a sudden, the knob turns, and the door swings open. His buddy stands, and together they look at the door and at each other.

"How the fuck?" Harry asks in a whisper.

"I have no idea," his buddy replies with a grin.

In the stadium's main entryway, a bunch of clothing store dummies are lined up, part of a traveling exhibit tracing the evolution of college football uniforms over the last century. Harry quickly strips to his skivvies, and swaps his slob wear for a vintage 1930s Ohio State uniform he eyeballed the day before when he was part of the crowd.

It's not as easy as he imagined when the idea first occurred to him. Old Double Zero, according to the back of his jersey, had been taller than Harry and slimmer, a twenty-eight-inch waist to Harry's expanding thirty-four. Even so, the pants almost fit if Harry leaves the top button undone and rolls up the cuffs.

With his friend's help, he manages to wrangle the shoulder pads into place, then dons the jersey, which requires straightening the pads again and rolling up the sleeves, which otherwise droop down past his fingertips. The cleats are clodhoppers and make Harry feel like he has clown feet, but he can at least walk in them.

That leaves the helmet, a hard leather shell crusted with sweat and hair cream. The whole uniform is tight, but the helmet is tight as hell. Maybe it's shrunk over time or Double Zero had a small noggin. Nonetheless, Harry manages to cram his head into it.

The helmet couldn't have offered much protection. It cuts across the middle of Harry's forehead and leaves his face completely exposed. Wide leather ear straps buckle under his chin to hold the helmet in place, but he doesn't need to fasten them. As tight as the helmet is, it's not going anywhere.

This may not make such a great Halloween costume after all, Harry thinks. Now would be a good time to abort the mission and leave. Instead they wander onto the field. The weather has turned exuberant, an apple-crisp October morning with a few clouds in an azure sky.

Encircled by empty bleachers, Harry lines up on the fifty-yard line, drops into a lineman's three-point stance and arches his back as though he's about to explode across the line of scrimmage and hurl himself at an opposing quarterback.

Meanwhile, Harry's buddy clicks away, running through a whole roll of film, ending with Harry pretending to stride down the field, about to score, his left hand extended to stiff-arm would-be tacklers. He's posing for his Heisman moment. Too bad they didn't think to bring a football.

Of course, they got caught. A security guard saw Double Zero, stripped out of his uniform, wearing Harry's red stocking cap, and investigated. Harry and his buddy spent a day in jail before their fraternity brothers managed to raise bail. Eventually they got probation and had to pay to repair the fence they snipped. It was just a prank, no real harm done.

They were graduating seniors with their lives in front of them. Harry's buddy was going to dental school, where presumably he'd use his hand skills for something better than breaking and entering, and Harry had a job lined up with a newspaper in Kentucky.

After graduation, Harry and his buddy lost touch, no particular reason. But that Sunday morning is at the top of Harry's highlight reel. Neither of his exes could understand what made it so special, and number two wondered why he'd want to wear a dead man's clothes anyway.

"It was a joke. It's not like I ripped them off his cold, dead body," *Just like her to spoil a good story.*

The Vicodin was kicking in. Turning on his side, Harry planted his cheek on the pillow. *The old Harry*, he thought. *I miss him.*

CHAPTER 11

Nora woke with her bracelet arm dangling off the bed. Wearing the bracelet to sleep was uncomfortable, but with everything that had happened recently, she was inclined to keep her tattoo concealed even from herself. Maybe she'd change her mind, but for now the bracelet was staying put.

Hitting the alarm, Nora coaxed herself out of bed and headed to the bathroom. She emerged twenty minutes later draped in a towel, not ready for another Monday.

Two items highlighted her agenda. She needed to talk to Jack about her experience at the Empire Theater but also about the tracking device on her car. It had to go, the sooner the better. And, of course, there was Wyman. She was supposed to call him. Nora wasn't sure she would.

Meanwhile, it was getting late. Sunday's outfit, which was also Friday and Saturday's, was spread out on the chair.

Nora's standards weren't that high, but four days in a row was too much even for her. Opening her closet, she surveyed her dwindling collection of clean clothes. In the back, sealed in plastic with the dry cleaner's tag still stapled to it, a dress caught her eye: Jillian's dress, like the bracelet borrowed and never returned. Nora took it from the closet and held it up.

Jillian had suggested it, inviting Nora into her room and holding the dress by its hanger so Nora could inspect it. She had been reluctant. Jillian's clothing sense leaned to the provocative, but this dress was nice, light blue and high-necked with short sleeves and a hemline that swirled slightly above the knee.

"Perfect. You look great," Jillian had said when Nora modeled it for her.

Well, not great, but nice enough, Nora thought, ripping the plastic, mildly astonished to find herself slipping the dress over her head and smoothing it down.

Reluctantly, she looked in the mirror. The dress still fit, and it didn't look dated. *It's not me*, she thought, but she could wear it without feeling foolish. Nonetheless, just before she stepped out the door, Nora hesitated and went back into the bedroom for another look. It wasn't too late to change, or rather it was late enough it no longer mattered.

Reviewing her appearance in the mirror, she removed her hair clip and finger-combed her hair. There, that was how she'd worn it.

About fifty minutes late for work, Nora swung by her cubicle to park her things and turn on her computer, then headed to the break room for a cup of peppermint tea. Harry was already there, filling a mug with that brown sludge the *Sun* called coffee.

Nora hesitated and thought about coming back later. Why look for trouble? But she wasn't a coward. Anyway, he'd probably seen her. "Good morning," she greeted Harry, trying to sound cheerful, waiting to get at the box of herb teas by the coffee pot.

Finished pouring, Harry turned toward her. Nora was struck by how tired and irritable he looked. 'Rough night?' She might have asked if she didn't know better. More concerning was the way he was scrutinizing her, almost as though he was trying to make up his mind. Was this the moment she'd been dreading? Was Harry getting ready to fire her? Of all the days to wear the dress.

"Yes?" she asked, willing him to get on with it. *Don't hem and haw, don't try to sugarcoat it to make me feel better. If you're going to do it, just do it.*

Harry seemed to remember he was holding a coffee mug and

took a sip, then another. "How's that business profile coming?" he asked as he lowered his mug.

So they weren't having that conversation. A reprieve. But it felt almost as bad. Wyman—there was no escaping him. "We've already spoken. We kicked around a few ideas," Nora said, feeling her way. "He seemed pleased."

"No problems?"

"No, none." What was she going to tell him—that after her last encounter, she wanted nothing more to do with that preening egomaniac vampiring around his gutted theater?

"Well, carry on," Harry said, looking grim.

Puzzled, Nora watched him slowly walk away holding his coffee mug at chest level. *Something's bothering him,* she thought. *Is it me?*

CHAPTER 12

Harry closed his office door behind him and sank into his chair, still perturbed from last night's encounter with Ratdaddy. In its wake, the Wyman project, once just a paid profile with the emphasis on "paid," had begun to seem as though it might not be so straightforward after all.

Over the phone, Wyman had been very specific about whom he wanted to work with. "If it's not a problem. I'm not trying to tell you how to run your business," he'd said, doing exactly that.

"No, that's fine," Harry had replied, working to hide his surprise and a touch of annoyance. "Nora Stanfell's a great choice," he added. "But I'm curious. What brought her to your attention?"

"A recommendation from one of my board members, Paul Tsitak. Paul worked with her a few months back on the historical society story, and he's been singing her praises ever since."

"I see." Harry vaguely recalled the story. No knock on Nora, but it was nothing special, a routine assignment handled with routine competence—not that Harry was complaining. Routine competence was plenty good. "Okay, I'll let her know."

"Thanks. Could you ask her to get in touch with me as soon as possible? We're eager to get started," Wyman had added, sounding pleased. And why not? He was getting what he wanted.

A tug-of-war, Harry thought. *Ratdaddy on one side, Wyman on the other. One despises her and wants me to fire her; the other's singing her praises and wants to work with her. I don't get it. She's young and bright, and she's attractive enough—the dress today was a nice change—but that doesn't begin to explain it.*

Her résumé—had he looked at it? He must have. Chances were it wouldn't stand up to scrutiny. They hardly ever did. A pretext if he wanted it. With a sour smile, Harry reached for the phone and dialed his assistant Joyce's extension.

CHAPTER 13

Lunchtime rolled around, and Nora decided not to go home to change after all. The dress was a mistake. This odd compulsion to revisit her past was getting stronger and needed to be resisted, but for this afternoon she could live with it. Besides, it might seem odd to reappear in a different outfit, if anyone was paying attention.

Nora left her bugged car in the parking lot and set out, heading to a stretch of shops and restaurants in Goldmont's downtown district about a half mile away. After the previous night's rainstorm, the sky was clear, and a light breeze swirled her skirt and caressed her bare legs.

On the corner across the street from her destination, Hambones came into view, a two-story art deco–ish building. Nora was passingly familiar with it.

"Goldmont's oldest and baddest club is loaded with scuzzy charm and regularly showcases some of the region's hottest bands," she'd written for a Weekend Capsule. "The drinks are cheap and strong, and be sure to check out the bathroom graffiti. It's choice." Someday she'd have to go and see for herself.

While she waited for the light, Nora glanced at the marquee. Curse the Dark was performing Saturday, An "End-of-the-World Concert," one show only, starting at midnight. The rest of the week it was a band called Bliss. Which reminded her: *Curse's pop-up—did he ever show for it?* Nora hadn't seen anything in the paper, but that wasn't surprising. Ironic loafing wasn't that newsworthy.

The light turned green, and Nora stepped off the curb. Across the street, her restaurant waited. She ordered a chicken Caesar. "Hold the anchovies." She was almost certain it didn't come with them, but just in case. "And a glass of hibiscus tea, please."

The food was decent and reasonably priced, a nice alternative to eating at her desk, but it was a salad, not an antidote. Midway through the meal, Nora's anxieties resurfaced—that same on-edge feeling she'd had in the break room with Harry, but this time stronger. *It's the dress*, she thought. *I never should have worn it. It's messing with my mind, taking me places I don't want to go.*

The bill was already on the table. Nora paid it and exited. As she crossed the street, her attention went back to the Hambone marque. Back in the day, it was the kind of place she and Jillian would've hung out. *Slut and Mutt*, she thought with a half-smile, recalling her private nickname for their not-so-dynamic duo. *A joke, but it had an element of truth.*

The walk was helping to clear her head. By the time she got back to the paper, Nora felt better. Even so, she briefly considered going home to change, but she knew she wouldn't. *I'm fine*, she told herself, glancing at her car in the lot and continuing to the building.

In her cubicle, a sheet of paper lay folded in half on her chair. With trepidation, Nora picked it up. It was a note from Joyce. "See me as soon as you get back" was all it said.

Nora's stomach lurched. *Busted*, she thought. Her time bomb of a résumé had finally ticked down to zero. *Not necessarily. It could be something else*, she tried to reassure herself as she navigated the warren of cubicles to reach Joyce's. She took a deep breath and stepped into the entryway.

Joyce was seated at her desk with her head bent over some document. She was in her forties and heavyset with a perpetually annoyed expression. Nora had the impression Joyce didn't like her, but she didn't think it was personal. Joyce didn't like anyone very much. And if it was what Nora expected, it didn't matter anyway.

"You wanted to see me?" she asked.

Looking up, Joyce swiveled in Nora's direction. Behind her tortoiseshell glasses, her eyes were dark brown discs, large and inscrutable.

"Come in." she said. Nora entered slowly. Alongside Joyce's desk, there was a chair. Joyce didn't invite her to sit down, so Nora stood next to it.

"Harry wanted me to talk to you. He seems to think we're not fully utilizing your talents."

"Oh," Nora said, not relaxing. *Too soon. There might be a catch.*

Joyce picked up the document she'd been looking at and extended it in Nora's direction. Nora took it and glanced at it. It was a spreadsheet, two pages long, stapled together, with her name on the top of both pages.

"Your updated project list," Joyce said. "Everything currently assigned to you is on it with working titles, due dates, and billing codes. The jobs are over there," she added, nodding toward a work table across from her desk.

On the table, Nora saw a stack of dark-green job folders. It looked like six or seven inches of new projects. "Great," she said, still processing this development, not sure what to make of it, but it had to be a good thing.

"The folders are arranged in the order we'd like you to do them in, so no shuffling, please," Joyce continued in a no-nonsense tone of voice. "It took a lot of effort to pull all this together. Do you have any questions?"

Nora glanced at the spreadsheet, then at the stack on the table. A thought occurred to her, and she turned back to the spreadsheet, scanning it, looking for one item. "I don't see Wyman," she said at last, flipping the page back.

Joyce regarded her with genuine-looking bewilderment.

"The Oceanfront Renewal story, Wyman and Associates," Nora clarified. "I don't see it on the list."

"Oh, that. Harry said to do it around everything else as you see fit. As far as he's concerned, it's a side project."

Nora nodded. More to process, but it sounded like good news. Apparently she could take her time calling Wyman or not do it at all.

"Good luck," Joyce said, dismissing her. "Take the folders with you. If you run into problems, let us know, preferably before the drop-dead date."

Going to the table, Nora lifted the stack, balancing it in both hands along with the spreadsheet. "Tell Harry thanks," she said with a quick glance in Joyce's direction.

Joyce grunted a response, already moving on, busy, no doubt, with whatever was next on her own to-do list.

Back in her cubicle, Nora eyed her pile of new projects, preparing to dig in. It might be interesting to do them Joyce's way—in strict top-to-bottom order, one at a time, no cherry-picking, no peeking ahead. Let each project be its own small surprise, like an award show where the master of ceremonies holds up the envelope. Nora picked up the top folder. *Drumroll please—and the winner is . . .*

Extracting pages, she leafed through them and set to work translating a press release from the mayor's office about a new dog park into something that resembled a newspaper story. Not exactly riveting stuff, but at least it wasn't another society party or a kitchen appliance.

As the afternoon wore on, Nora got into a rhythm, a loop in which the stack of projects on her left slowly shrank and a new stack on her right slowly grew.

After each transfer, Nora recorded her time in a notebook she kept for that purpose and walked to the break room, the bathroom, or the kiosk on the first-floor lobby, a less-attractive alternative given its proximity to the funeral museum. Then, reversing her steps, she picked up where she'd left off.

By four o'clock, Nora had succumbed to fatigue and a feeling that words were heavy, dull things you lugged around, and when you'd finished smithing and polishing, had finally stripped away everything extraneous and gotten down to the who, what, when, where, and why of it, what you were left with was likely to be "New

Dog Park Set to Get Tails Wagging." Not that there was anything wrong with that. People needed to know.

Abandoning her current story—an article about vertical gardens, which she'd tentatively titled "Time to Grow Up"—Nora stood and stretched. She'd given up on Jack. He wasn't coming in, or he had and he was avoiding her. After Junior's he might be too embarrassed, but his tip had panned out. And she still wanted him to un-bug her car.

What to do? If she left now, where would she go? Home to change out of her dress? Then what? She could call Wyman. It wasn't too late. *No*, she decided, and sat down again. *Tomorrow*.

CHAPTER 14

In line for the eight o'clock show at Hambone's, Nora extended her ID and a five-dollar bill to the security guard working the door. She'd left the *Sun* around six. Tense and too wound up to go home, she'd grabbed a bite to eat and meandered, one turn leading to another, until she found herself pulling into Hambone's parking lot, which was what she'd intended all along. She was still wearing the dress.

"Sorry, sweetheart, I'm not buying it," the security guard said, dismissing Nora's ID. The guard was tall and wide and dressed in a torso-hugging black T-shirt. A snuffed candle with wisps of smoke coming off the wick decorated the T-shirt's front—advertising for Curse's end-of-the-world show, no doubt. At the moment, the candle was barely visible behind a pair of massive forearms folded across his chest.

The situation was plainly ridiculous. Back in her college days, she and Jillian never had any trouble getting into clubs. Meanwhile, in the here and now, people with presumably less-suspect credentials were piling up behind her. Nora was about to give up when a hand from behind lightly gripped her upper arm and a male voice said, "Hey, Neil, quit hassling the lady. She's with the band."

Startled, Nora turned to look. The person attached to the voice was pale and pleasingly lean. He had long, center-parted blond hair and a scruffy Jesus beard. In his right hand he held a guitar case.

"Hi, Curt, great to see you, man. How was Seattle?" The security guard lowered his arms.

"Awesome, we killed." Curt grinned. "Good to see you, babe," he continued, turning to Nora, confounding her with soulful blue eyes. With a conspiratorial wink, he added, "I was beginning to think you weren't coming. Nice dress. Is it new?"

"No, I haven't worn it in a while," Nora said, aware she was being played. Within her, something was stirring. It had been a long time. She gave him another look and thought, *Maybe*.

"Well, you look terrific," he replied, his hand still on her arm.

"Okay, man, have a great show," the security guard said, pretending to relent and waving them through.

Past its art deco facade, Hambone's was long and narrow with unadorned brick walls and a concrete floor. To Nora's right, the bar ran most of the length of the wall, staffed by two female bartenders wearing the same promotional T-shirt as the security guard.

A stage with a midnight-blue backdrop took up most of the back area. A mismatched jumble of tables and chairs filled the remaining space to the fullest extent allowed by the fire code—which, according to the sign posted across from the bar, was 360 occupants. About half that many were already inside, and people continued to file in.

"Thanks for the assist," Nora said, still sorting out her feelings. They were standing at the back of the room while she tucked her money and ID into her wallet "I guess if you want to get anywhere, the magic phrase is 'I'm with the band.' That's good to know."

"Glad I could help," he replied, unleashing a killer smile. "In case you're wondering, I'm Curt. That's with a *C*, not a *K*, and I really am with the band." He held up his guitar case.

"Pleased to meet you, Curt," Nora said, puzzled about the "*C* not a K" business but not so mystified she wanted to ask. She should probably make up a name. Jillian always had. It was part of the game. "I'm Nora," she said, deciding not to add to the air of unreality already surrounding the moment.

"Lovely name; it suits you," Curt said, and reached for her hand.

Gun-shy after her experience with Wyman, Nora tensed, but it was her left un-braceleted hand, and nothing happened. Her wrist remained quiet.

Fingers intertwined, they wended through the room toward the stage. It was slow going, with frequent stops to greet fans—mostly middle-aged but not exclusively. Occasionally Curt grinned in her direction, but he didn't introduce her or make any effort to bring her into the conversation, which was fine with Nora. Whatever role she was playing, it wasn't a speaking part.

From the conversations going on around her, she realized that Bliss was a tribute band, a close copy of Nirvana, whose lead singer was also named Kurt, but with a *K*, not a *C*. Her Curt bore a strong resemblance to the original, Nora decided, doing a side-by-side comparison of the flesh-and-blood one beside her and the one peering from faded T-shirts and other fan gear.

As they approached the band table, Nora got a shock. Two blondes were seated at the far end, cuddled together, softly cooing. Both had platinum hair, one's cut in a short asymmetrical slash, the other's long and curly, cascading to her shoulders in ringlets.

They were young, probably too young to be here, and she resented being lumped in with them. Swiveling their heads, they registered Nora's presence and quickly looked away.

Nora stopped. "I know," she said and let go of Curt's hand. "They're with the band."

They came back with us from Seattle," he replied, gazing at Nora. His eyes were very blue. "Just ignore them," he continued, his voice a seductive purr. "Tonight's all about you. After the set, why don't you come backstage? We can get to know each other better."

They were moving again. Nora didn't respond.

"So, are we good?" he asked as they approached the band table.

"I don't know." Tonight was beginning to feel like a mistake.

Tight-lipped, Curt started for the stage door, his guitar case swinging as he walked.

"Hey," Nora called after him.

He turned toward her.

"Have a great show."

Curt grinned, gave her a nod and started walking again. *So apparently I'm staying*, she thought. *It would be really crappy to leave now.*

Seating herself at the other end of the table from the blondes, Nora adjusted her chair so they weren't in her direct line of sight. Eventually a waitress came around, and she ordered a gin and tonic, her old college standby. She was pleased to discover the drinks were free if you were with the band, and apparently no one got carded, not even underaged blondes.

Let it go, Nora told herself, glancing at the junior end of the table, then self-consciously down at her dress, thinking, *The last time you wore it, you weren't much older than they are. You really should leave. Nothing good can come from this.*

She took a sip of her drink. Her Weekend Capsule had gotten it right. The drinks at Hambone's were large and potent. As for the graffiti in the bathroom, that could wait for another time.

Nora was working on her second gin and tonic when the house lights dimmed and Bliss came out, Curt on lead guitar, flanked by another guitarist with a drummer behind him. The band might have been a copy, but they delivered.

Buzzed, Nora let the music possess her, felt Curt's vocals and amped-up guitar chords crash against her. It was so loud that even the surface of her drink rippled, and when she reached for her glass, she could feel the vibrations in her fingers.

Their set ran about seventy-five minutes with a finish that smelled like teen spirit. The applause subsided, and the house lights came on. The blondes rose, clip-clopping in their stilettoes toward the stage door. The moment of truth. Nora stayed put. She picked up her gin and tonic to polish it off.

By now the fizz was mostly gone and the ice cubes had melted. Even watered down, she could feel the alcohol's bite on her tongue, and her lips and cheeks tingled. She was still sitting, trying to decide what to do when Curt came back onstage. Conspicuously ignoring her, he picked up his guitar and held it up, scowling as he examined it.

Nora rose, paused for a moment and headed out with a quick glance back. Part of her, the sane part, hoped he wouldn't follow. She was standing by her car as he approached. His untucked shirt flapped up and down, playing peekaboo with his belly button.

"Are you taking me for a ride?" he asked, a sheen of sweat on his face from his on-stage exertions.

"Don't you have another show to do?"

"Not for twenty minutes. It's okay if I'm late. They'll wait."

Nora took a deep breath and looked down, touching her bracelet, reassured it was still in place. Her tattoo was shielded.

"Scared?" he asked.

"A little." The key fob was in her hand, and she chirped the car, watching as he went around and opened the driver's side door for her. She got in. Her heart was hammering. Around her, the air felt hot and thick. Something was stirring.

People were arriving for the next show, and it took a while to exit the parking lot. Nora took a right past Hambone's, turned right again, and pulled into a bank drive-through. Drifting into the far corner of the lot away from the security lights, she killed the engine.

They met over the gearshift. Curt's breath hissed in her ear, and his hands groped for her, urgently grappling with her dress to tug it down. Seams ripped, and the dress gaped open.

"Hey, slow down. Take it easy." Nora pushed him away.

With avid eyes, Curt watched her slip the torn dress from her shoulders and down her arms. Reaching out, he took her hand and guided it toward his lap. Her bracelet snagged on his waistband and continued inside.

Curt screamed. Violently recoiling from her touch his shoulder struck the door. Horrified, Nora watched him grapple with the handle. The door lurched open, and he tumbled out, struggled to his feet, and hobbled off.

Heart still racing, Nora sat there, trying to make sense of what had just happened. She'd felt something too, but it was mild, a mere tickle. Poor Curt. She was wearing her bracelet, and it hadn't done any good. This was much worse than her experience with Wyman.

Should she go after him? She couldn't, not in her ripped dress. And besides, he was afraid of her. She couldn't blame him. Lifting the dress, she held it in place as she reached across to close the passenger-side door. *Get out*, she thought. *Go home. You've done enough damage for one night.*

CHAPTER 15

One hand hovered over the keyboard; the other propped up her head as Nora tackled the next story from the stack on her desk. It was another one on gardening—specifically, garden walkways. So far all Nora had managed was the headline. "Choose the Right Path" struck the appropriate note and was indisputably sound advice although clearly something she'd never done.

Her mind was still stuck on the previous night's debacle. Jillian's dress, damaged beyond repair, was currently draped over her bedroom chair, haunting her apartment with its reproachful presence. *I should never have worn it. What was I thinking? Wait, are you blaming the dress? What you wear changes who you are. Yes, but not completely. You're still responsible.*

Dress or no dress, she couldn't deny she'd been attracted to Curt. It was meant to be a meaningless fling, a let-yourself-go time-machine trip into the past. The dress may have facilitated that, but it hadn't attacked Curt. That had been Nora—or, rather, her tattoo. She glanced at her wrist. After last night's debacle, she'd switched bracelets and was wearing Jillian's enamel-and-gold one again.

Maybe it was time. She was tempted to call Wyman, caught herself reaching for the phone, and hesitated. *No,* she decided, *I'm not ready.*

With a sigh, Nora forced herself to sit straight and focus on the screen. Rereading her headline, she tabbed down a line and wrote, "Pathways can be straight and narrow, broad and winding or elaborate and branching, but whatever shape they take ..." She paused and, after a moment's contemplation, added, "... the right one can add interest and intrigue to any setting."

Interest and intrigue on a pathway? A new low, even for her. The world wasn't mocking her. It was snickering in disbelief. Gloomily, she deleted everything she'd written and started over.

Nora was unproductively pecking away when Harry's email arrived, subject line "Jack Switzer."

Harry's message was reassuring, downplaying Jack's misadventure and reducing it to a stumble in the dark. Jack would be out for a while, but he was expected to make a full recovery. Details followed for anyone who might care to visit him in the hospital or send flowers.

Agitated, Nora reread it, one more thing to feel guilty about. She'd known Jack was drinking himself into a stupor. She should have offered him a ride home, but she'd been angry and anxious to leave, and he would never have accepted it anyway.

No good, it didn't exonerate her. Too restless to sit, Nora headed to the break room and poured hot water into a Styrofoam cup. Rummaging through the box of herb teas, she found a packet of lemongrass and vigorously dunked, sending worried ripples through the hot liquid.

The rest of the newsroom seemed to be taking the news in stride. "Good old Jack," the consensus seemed to be. "If you're going to fall down a hill, dead drunk is the best way to do it."

Finally, Nora packed up her laptop and headed to the hospital, impatiently maneuvering through the early rush hour traffic. As she passed the hospital information desk, she was tempted to ask if anyone named Curt had been admitted recently.

Too weird. Besides, I don't even know his last name. Stopping instead at the flower kiosk by the elevator, she bought a dozen tulips. *A bit past their prime,* Nora thought as she examined them in the elevator, *but good.* She wasn't coming empty handed.

Jack's door was open. "Hello," Nora called out. She waited for a response, didn't hear one, and cautiously entered. Plumped up in bed, Jack turned his head in her direction and managed a small welcoming nod.

"Hi, Jack, sorry to hear about your accident." Nora shyly advanced, taking in his swollen, battered face. His forehead and nose were swathed in bandages. He had two black eyes and more bandages on both arms.

"Hi, Nor. 'ood of you to come," Jack said with a wince. "I 'it off a piece of my tongue." He opened his mouth as though he was about to show her, decided against it, and closed it again.

"I brought you some flowers," Nora hastily said before he could change his mind. She lifted the tulips into Jack's line of sight.

"'ice," he said with a fleeting smile as painful to witness as it must have been to produce.

Eager to move on, Nora scanned the room for a vase. The only one in sight was on the dresser across from the bed, and it already held a showy bouquet of red and blue flowers with sprigs of greenery. She placed her flowers down beside it.

A card was propped against the vase, and she leaned forward to read it. "Get well soon. No more falling off cliffs," the card said. "We need you in one piece." It was signed, "Your colleagues at the *Sun*."

"Cool. Everyone's concerned about you," Nora fibbed, turning toward Jack.

"'ucky me," he said. The bitterness in his voice surprised her, but she could understand it. According to the police report, which she'd checked before she came, Jack had spent the night by the creek. A young boy, wandering down to catch minnows, had discovered him. Jack's pickup truck left overnight in the parking lot apparently hadn't raised any concerns.

There was an armchair beside the bed. Recrossing the room, Nora sat down. On the other side of the bed, a dinner tray rested on a stand. On it, a slab of meatloaf, some mashed potatoes, and a mound of peas sat untouched—a troubling sign in someone who until now had been so omnivorously, insatiably hungry.

"Sorry, I should have offered you a ride home," Nora said, finally getting it off her chest. "I should have offered you a ride."

"'ouldn't have made a difference."

"Why not?"

"Just a matter of time. I didn't fall. I was 'ushed."

"Why would someone push you?" Nora asked, not sure she believed him. Jack could be annoying, but to throw him down a hillside and leave him for dead took vexation to a whole new level.

"Hello, coming in," a voice interrupted, followed immediately by a nurse in scrubs carrying a flower arrangement. She appeared to be in her early thirties, tall and thin with lank brown hair. Her hazel eyes projected niceness, and seemed oblivious to the irritated-at-being-interrupted glance Nora cast in her direction.

The flower arrangement she was holding hid her name tag, but there was a whiteboard next to the dresser, listing on-duty staff. Nora looked at it and decided she was probably Wendi—small circle over the *i*—Capehart.

"These just came. Aren't they lovely?" Nurse Capehart enthused, holding up a straw basket filled with yellow carnations. A wide yellow ribbon twined around the basket's circumference and concluded in a large bow with drooping tendrils.

With effort, Jack turned his head to look. Given the state of his face, his expression was hard to read. It could have been a smile or a grimace. Personally, Nora found all that yellow off-putting. *Cowardice, disappointment, and disease, they're all yellow. Caution, too, come to think of it. That might not be so bad.*

Nurse Capehart put the basket down on the dresser. "Oh, look, there's a card," she said, spotting a small yellow envelope camouflaged among the carnations. With the panache of a game show host about to announce the big prize, she removed it. Would you like me to read it?" she asked.

Jack lifted his hand and lowered it again as if to say, 'Be my guest.'

Careful not to tear the envelope, Nurse Capehart removed the card. Nora would have let it rip. With a puzzled expression, she examined it and wordlessly gave the card to Jack.

"'hit," he said. The hand holding the card dropped to the bed.

Reaching out, Nora took it from his slack fingers. A cartoon rat had its tail caught in a trap. His eyes bulged from his head, and a long red tongue speared out of his mouth while his paws frantically windmilled the air and a triangular wedge of sprung cheese arced overhead. Underneath, printed in scratchy letters, Nora read,

Snap! Better watch your step, Jack. Not every rat gets a reward.

The card was unsigned, and the back was blank. Perturbed, Nora handed it to Nurse Capehart, who reluctantly accepted it and put the card down beside the basket.

To Nora's dismay, Nurse Capehart didn't seem to be in any hurry to leave. First she took Jack's temperature and blood pressure. Then she plumped his pillows, and then she picked up his fork and cut his meatloaf.

"At least try it; you need to keep your strength up," she said, holding up a forkful. Jack's mouth remained defiantly shut. Since the carnations had arrived, his mood, none too cheery to start with, had turned increasingly glum.

"How about a milkshake? I bet something cool would feel good," Nurse Capehart coaxed.

"'nilla," Jack relented. That was all it took. A moment later, she was gone.

Nora had been biding her time, reexamining the card. She put it down and sat beside Jack.

"What gives, Jack?" she asked. "Who pushed you?"

He shook his head.

"Does it have something to do with me?"

"Please go," he said. In his blackened eyes, Nora saw fear.

"Can we at least talk about it?"

"No." He grimaced and turned his face to the wall.

As Nora waited for the elevator, she saw Nurse Capehart returning with a vanilla milkshake and a plastic vase. *For the flowers I brought*, Nora thought, touched by her thoughtfulness.

"Thanks for visiting," Nurse Capehart said, stopping in front of Nora. "I know he appreciates it."

"I'm glad he's in good hands. Jack can be ..." At a loss, Nora paused. "... difficult," she decided. "He's a character."

"Oh, he's not so bad." Nurse Capehart smiled. "He just needs time to settle in. That card was strange though."

"Yeah."

There was an awkward silence.

"Well, thanks again," Nurse Capehart said, looking ready to move on. "Hope to see you around."

Not sure what to say, Nora flashed a goodbye smile, thinking, *Not likely, not after the way Jack dismissed me. He's scared*. She pressed the button for the elevator. It came, and she stepped in.

Snap. Jack didn't fall; he was pushed.

CHAPTER 16

The Goldmont Marketing Association Lunch and Learn takes place the first Wednesday of each month (summers excepted) and according to the organization's website, "provides a lively forum for networking and professional development with presentations by some of the industry's foremost movers and shakers."

Arriving as part of a delegation and with twenty minutes to kill, Harry headed for the drink line. He hadn't attended in a while and was here only because the *Sun's* general manager was the guest speaker. His topic, successfully managing a newspaper in a changing media landscape, struck Harry as rich.

The paper was losing money, subscriptions and advertising revenue were down, and Harry had heard rumors a major reorganization and layoffs were in the works. Hang on or look for another job? Today's presentation might help him decide.

Stuffing a dollar in the tip jar, he took his drink, sipping as he surveyed the room. A woman started toward him, smiling with anticipatory pleasure. She appeared to be in her early thirties and was wearing a cream-colored blouse, a black pencil skirt, and red high heels.

Around her neck she wore a silk scarf, the boldness of its pattern jumbled by the elaborate way it was knotted. Max Rage would have welcomed her with open arms; she was definitely a babe. Harry clutched his drink and wondered what she wanted.

"Hi, Harry. Finally," she greeted him. In the noisy room, he couldn't quite catch her name. *Presley*, he thought, *something-Presley or Presley-something.*

"If you have a moment, I'd love to get your advice," she continued in a flirty voice.

Harry cautiously nodded.

"A client in Portland is looking for a media heavyweight. Someone in your mold. Her hand fluttered, landed on his forearm and lingered. "It's a brand-new position, and it needs a real go-getter, someone who can grab the reins and hit the ground running. Do you know anyone who might fit the bill?" Her expression said, 'I'm looking at him.'

A headhunter. The usual bullshit. "How did you find me?" Harry asked, annoyed and slightly alarmed. He wasn't job hunting—not yet, anyway. And even if he were, her timing was terrible.

This was a public event intended to show confidence in the company he worked for, not a job fair. There were about sixty people here, eight of them from the newspaper. Someone watching could get the wrong impression or the right one, depending.

"Oh, I have my sources," Presley replied. She lifted her hand from Harry's arm and dipped into her purse. It emerged, holding a business card. "In case you know anyone," she added, extending it to him.

Harry quickly took the card and stuffed it into his jacket pocket. He could dispose of it later. "I'll think about it," he said.

"Thank you. It was a genuine pleasure talking to you, Harry. Ciao." And with a conspiratorial smile, Presley moved on.

Taking another sip of his drink, Harry went back to surveying the room. Robin was bound to be here. *Might as well get it over with*, he thought, and glanced at his watch. *Ten minutes until lunch. Good, I can keep it brief.*

Unmistakable in her light-blue pantsuit, she was standing by the hors d'oeuvre table. As he watched, she picked up a bunch of grapes, popped one in her mouth, and vigorously chomped.

"Well, hello, stranger. Long time no see," she said with a toothy grin as Harry approached. "Did they have to drag you here kicking and screaming, or did you voluntarily turn yourself in?"

"Hello, Robin. Good to see you. Looks like a decent turnout."

When he'd worked at *Motherlode,* they'd come to these events together. As a newcomer, Harry could use the exposure, Robin had insisted. He suspected she liked having a chauffeur—one who never asked for gas money. Back then, she was the organization's president; now she headed up the program committee.

"Our best turnout this year," Robin said. "A lot of people are interested in what's happening to the *Sun.*"

Harry caught the insinuation. "How's *Motherlode* doing?" he countered. "I haven't seen it in a while, but maybe I'm not shopping at the right stores." The magazine was distributed from racks by the checkout counter, where it shared space with other free publications. Advertising and personals paid the freight, or used to. That might not be enough anymore.

Robin's grin, which had gradually subsided, reemerged. It was an enigmatic grin. It seemed to suggest there were things she could say if she chose to. Harry had seen it before and waited.

"I hate to bring it up, but there's something you need to know," she continued with the air of someone who had wrestled with her scruples and emerged victorious. "One of your reporters pitched me a story. Unsolicited, of course."

"Is that so?" Harry said, suppressing his annoyance. Most of the articles in *Motherlode* were written by freelancers, some of whom were also employed by the *Sun.* The paper discouraged but didn't prohibit the practice unless it was an obvious conflict of interest.

As a matter of professional courtesy, Harry ought to have been consulted. Otherwise, he might get blindsided. Like now—and by Robin, of all people. On the other hand, for Robin to bring it up when her livelihood depended on the willingness of people like Harry to look the other way was odd.

"I'm afraid so," she said and paused so he could coax out the details. Harry took a sip of his drink and waited. He was certain the details didn't need coaxing.

"I believe her name is Nora Stanfell," Robin continued. "It was a history piece. She seemed to think she'd solved a local mystery—something everyone else had missed. It was a lot of speculation, some of it wild. Of course, I couldn't use it. But I thought I might be able to offer her some guidance, as I'm sure you've been trying to do." Robin made a face. "Apparently I was mistaken."

Harry kept his face carefully neutral. *Nora again.* "Sorry to hear that," he said. Around them, people were sitting down.

"Oh, I don't care. If it were only me, I wouldn't mention it. I'm concerned with how she might be impacting the paper, the reputational harm she could be causing you. I don't want to tell you how to run your department, but you might want to sit her down and give her a talking to."

"I see," Harry said. By now they were the only ones standing.

"Well, take care. I'm glad we've had a chance to talk." Robin plucked the last grape from the stripped stem and dropped it on the hors d'oeuvre table. "You should come more often."

Remembering his drink, Harry took a healthy swallow, with his eyes following Robin to the front of the room and the empty seat next to the *Sun's* general manager.

It's no big deal. She's head of the entertainment committee; he's the guest speaker, Harry told himself. His hand went to the jacket pocket with Presley's card in it, feeling for it through the fabric. *Maybe I should hold onto this for a while.*

Two days later, the card had migrated to Harry's desk. Outside his office while he talked on the phone, Nora idly observed Harry's posture—the way he hunched forward in his chair, and how his hand curled around the telephone receiver to screen the lower part of his face from view. *Standard office paranoia,* she thought. *People whisper and act like they're hiding something even if all they're doing is making lunch plans.*

Irresolutely shuffling her feet, Nora considered leaving. She needed Harry to approve her time sheet, but it could wait. The newspaper was now taking forty-five days to pay. An extra weekend hardly mattered.

She was still making up her mind when Harry looked in her direction, smiled apologetically, and raised an index finger so now she was committed. She had to stay. Time passed slowly. One minute became two, became three. Finally, Harry hung up the phone and motioned for her to come in, simultaneously picking up the card and tucking it into his shirt pocket.

"My time sheet," Nora said, getting right to it, holding it up as she advanced.

Harry took the time sheet from her, placed it on his desk, and appeared to study it. "Looks like you're staying busy. Good," he said, and signed it. "Anything I should know about?"

"No," Nora answered, not sure where she'd even start.

Harry nodded. "Tough news about Jack. Have you seen him? How's he doing?"

"Oh, you know Jack. He's grumbling and complaining, but the hospital's taking good care of him. It was nice of us to send flowers. I didn't know the paper had a budget for that."

"It doesn't. That was me," Harry said with a slightly embarrassed smile. His voice dropped to a whisper, and he added, "Shut the door."

Alarmed and trying not to show it, Nora complied.

"I understand you've been working on a side project," he continued when she was seated again.

Nora looked at him mutely. There was only one way he could have known about that—only one person who could have told him.

"A history piece, I gather. Something about our little town," he prompted her.

"Yes," she said reluctantly.

"Is it any good?"

"What?"

"Your story. Is it any good?"

"I think it is."

"Think or know? History stuff tends to put our readers to sleep, in some cases permanently. We really can't afford to lose any more of them."

Not sure where this was leading, Nora remained silent.

"Send it to me if you want," Harry continued. "No promises, but we might be able to use it in *Weekender*. You'll get a byline and some extra cash."

"I don't know," Nora said, hating how tentative she sounded. "I'm not sure it's a good fit."

"Well, it's your call. Whatever you decide is fine," he said, and leaned back in his chair. The conversation was over.

Back in her cubicle, Nora tried to make sense of it. Before she went in, Harry had been on the phone, possibly with Robin.

Why would she entice him to read my story? Nora scowled. *Obviously she expects him to hate it. Should I send it anyway? "My call," he said. I think I want him to see it, even if he can't use it. But first I'm going to reread it, polish it, and proof it one last time. After that, it's out of my hands.*

CHAPTER 17

With a parting smile, Harry stepped into the elevator. The job interview had gone well. Presley's client, a commercial real estate firm in Portland, needed a senior content editor to oversee a newsletter and series of technical booklets.

Harry had come prepared and was satisfied with his performance. He'd shown an appropriate level of enthusiasm, had asked the right questions, and had worked at looking thoughtful and savvy, making it clear he had plenty left in the tank.

The interviewer, a woman approximately half Harry's age, had seemed impressed, although of course she might be faking. As for her description of the job, it was hard to judge, but nothing she said seemed wildly inconsistent with the facts Harry had already uncovered. In short, he felt reasonably hopeful, and if the company came through with an offer and the money was good, he might accept. Then again, he might not.

Spinning through the revolving door, Harry exited the building, joining the throng of office workers heading to lunch. Impeded by his bad back, his pace was slow, and people streamed past him. At the first restaurant he came to, he opened the door and was assailed by the din of chattering diners and clanging cutlery. Too noisy. He wanted someplace where he could unwind before driving back to Goldmont.

Closing the door, he continued down the street. He was running out of options. His car was parked in the corner lot, and he didn't intend to walk any farther than that.

A voice behind Harry intruded on his thoughts. "Well, hello, stranger. Fancy meeting you here."

Startled, Harry stopped and turned. Ratdaddy was standing behind him, looking almost preppy in a navy-blue blazer, khakis, and a light blue dress shirt open two buttons down on his chest. He was carrying a gym bag.

"What are you doing here?" Harry asked, too surprised to hide it.

"This is my turf. I live here. You're the one who's out of place," Ratdaddy replied with one of his only-kidding, not-kidding smiles. "Come on." He slapped Harry across the shoulders. "I'll buy you lunch. I insist."

Damn. Now what? Harry ruefully glanced at his car as they passed the corner lot. *Better to know. Keep your enemies close. A good rule but painful to follow.*

Ratdaddy set a grueling pace, and Harry had a hard time keeping up. Three blocks later, he finally stopped in front of something called the Muscle-Up Café, a cafeteria-style restaurant located next to a twenty-four-hour fitness center.

Ratdaddy held the door open, and they entered, taking their place in line behind a small crowd of people who seemed to think they looked good in spandex. Some of them did.

"Nice to see you again, Mr. Ratskeller. How was your workout?" the counterman greeted them when it was their turn to order. The counterman was jowly with a belly that pressed roundly against his restaurant-logo T-shirt—a hopeful sign in an eatery whose mission statement, posted on the wall, proclaimed its commitment to "healthy and nutritious" but didn't mention "tasty" or "filling."

"Not yet, Mike. Change of plans." Ratdaddy sounded almost genial. "I'll have my usual, and see what my friend wants."

Scanning the menu board for something he wouldn't mind ordering, Harry settled on the Yup-a-Doo wrap, which consisted of steak and turkey bacon with a special sauce and a side of hash browns. His selection principle was simple: it was the heftiest item on the menu, weighing in at 652 calories. Ratdaddy's Chick-Chick wrap was a mere 420.

Ratdaddy pulled out a money clip and peeled off some bills, and together they staked out a table at the back of the restaurant, busying themselves with collecting utensils and napkins and pouring drinks from a large glass urn containing filtered water on a bed of sliced cucumbers.

Finally settled, Ratdaddy dug into his gym bag, pulled out an object, and placed it in the middle of the table. "Yours?" he asked with an inquisitive air.

It was a beat-up copy of *Dead Certain*. The spine was cracked, pages had come unglued, and the cover was ripped down the middle and bandaged with clear tape.

"I wrote it, if that's what you mean," Harry replied cautiously, glancing at his battered book. It wasn't much of an admission. His name was at the top in big white letters.

Below that, an anxious-looking blonde, dressed in a bath towel, pointed a gun at nothing in particular. After all this time, her presence continued to rankle. She didn't have a damn thing to do with the story. She didn't even look as if she'd just taken a shower.

"I thought so," Ratdaddy said, sounding pleased with himself. "I saw it lying around."

"Did you like it?" Harry asked. It seemed safer than enquiring where Ratdaddy had picked it up or how the book had gotten into its present condition.

Ratdaddy looked thoughtful. "I liked the fight in the poolroom," he finally said. "The fat guy who gets thrown out the window, does he live?"

"Yes, he lives," Harry said, disappointed, but it was his fault for asking. The fight took place in chapter 1, somewhere around page six, and the window was on the first floor.

"Good There's no point teaching someone a lesson if they don't survive it."

With a smile, Ratdaddy put his hand on the book and slid it the rest of the way across the table.

It was a pleasant smile, agreeable even, and for a moment, Harry thought it was directed at him, but then he saw a young woman in a Muscle-Up T-shirt and tan shorts bustling toward them, bringing their order. Maybe it was a case of don't crap where you eat, but Muscle-Up Ratdaddy seemed a lot better mannered than the Goldmont version.

"Hey, Emil, good to see you." Their server smiled back.

Interesting, Harry thought. *So around here, he isn't Ratdaddy.*

"One Chick-Chick," she continued, putting a plate down in front of Ratdaddy. "And one Yup-a-Doo." She set down Harry's. The wraps were big and squat and sealed in aluminum foil.

"Thanks, Darla," Ratdaddy responded, but it was to her back. She didn't have time to dawdle. The place was filling up as worked-out bodies from next door continued to pile in.

At 652 calories, Harry's Yup-a-Doo felt substantial and had good hand heft. The first bite wasn't bad, just slightly hollow. The second bite pleased him less, providing the semblance of substance without the pleasure he associated with eating.

Ratdaddy obviously didn't share his qualms. He vigorously chomped his white meat and reduced-fat cheddar Chick-Chick, washing it down with cucumber water.

Finished, he swiped a napkin across his lips, crumpled it into his plate, and, in a getting-down-to-business voice, said, "Okay, Harry, time to talk. What's going on with your star reporter? Have you checked her credentials like I suggested?"

Stalling, Harry took a bite of his Yup-a-Doo, slowly and thoroughly chewing. "There's nothing to check. She's a model employee," he answered.

"I see, and the fact that she lied to you, doesn't have a journalism degree, never even graduated from college, and has all kinds of dubious associations doesn't bother you? You're perfectly okay with all that?"

Harry shrugged. It bothered him, at least some of it, but it was none of Ratdaddy's business.

He was still holding the Yup-a-Doo, and he set it down. "I've been wondering," he said, looking up, deciding to chance it. "What makes her so interesting? Why do you care?"

If Ratdaddy was annoyed, he didn't show it. "Just trying to be helpful," he said. Reaching down, he picked up his gym bag and stood. "It was good seeing you, Harry. We'll talk again in Goldmont."

Troubled, not looking forward to the walk back to his car, Harry watched Ratdaddy wave to the counter guy on his way out. The book was still on the table. Harry picked it up and tucked it tenderly into his briefcase. Abandoning his Yup-a-Doo, he waited a few minutes to make sure the coast was clear, then left.

CHAPTER 18

Dr. Silverblatt leaned forward in her leather chair, and impassively listened as Felony ran through her "Where I Go from Here" exercise. Her decision to share it had been last minute and impulsive. On her way out the door, she'd walked past the notebook lying facedown on the coffee table. Hesitating, she'd backtracked, stared at it, and, undecided, slipped it into her purse.

Finished with her recitation, certain she'd made the wrong decision, Felony waited. Dr. Silverblatt slowly stirred. Her hands had been loosely resting in her lap, and she took a moment to smooth her skirt, which was long and rust-colored.

"It's a good start. It's important to sort out your thoughts," the doctor said with a gentle smile. "A wise person once told me you can't plow a field by turning it over in your mind. Now that you've surveyed yours, what's next? Where does Jillian go from here?"

Felony's face tightened. She reminded herself that Dr. Silverblatt was allowed to use her real name, but that didn't mean Felony had to like it. Taking a moment, she shut the notebook and rested her purple fingernails on its chartreuse cover. The clash of colors annoyed her, made it obvious it wasn't a serious notebook.

"Good question. I wish I knew," she said with a grimace.

Not letting her off the hook, Dr. Silverblatt placed her hands back in her lap and waited.

"The truth is I'm done," Felony continued when the pause had lasted too long. "I can hang on for a while. I still have fans, but it's only delaying the inevitable."

Dr. Silverblatt cocked her head, her expression questioning.

Felony's mood, already dark, turned darker. "I don't know." She scowled. "Something's got to give. This can't go on much longer. It just can't."

That same evening around nine o'clock, Felony was hurrying out of Whole Foods when a male voice somewhere behind her shouted out her name.

She kept walking. *Probably a fan. Pretend you didn't hear.*

Felony had been soaking in the tub when she remembered she needed coconut oil for the shoot tomorrow morning. *It's a bad sign when you start forgetting the important stuff.* Shaking her head, she stepped out of the tub and threw on some clothes: an old Sleater-Kinney band T-shirt, baggy shorts, flip-flops, and the Indianapolis Colts cap. No makeup, but that was okay. It was going to be a quick in and out.

Her pursuer was closing fast. *Please don't be crazy,* Felony silently prayed as she turned to face him. It would probably be okay. The parking lot was well lit, and there were people around.

"You're Felony Foster," he said, pulling up alongside her, making it sound like an accusation.

Not speaking, she took him in. He was tall and muscular. His hair was tugged into a rat tail, and he was wearing a black warmup suit with white stripes running up each leg.

"I thought I recognized you." He flashed a toothy smile. "I do *Before She Broke Her Mother's Heart.* You've probably seen it. I need to verify a few facts for an upcoming segment."

Felony scowled. He was probably lying. She hadn't seen his show or even heard of it, and the so-called journalists covering the industry never let facts get in their way.

In the last year, Felony had seen stories claiming she was HIV positive, had gotten an abortion, and had just been dumped by a rock star whose popularity had peaked in the early 90s. Only that last item was kind of true. It had been a couple dates, and his music sucked.

"Your real name's Jillian Wexler," her pursuer continued in a down-to-business voice. "You're from Evansville, Indiana. You grew up in a good salt-of-the-earth family. I've seen your prom pictures. Very sweet. And oh—I almost forgot—you have a couple arrests for shoplifting. Did I miss anything?"

Felony looked at him with unconcealed loathing. *He's trying to intimidate me. It's working.* Her car was about fifty feet away. She started walking toward it.

"According to my sources, you left college midway through your senior year," he said, his voice at her ear, keeping pace. "You had a roommate, Nora Stanfell. I've seen her photo. You were lovers, right?"

Felony kept walking, faster, with her head down.

"What happened? It must have been something."

She stopped; they were beside her car. "Listen, I don't know what your game is, but leave Nora out of it." Her voice was shaky but defiant.

"So, it's all perfectly innocent. Nothing to hide. Or are you feeling guilty?"

"I'm feeling it's none of your business. We haven't seen each other in ages," she said, immediately regretting it. Better to stay silent.

"You might want to keep it that way. You seem like a bright girl, Felony, Jillian, whoever the hell you are. A storm's coming, and believe me, you don't want to get caught in it."

"Is that a threat?"

"No, of course not. You're free to do whatever you want. It was a pleasure meeting you." He smirked. "Now, if you'll excuse me, I have some shopping to do." And turning his back on her, he strode toward the store.

CHAPTER 19

God, what a farce. Felony's costar, who went by the name Ice Cold, had downed too many boner pills along with a Trimix shot—she could see the bloody dot on his penis—and couldn't perform. Ice's erection, lurid purple and swollen, jutted from his groin like a tuberous growth. Getting him dressed had been a challenge, and they had to leave him unzipped.

Still on the couch but sitting now and wearing a short robe, Felony watched a production assistant support Ice out the door for a trip to the emergency room.

"You don't have to go in. Just drop him off at the entrance," the director had told the PA, who was young, female, and trying hard not to look.

At least she'd get paid. For Felony, it was a wasted morning, not to mention how wounding it was to her vanity to have a partner who needed to swallow a fistful of pills and shoot up his dick to get hard for her.

In a way, though, she was relieved. Anal was always a trial, even with coconut oil, and last night's parking lot encounter was still troubling her. She'd checked when she got home. *Before She Broke Her Mother's Heart* didn't exist, or at least she couldn't find it. As she replayed the conversation in her head, she was surprised how much of it had focused on Nora.

What was Nora up to now? It was none of her business, and

Nora wouldn't appreciate hearing from her anyway, so that was settled.

On her way to lunch, Felony dutifully checked in with her agent Nick. She tried to sound unruffled, even amused by what had happened at the shoot, but she finished by telling Nick to add Ice Cold to her won't-work-with list.

Nick chuckled. Felony's list already included about half the guys in the industry and a significant number of the women.

"What about going on the dance circuit for a while?" he asked after a pregnant pause. "You know, get in front of your fans and build back the excitement."

"It's easy money," he continued when Felony didn't respond. "All you have to do is take it. You don't even need to do a full act. Just show up and flash some skin. The hicks will love it. Plus you can sell photos. They'll line up to have their picture taken with Felony Foster."

Felony had never toured, but she'd heard stories: club managers who ripped you off; customers who bought you drinks with god-knows-what in them; and those four in the mornings when you were too buzzed to sleep and you stood at the window, staring into the parking lot, hoping the sun never came up.

"Talk to me, Felony. What do you think?"

"Sorry, busy intersection. I needed to concentrate."

"Right, all I'm saying is it's time to refresh your brand."

"Got it. I'm a brand."

You know I only want what's best for you. How long has it been?"

"How long has what been?"

"Since we started working together."

"About a year and a half," Felony said without needing to think about it. He was her third agent. The first one had disappeared; the second one was serving three to ten—nothing to do with her, fortunately.

"Well, it's been a great run," Nick replied.

"Yeah." The restaurant was coming up on the left. Felony slowed down and signaled for a turn. "Let me think about it. I'll get back to you," she said.

"Good. Whatever happens, you know Felony Foster will always be number one in my book."

"Yeah, I know."

She turned.

CHAPTER 20

Jack was going home. His face had gone from swollen and raked raw to scabby and healing under a coating of antibiotic ointment, and his various body parts were functioning more or less as nature intended. They just needed to find something he could wear. The clothes he had on when he came in were shredded beyond repair, and Nurse Capehart had told him days ago he needed to make arrangements.

Finally, after too much running around, she'd managed to scrounge up a set of surgical scrubs. They were tight even with a drawstring waistband, but at least they were decent, covering up all the things that needed covering. Now she was distressed to learn no one was coming to pick him up.

"Isn't there anyone you can call?" she asked in a calm-under-duress voice. The young woman, who had visited at the beginning of his stay, hadn't returned, so probably not her, but Jack had a sister. She'd stopped by two or three times. Nurse Capehart had been struck by the family resemblance. "What about her?" she asked.

Sitting on the side of the bed, Jack compressed his face into a pout and folded his arms across his chest. "She can't afford to miss work," he said carefully, still learning how to articulate with a truncated tongue. "She's a single mom with three kids. What about a cab or an Uber?"

"No." Nurse Capehart shook her head. It was strictly against hospital policy.

Jack's only other visitors had been three guys, one of them

sporting a Mohawk. Awkward and solemn, they'd trooped behind her to Jack's room and grouped themselves around his bed, looking more like a delegation than a gathering of friends.

When she came by on her rounds, not that much later, they were gone. A white T-shirt with "Old Farts Club" blazoned across the chest in an antique typeface bannered the back of a chair. Below the text, a codger, bent double, supported by twin canes, smirked as a billowing green cloud emerged from his ample buttocks.

"What would you like me to do with it?" Nurse Capehart had asked, holding out the shirt as if there might be some doubt about what she was referring to.

"'urn it," Jack had said. "Burn it," he corrected himself, glaring as she folded the T-shirt and placed it in the closet. Since then, the shirt had migrated, and it was now tucked into a plastic bag with his shredded clothes and a few other personal effects.

"No one you can call? Maybe someone you work with," Nurse Capehart asked.

"No," Jack said, looking defiant. "No one."

"Okay, a cab it is," Nurse Capehart decided. The rules were important, but sometimes you had to bend them.

A knock sounded on the door, and an orderly entered pushing a wheelchair, which he parked beside the bed. Jack stared at it in disbelief at this new indignity being visited upon him.

Enough, Nurse Capehart decided. She didn't know why he was behaving so badly, but the wheelchair wasn't negotiable. Everyone who wasn't dead left in one. She was about to tell him so when the orderly turned to her and said, "His ride's here, a black Chevy Tahoe."

Jack instantly deflated. Exhaling sharply, he lowered his head and let his hands dangle beside him. Alarmed, the orderly moved toward him, but Jack waved him off. With a grim smile, he stood, positioned himself and dropped into the wheelchair. Crouching beside him, the orderly lifted Jack's feet into the stirrups.

"Okay." Jack gripped the armrests. "Let's get it over with."

In silence, with the orderly pushing and Nurse Capehart walking beside Jack, their little procession started down the corridor toward the service elevator. The bag containing his personal effects rested in his lap. Alongside it was a goody bag with a tin of Johnson's Baby Powder, Hope-in-a-Jar skin cream, some Neosporin ointment, and a package of Depends.

"Goodbye and good luck," Nurse Capehart said with a parting wave as the elevator door opened. "It was a pleasure caring for you."

Jack responded with a glum smile and lowered his head.

Strange, Nurse Capehart thought as the doors closed and the elevator descended. *If he had a ride coming, why didn't he say so?*

CHAPTER 21

In a coffee shop a few miles down the road, Nora interviewed the hospital's Good Samaritan of the Year for a story on volunteerism—another small assignment from Harry's seemingly endless story carousel. As promised, she'd sent him the history piece. That had been three days ago. So far, he hadn't responded. If he never did, that would be okay. She was ready to move on—unless, of course, he loved it.

It was time to end the interview. Her Good Samaritan was very grandmotherly, but Nora had spent more time than she could justify and certainly more than she could bill. Currently she was looking at a phone photo of the Samaritan and her therapy dogs, three friendly-looking fluff balls that got wheeled through the hospital in a miniature baby carriage.

"Very nice," Nora said, handing the phone back. "Why don't you send me the picture? I can't promise, but we might be able to run it with the story."

They were still sitting when a pinging sound came from Nora's purse.

"Do you need to check your messages, dear?" the Samaritan asked, looking up from her phone. She wasn't having any luck with the picture.

"It can wait," Nora said. Text messages were never good news. The night her father died, she'd texted him and hadn't gotten a response—her first inkling something was wrong. Since then, she'd been broken up with and fired by text. If she was lucky, the current message would be nothing worse than an e-coupon from her neighborhood dry cleaner. Another ping followed a few moments later. This time they both ignored it.

Back from the interview, sitting in her car in the newspaper parking lot, Nora finally checked her phone. Her Samaritan had managed to send the photo. *Good for her.* Nora thought. It was sappy but sweet. She was glad she'd remembered to ask. Harry would probably appreciate her diligence, not that he was likely to say so.

She was about to put her phone away when she remembered those text messages. Letting her thumb hover over the app, she reluctantly tapped.

"Hi, it's Jillian ..."

Nora lowered the phone. Bad news, but bad from a long time back. Steeling herself, she raised the phone again and read: "Hi, it's Jillian. Hope you don't mind hearing from me. I'm coming to Goldmont on business and would like to see you. It's probably too late to make amends, but we can at least clear the air. If you don't want to, I understand. BTW a couple nights ago I was ..."

The message broke off. Nora quickly scrolled to Jillian's follow-up message.

"... accosted by some weirdo. He seemed to be obsessed with you. Something about a coming storm. Scary-looking motherfucker, tall and muscular. I don't know his name. You might want to watch out."

Incredulous, Nora lowered her phone. *Now what am I supposed to do with that?* she thought, instantly alarmed. *Call Wyman? What if it's Wyman or even Hector?* Putting her phone away, she stepped out of the car and nervously glanced around. As far as she could tell, she was alone. No one was following her.

"Yes, I'd like to see you," Nora hastily wrote when she got to her cubicle. "What else can you tell me about this stalker? It might be important."

"Honestly, not much" Jillian immediately responded. "Like I

said, tall and muscular, beady eyes, and his hair was pulled into a small tail."

So not Wyman or Hector, which was some comfort.

⟋⟍⟋⟍⟍

In his office in front of his computer, Harry was finishing his critique of Nora's history piece. Asking to see it had been a mistake. He'd been curious, but mostly he'd wanted to one-up Robin by publishing a story she'd foolishly rejected. Except he couldn't use it either. Not that it was terrible.

Leaning forward, hands steepled at chin level, Harry reread his note:

> I like your story, but you didn't finish the job. If you're going to dig up a body, dig it all the way up. You're suggesting Tony Goldmont was murdered by local business interests with the likely involvement of our newspaper. One-hundred-year-old murders are notoriously hard to solve. Those involving our town's founder and your employer require even more spadework. If you want to pursue this story, you need to keep digging. But remember: no matter how much research you do and how strong the case you make, it's not likely to be bulletproof. Think it over and let me know what you want to do. No rush.

Pondering, Harry skimmed through his message again and deleted "No rush." It sounded too much like a kiss-off. Satisfied, he pressed send and watched the message disappear from the screen. He hoped, really hoped she'd drop it.

CHAPTER 22

Saturday afternoon at a table at the corner of Home Improvement Avenue and Remodelers Lane, Nora sipped iced tea for the caffeine boost and checked the time on her phone again. She'd been at the home and garden extravaganza for almost four hours, and she had one more event to cover.

On the table, notes from a manufacturer's rep extolled the wonders of precision multi-LED cook technology. A canvas tote bearing the extravaganza's logo lay at her feet, stuffed with brochures, press kits, and product samples Nora had accumulated throughout the day.

She shut her eyes for a moment and let her mind drift. She saw herself trudge up the steps to her apartment, dump the contents of the tote on the kitchen table, then wearily sift and sort the pages she'd dog-eared and annotated. Dull, very dull, but that was the point. Staying busy was a good way to avoid thinking about things.

At least she wouldn't be wasting more time on the history piece. Not after Harry's critique. Rejection hurt, even when it was sugarcoated, but Nora could see Harry's point; she had even tried to warn him it wasn't a good fit for the *Sun*. To her relief, there had been no follow-up discussion, and it didn't appear to have changed their relationship. He was still feeding her work.

Nora sighed and took another swallow of her tea. In the three days since Jillian's warning, she'd gone from agitated and anxious to jumpy but resigned because realistically what could she do?

Contact the police and tell them what exactly? That someone might be stalking her? *No, I haven't seen him, but I've heard he's out there.* At best, they'd humor her and file a report, which might be useful after the fact but would do nothing for her in the here and now. That left Wyman, except she still didn't trust him. Nora sighed again.

"Hello," a deep voice rumbled, startling Nora out of her thoughts.

She looked up. Hector, large and towering, was standing across from her.

"Oh," Nora replied, surprised but not entirely displeased. Today Hector was wearing what looked like a vintage chauffeur's outfit. A jaunty gray hat with a black brim was tucked tight on his very large forehead. A gray double-breasted jacket covered the immensity of his chest with rows of shiny black buttons.

"You'd better sit down." Nora said, indicating the chair across from her. They were attracting attention. People were doing double takes, and the rent-a-cop at the cafeteria exit kept shooting glances in their direction. Moving the chair aside like so much dollhouse furniture, Hector lowered himself to his knees and leaned forward.

"What brings you here? You don't seem like the home and garden type," Nora asked, trying not to look too deeply into his eyes.

"I've come to fetch you. We need to leave." Reaching across the table, he extended a huge slab of a hand toward her. Nora hesitated.

"Don't worry; I'm wearing gloves," he said, apparently misunderstanding her reluctance.

Do I or don't I? Nora placed her left hand in his and felt his fingers close around her. His grip was snug but not painful.

The extravaganza was in the event space at the local shopping center. To leave, they'd have to travel the entire length of Home Improvement Avenue, pass through a set of double doors, and exit through the food court.

Together they rose and set out. Hector's pace wasn't fast, but his strides were long, and Nora had to work to keep up. *The canvas tote,* she remembered. She'd left it by her chair. *All that work. Too late now. I'm not going back.*

As they continued along the avenue, people scurried to get out of their way. The rent-a-cop had abandoned his post by the cafeteria exit and was following them, keeping his distance. They'd almost made it when a figure emerged from the crowd and planted himself in front of the double doors.

Nora froze. It was him, tall and muscular with dark brown hair fastened in a short tail, the stalker Jillian had warned her about.

"Get away from that girl. Leave her alone," he bellowed in a voice calculated to incite. "Now, if you know what's good for you."

Stirred by his call, people crowded around them, a posse of concerned citizens, their interest in bathroom fixtures and major appliances subsumed by outrage at this brazen abduction occurring before their eyes. On the periphery, the rent-a-cop continued to monitor the situation. It appeared Nora was in imminent danger of being rescued.

"It's all right," Hector said, his voice deep and unfazed. "Take off the bracelet and keep moving. Head for the exit. I'll back you up." He let go of her hand.

Back me up? Startled, Nora looked at him.

"Go on," he encouraged her. "Let him see your tattoo. He's afraid of it. We all are."

Reluctant, hands shaking, Nora shrugged off Jillian's enamel bracelet. *Now what?* She shot a quick glance at Hector—he was still guarding her back—then turned to face her stalker again.

Fists balled at his sides, he was staring at Nora's naked wrist. His expression hardened, and he slowly started toward her. In a panic, Nora threw the bracelet at him. It struck his chest, clanked to the floor and rolled away. *Damn.* After all this time, she hated to lose it.

Hector had told her to head for the exit, but to do that she would have to go toward the stalker. Instead Nora juked to the right and was stymied by the crowd and an elaborate plumbing display. He was still coming. Nora braced herself.

Alongside her now, he raised his arm and draped it across Nora's shoulders, avoiding her tattoo, getting ready to lead her away. Nora's pulse was pounding, and under her tattoo, her wrist felt as though it was on fire. She raised her arm and swung. He was too quick for her. He ducked, and her wrist lightly grazed his cheek.

Nora's world exploded. Pain, ferocious and scalding, shot up her arm and engulfed her in waves of flowing scarlet. Around her she heard shouts and screams, the sound of things smashing, and then nothing—nothing at all.

PART II

Three Years Earlier

May you never, oh never behold me
Sharing the couch of a god.
May none of the dwellers in heaven
Draw near to me ever.
Such love as the high gods know,
From whose eyes none can hide,
May that never be mine.
To war with a god-lover is not war,
It is despair.

—AESCHYLUS, *PROMETHEUS BOUND*

CHAPTER 23

"Are you sure you're old enough, sweetheart?" The tattoo artist asked with a self-amused grin, barely glancing at Nora's college ID. The artist was pale and thin, almost emaciated, with white-blond hair down to his shoulders, and he had a billy-goat tuft of beard. Above his right eyebrow, a jagged line of metal Xs made his forehead look as if it had been crudely sutured. From his nose, a small ring dangled, and another ring hung from a corner of his upper lip.

"Yes, I'm sure," Nora replied, on edge but trying not to show it. Coming here tonight was a big deal. It had taken a long time to work up the courage. For the occasion, she'd dressed in an old pair of jeans and an oversize work shirt, and she'd pulled her hair, which was mostly chestnut brown with residual splotches of purple, into a messy ponytail.

Catching her reflection in the mirror behind the counter, Nora realized she might have miscalculated. In her attempt to appear sexless, she'd managed to make herself look about fifteen years old. Some guys might find that a real turn-on.

And what about you?" the artist asked, directing his attention to Nora's friend Anita, stationed by the door with her arms folded in front of her. "Are you getting inked, too?"

Visibly startled, Anita shook her head. Squat and pudgy, she was dressed as usual in khakis and a fully buttoned-up long-sleeved shirt. Around her neck, a small silver cross dangled from a chain. She and Nora sat next to each other in Psych 225—Principles of Abnormal

Psychology—and they were in the same study group. Anita had hesitated but had finally agreed to accompany Nora here tonight.

"So just you." The tattoo artist said, focusing on Nora again. "What can I do to you?"

In her left hand, Nora held a small manila envelope. She nervously opened it, removed a three-by-five notecard, glanced at it as though to reassure herself, then extended it to him. "This," she said, "I want this."

Her mark, unique and individual. She'd worked on it for almost six months after her father's death, adding and stripping away details, deliberating over matters of color and form, putting the drawing aside and coming back to it until finally, when she was most frustrated, she realized there was nothing left to add or subtract.

It was what she'd been working toward all along, only she hadn't known it. Not some dippy, misconstrued Chinese characters to be inscribed on a shoulder or a pseudo-Latin profundity to run the length of her forearm so everyone could see what a serious, thoughtful person she was. This was all hers, unique and individual, and now, finally, she wanted it inscribed on her skin.

The artist took the card and glanced at it, started to put it down, changed his mind and looked at it again. "Interesting," he said, finally laying the card on the counter.

"But can you do it?" Nora asked. Everyone said it was the best tattoo parlor in town, and the sign out front promised "Free tattoos for ladies. $5 piercings," so the price was right.

"Yeah, but not for free, if that's what you're thinking. Those are the free tattoos." The artist pointed to a display behind him where butterflies floated, hearts fluttered, and Tinkerbells waved wands full of pixie dust. "Flash sheet stuff," he added in a dismissive voice. "Just slap it down and color it in. Ten minutes tops and you're done. What you have in mind isn't going to be quick or easy."

"How much?" Nora asked, swallowing her dismay. Money was tight, and she'd been counting on it being free, minus a generous tip of course.

"Since you've got a college ID, let's say three hundred. It's a good deal. Normally, I charge three seventy-five."

"Okay," Nora reluctantly agreed. That long-deferred haircut would have to wait a while longer, and she'd need to make some budget cuts. What cuts she didn't know; her budget was already pinched.

"Great. You won't regret it," the artist said. All business now, he lowered his head and took another look at Nora's drawing, studying it.

The moment of truth. I'm putting myself in his hands. Do I trust them? Nora asked herself, focusing on those hands spread out on the counter.

The word "HELL" was tattooed on the fingers of his right hand; on his left was "FIRE," one letter per finger, mirror-reversed for easy reading. Starting at his wrists and extending up his bony arms, an inked jumble of ghosts and ghouls tussled, disappeared beneath his T-shirt sleeves, and reappeared on his neck amid tongues of fire. *Yes,* Nora decided, *I trust him. I'm not sure why, but I do.*

"Your drawing's cool," the artist said, looking up. "All those curves and swirls. You don't have a single straight line. But are you sure about the colors? Pink and purple aren't exactly a fashion statement."

"I don't care," Nora said, too sharply. It had surprised her, too. She'd tried a lot of combinations and had kept coming back to that one.

"And where are we putting this little number?" the artist asked, moving on.

"Here." Rolling up her sleeve, Nora extended her right arm to expose her wrist, slight and slender with a pale tracery of veins and nerves near the surface.

"Are you sure?" the artist said. "I put it there, it's gonna hurt like hell. You'd be better off somewhere where you've got some padding."

"I don't care. That's where it goes. On my right wrist. Do we have a deal?"

"Indeed we do," the artist said, raising his hands in mock surrender. He came out from behind the counter, picked up the drawing, and headed toward the back of the studio with Nora close behind. Anita trailed after them, reluctantly abandoning her post by the door.

The tattoo parlor had two workstations. Stopping at the first one, the artist gestured to a large reclining chair—it looked like something you might find in a dentist's office—and waited while Nora eased herself into it.

Beside the chair, there was a round stool with a padded seat, and next to that a portable table laden with the tools of his trade. The artist placed Nora's drawing on the table, then sat down. Positioning her wrist on the armrest, he stared at it then ran his fingertips over the wrist, lightly stroking.

"I'm ticklish," Nora said, resisting the urge to jerk her arm away.

"Don't worry; I'm not going to tickle you," the artist replied. Tugging on a pair of surgical gloves, he swabbed her wrist with an alcohol wipe, then carefully shaved and dried it. Finally, he picked up a marker.

"Hold still. Try not to fidget," he said and started sketching, going back and forth between Nora's wrist and the drawing, slowly mapping it onto her skin.

Nervous, Nora turned toward Anita. Her friend was seated about ten feet away, balancing a textbook in her lap, apparently too absorbed in it to look up. Her right hand, pressed against her collarbone, covered her silver cross, hugging it close.

So much for moral support, Nora thought, and turned away. The artist was still sketching. Too anxious to watch, Nora closed her eyes and let her mind wander.

"Got it. Take a look," she heard him say. Unsure how much time had passed, she opened her eyes. "It was a bitch to place," he added, looking pleased with himself. "It had to be exactly right or it would have looked wonky. What do you think?"

Raising her arm, Nora peered at her wrist, examining his sketch. "It's good," she said at last, satisfied. She allowed herself a quick glance in Anita's direction. *Still studying. So be it.*

"Now the fun begins," the artist announced. He removed a

needle from the autoclave, and let his fingers travel over the assembly, making miniscule adjustments that seemed to Nora like a mental deep breath before he plunged in.

"Try not to move. If you need a break, let me know. It shouldn't be that bad."

Nora heard the needle buzz and gasped as she felt the sting of it piercing and repiercing her wrist. It hurt. God, did it ever. It brought tears to her eyes. Nora concentrated on her breathing—slow, deep, in and out. It helped, but not enough.

It took about fifty minutes, with periodic pauses, to refill the ink tank and swab away droplets of blood. And when it was over, she had to max out her credit card to pay for it, but it was worth it. He'd done what she wanted—rendered her intentions with absolute fidelity.

As Nora put her wallet away, she started to feel dizzy. "I'm … I don't know. Everything's spinning," she murmured, leaning against the counter to support herself.

"Tattoo shock," the artist said knowingly, standing on the other side of the counter from her. "I jabbed you about a thousand times a minute. Your body thinks it's being attacked. All that adrenaline piles up and fucks with your system. Don't worry; it'll pass. There's a cool lounge upstairs. Why don't we go up? Maybe listen to some music, smoke a little dope, and drink some wine."

Still shaky, Nora watched him stroke his billy-goat beard and imagined a ghost-and-ghoul tattooed arm around her waist, supporting her up the stairs. Anita trailed after them, scowling over her textbook.

"Nora, are you coming?" Anita's voice cut through her fantasy. She was standing by the door, holding it open, staring daggers at Nora.

"Sorry, she's my ride home," Nora said with a woozy smile. Beneath the bandage, her wrist was starting to throb.

"Next time," the artist said with a philosophical shrug.

"Nora!"

"Coming," she said, not quite ready to move. On the counter, a stack of pamphlets sat, "HOW TO CARE FOR YOUR NEW

TATTOO" on the cover, white block letters against a dark green background. She took one and stuffed it into her back pocket.

The ride back to campus was short and jerky. Anita stared ahead, driving slowly, braking with exaggerated care at every stop sign and light almost turning red. For her part, Nora looked out the window and watched the world lurch and flow. The throbbing in her wrist had grown more intense. It almost felt as though her heart had migrated underneath her tattoo and was beating there.

"Well, that was interesting. I don't believe you," Anita said, finally breaking the silence. They were in the dorm parking lot, sitting in her idling car.

"Why are you so angry?" Nora asked in a voice that felt as if it were coming from far away but was recognizably hers.

"I'm not angry. I'm disappointed. I didn't think it would bother me. Live and let live, but what you did back there is wrong."

"I got a tattoo. That's all," Nora managed to say. The stream of cool air blowing from the car's vents was soothing, and she tried to focus on that.

"It's wrong. Cutting your flesh is wrong; it's ungodly," Anita replied in an aggrieved voice. "Your body's a temple for the Holy Spirit. It comes from God. It's for his glorification, not yours."

Nora frowned. She'd known Anita was religious, just not that religious. *My body belongs to me,* she thought. *It's mine. I can do what I want with it, and no one can tell me otherwise.*

Turning off the engine, Anita thrust open the door. "Are you coming?"

"In a moment," Nora said, and let her head fall back on the seat.

"You're not going to be sick, are you?" Nora heard concern in Anita's voice, but mostly for the upholstery.

She opened the door, rocked forward to free herself, then leaned back against the side of the car, and waited for this latest wave of dizziness to pass. About five feet away, Anita glowered. Monday's abnormal psych class was going to be more abnormal than usual.

"Good night, thanks for the ride," Nora said. Shutting the car door, she set out not toward the dorms but in the other direction. She was weaving, but that was okay. It was Friday night. Anyone who saw her would think she was drunk.

"Hey, where are you going?" Anita shouted after her.

"I don't know," Nora called back, or perhaps she only imagined it. She was setting out, finally going to seek her destiny. That she had a special one, uniquely her own, had long been an article of faith not supported by her teachers, school counselors, or any of the other responsible adults in her life.

Eventually she'd learned to keep the destiny business to herself, had discovered that once you got past the "Hi, sweetheart, how's my little princess?" stage, people no longer were willing to humor you.

It didn't matter. Destiny was private and personal, a path no one else could follow but anyone could despoil. It needed to be fiercely guarded until one day after a long winter, the first tender shoots broke through. Someone would knock on your door with an urgent summons. A shaft of light would blaze forth and bathe you in its glow. But until that glorious day, you had to blunder and seek, weaving around parked cars with a throbbing wrist and a headful of thoughts you couldn't share.

The parking lot became a sidewalk, then a street, followed by an illuminated greenspace with groves of trees casting shadows across the grass. A cluster of school buildings fronted the area on one side. Between the two center buildings, a narrow cement walkway ran.

The walkway ended in a small cobblestone courtyard confined behind a chain-link fence. Through its links, Nora saw a circular pool with jets of water arcing into the night sky. The gate was unlocked, and she entered.

In the center of the fountain, through the spume and spotlights, a towering bronze figure stood, nude except for a drapery strategically placed around his neck and flowing down his thighs. Nora approached, marveling at the fury concentrated on his bearded face, the power in his upthrust arms and clenched fists, a battering ram to shatter the sky if only he could break free.

Easing herself down at the fountain's edge, she dangled her feet, not bothering to remove her sneakers. The water felt cool and welcoming. Taking out her wallet, keys, and the pamphlet, she placed them on the grass then slowly lowered herself, letting the spray from the fountain rain down on her.

At first she kept her wrist elevated, but by degrees it, too, descended. The throbbing had become less intense. The water was helping. Leaning back on her elbows, Nora drifted, occasionally glancing up at the bronze figure above her. Was it her imagination, or had his expression changed? He was almost leering. It had to be an illusion, a last vestige of tattoo fever.

After a while, she became aware of a whirring sound. At first barely audible over the cascading water, it grew louder and more insistent. Nora stood and turned. A spotlight shone on her, narrowing and intensifying as it approached, holding her in its glare. Raising her left hand, she attempted to shield her eyes.

Two figures appeared, backlit by the beam and glowing around the edges. "Well, well, what do we have here," a male voice jeered. "Looks like there's a fish in the fountain. Or is it a mermaid?"

"Easy, Larry," the second voice, higher pitched and female, answered.

"Want I should get the net?" the male voice continued, punctuating his words with a harsh laugh.

After a moment, the spotlight cut out. Lowering her hand, Nora stepped from the pool and grabbed her things. Two figures were advancing toward her. As they got closer, she saw their uniforms. The campus cops had arrived.

"Are you all right, miss?" the female cop asked, standing close enough for Nora to see her badge and read the name tag pinned to her shirt. Officer Tameka Copeland was heavyset with short, enameled-looking hair curled in a tight wave. She wore hoop earrings, and her fingers were studded with long nails, buffed and polished to a pearlescent white.

"You scared me," Nora said in a reproachful voice. Her hair was plastered to her head in long, limp strands, and now that she was out of the water, her teeth were beginning to chatter.

"Goddammit it. How in hell did you turn the water on?" Officer Larry Roach exploded onto the scene. Middle-aged and burly, he had a ruddy face and an abrasive-looking mustache that bristled when he spoke. "If this is a sorority stunt, it's a stupid one. You're lucky we came when we did," he scolded. "It's dangerous to go wandering in the dark."

"Take it easy, Larry, she's a kid," Officer Copeland said in her good-cop voice. "Why don't you check out the scene? I'll take her statement.

"You're shivering," she continued with sudden awareness, turning her attention to Nora again. "Come with me."

She took Nora by the arm and led her to a golf cart parked on the other side of the fence. From a compartment in the golf cart, Officer Copeland pulled out two blankets. She spread one blanket across the bench seat at the back of the cart for Nora to sit on, then draped the other one over her shoulders. The blanket was snug and came down below her knees. "Better?" she asked.

"Yes, much," Nora said, hugging the blanket close, burrowing into it for warmth. Her tattoo shock had passed.

"Did something happen tonight?" Officer Copeland asked, looking at her intently. From somewhere she'd produced a clipboard with a pen attached to it by a chain. "Is there anything you'd like to tell me?"

"No," Nora said with a shake of her head.

"You do know you're trespassing, right?" Officer Copeland said, her voice a little less friendly.

"I didn't know. The gate was unlocked. I just walked in."

"And the signs on the fence warning you to keep out?"

"I didn't see them," Nora said. Her teeth had finally stopped chattering

Officer Copeland clicked her pen and wrote something down. "This site's been condemned. The fountain hasn't been turned on in ages," she said when she was finished. "Yet the gate's wide open, the lights are on, the water's going full blast, and you had nothing to do with it. Is that what you're telling me?"

"Yes," Nora replied, waiting while Officer Copeland made another note.

"That bandage on your wrist, what happened there?" Officer Copeland asked, pointing at it with her pen. "Did someone hurt you?"

"It's a tattoo. I just got it."

Sitting down next to Nora, Officer Copeland rested the clipboard in her lap. "I have one too," she said, lightly tapping her breastbone. "Me and my baby girl, matching tattoos."

"Nice. You must be close," Nora said, not sure where this was going but glad to change the subject.

"We are. She's my one and only, my wild child, always getting herself into trouble. Then a couple months ago, she came home and said, 'Momma, you're right. I need some discipline in my life. I'm joining the army.'

"'Hallelujah,' I thought, 'an answer to a mother's prayers.' The very next day, we went and got matching tattoos—overlapping hearts with each other's names."

Beaming, Officer Copeland touched her breastbone again.

"Nice," Nora managed, thinking, *March in someone else's army? No, thank you.* Her blanket had come loose. Reaching up with her bandaged wrist, she snugged it around herself again.

"What did you get?" Officer Copeland asked. "Something pretty, I bet."

Nora hesitated, not sure how to put it into words. "It's a design," she said, "sort of like a seashell, but from the inside."

Officer Copeland's smile wobbled. "I'm sure it's lovely," she gamely replied.

They were seated together in companionable silence when Officer Roach returned. "The control panel's locked," he reported glumly. "There's no sign of tampering. I guess it is a glitch in the controls."

Picking up her clipboard, Officer Copeland stood, clicked her pen, and made another note. "Time to take you home, sweetheart," she said.

Seated by herself on the back of the golf cart, wrapped in the blanket, Nora stared at the figure in bronze until it vanished in the mist. They turned, and the mist disappeared, too. Their trip ended at Nora's dorm. She hopped off the golfcart, wet, embarrassed, and anxious to escape. It was after eleven, and to her relief the area was deserted.

"What happens next?" Nora asked as she handed the blanket to Officer Copeland.

Lips pursed in disapproval, mustache bristling, Officer Roach intercepted the question. "That's entirely up to you. Keep your nose clean, stay out of trouble, and you're good. Next time, we throw the book at you."

"This report is now part of your official college record," Officer Copeland clarified her partner's statement. The clipboard had reappeared. "But don't worry; it's just a warning, and it's strictly confidential. No one will ever know unless you tell them." With her elaborately manicured nails, she pinched the bottom copy of the report, tugged it free and extended it to Nora.

Under "Offense," Officer Copeland had written, "Subject was discovered in the Courtyard Fountain at approximately 10:30 p.m. The gate appears to have been left unlocked, and the fountain was running. No evidence of tampering was observed. Subject claims not to have seen Keep Out signs posted at the site and cooperated fully with the investigation."

"We all make mistakes. The idea is to learn from them," Officer Copeland said with a sympathetic smile when Nora was done reading. Maybe thinking of her baby girl, she added, "Everyone needs to serve something bigger than them. You just have to figure out what that something is."

Nora nodded, waiting for her to finish. Without the blanket, she was getting cold again.

"Okay, I guess that's it. Good luck," Officer Copeland said.

"We'll be watching you," Officer Roach added, getting in his two cents' worth.

Not looking back, Nora climbed the steps and entered the dorm. Her suite was meant for two people, but the roommate assigned to her by the campus housing system had moved in with her boyfriend a few weeks into the school year.

No great loss. She and Jillian weren't exactly kindred spirits, and it was a lot easier to tolerate your own idiosyncrasies than deal with someone else's.

Closing the door behind her, Nora paused to shed her soggy clothes, leaving them in a pile behind her as she headed to the bathroom. She turned on the shower, waited for it to heat up, and stepped in. Water flowed over her, running in torrents down her breasts and back.

I'm going to be waterlogged, she thought as she reached for the temperature control, inching it up a little and then a little more, wondering how hot she could stand it. Very hot, as it turned out.

She was thinking about the statue again. With her hands at her sides, head bowed, eyes closed, Nora slowly descended until her bottom rested on the tile floor. Raising her hands in front of her so her palms touched, she let the water hold sway, reveling in its caress. By now her bandage was a soggy mess, sagging away from her wrist, but it somehow remained intact.

At last, languid and warmed, Nora slowly stood and dialed back the torrent until it was a trickle and finally nothing. She'd forgotten to turn on the vent fan. The air was steamy, and fat droplets of water pocked the walls and ran down to the floor in rivulets.

Nora reached for a towel, wrapped it around herself, and padded to the bedroom, leaving a trail of wet footprints behind her. As she reached the bed, she let the towel drop and fell back, lying on top of the sheets, dangling her wrist over the edge. She didn't even bother to turn off the lights.

CHAPTER 24

Daylight streamed through the window, bombastic and overbearing, like a salesman who won't take no for an answer. Nora tried turning her back to it, but it didn't help. She was awake. She threw on a cotton robe and made her way into the suite's common room. Somehow her bandage had made it through the night.

Worried about what she'd find when she unwound it, Nora procrastinated, busying herself with boiling water for tea. She poured a bowl of granola from a plastic storage container her roommate had left behind, then remembered there was no milk. She could eat it dry, she decided, carrying the bowl and a mug of ginger-root tea to the table. It wasn't a good combination. The granola was cloyingly sweet, and the tea wasn't one of her favorites, which was why she had so much of it.

Nora put down her spoon and looked at her bandaged wrist resting in her lap, and now she was in a hurry. She headed to the bathroom, quickly unwound the dressing, and tossed it in the wastebasket. Steeling herself, she raised her arm, thinking, *Please, please, please, don't be hideous.*

The intricate tracery of ink on her wrist was dotted with dried blood, and the skin around her tattoo was red and puffy, tender to the touch. But once she washed it, her tattoo looked exactly the way she'd envisioned it. Ignoring the discomfort, Nora held out her arm with her fingers flexed and gazed almost reverently at what she'd wrought. The blood, the pain she'd felt, and the dull ache that persisted, made the moment almost sacramental.

Remembering the tattoo-shop brochure, Nora returned to the mound of clothes she'd left by the door, extricated it from her soaked jeans and peeled it open.

"Your New Work of Art Is Beautiful, but It Is Also an Open Wound," she read. "Give It Time to Heal." For the next two weeks, Nora followed the brochure's instructions to "Regularly Bathe Your Tattoo. Blot It Dry with a Clean Towel. Protect It Under Long Sleeves, and Avoid Exposing It to Sunlight."

One Sunday morning as she healed, Nora returned to the courtyard, concerned that by daylight all she'd see was a concrete basin with a kitschy statue in the center.

The reality was much worse. The statue and the pool were gone, and the ground was hacked and rutted, scored with tread marks. A bulldozer was parked on the far side of the courtyard and next to it, a large dumpster overflowed with chunks of concrete, broken cobblestones, and mangled pipes.

Where the statue once stood, only the pad remained. Nora tried the gate. It was locked, and three signs posted along the fence, obvious enough now, warned her to stay out. She turned away, heading back to the dorm while she tried to sort out her thoughts.

Up ahead was the parking lot. "Tattoo shock," the artist had said. "I jabbed you"—Nora concentrated, trying to remember—"a thousand times a minute. Your body thinks it's being attacked. All that adrenaline piles up and can fuck with your system."

Was that it? Had her experience been nothing but tattoo shock? She'd never know. The statue was gone, and the fountain had been demolished. Nora stopped and retraced her steps back to the courtyard.

The fence was about six feet high. She looked to her left, then her right, then behind her. She was alone. No one was coming, no campus cops. She gripped the metal bars, climbed, and swung herself over, landing in a crouch on the other side. Apprehensive—no excuse now, she was treading on forbidden ground—Nora paced the courtyard and scrutinized its muddy, hashed-up surface.

Approaching the concrete pedestal where the statue had once stood, she hesitated, glanced toward the fence—still no cops—and stepped onto the pedestal with her hands at her sides.

Nothing. She felt nothing: no stirrings, no emanations, however faint. Nothing. Her destiny wasn't here after all. She needed to move on or risk getting caught trespassing again. *Well, at least you tried,* she consoled herself as she scaled the fence. As if that was supposed to make her feel better.

CHAPTER 25

"Hey, roomie, are you eating my cereal?" a too-cheerful voice called out, catching Nora by surprise.

It was a Saturday morning about a week since her return visit to the courtyard, and Nora was sitting on the couch with the TV on—nothing special, just background noise. She'd solved the dry cereal problem by making a quick run to the cafeteria for a carton of milk. The cereal was still cloyingly sweet, but at least she could eat it.

Nora reached for the remote and flicked off the TV. "Sorry, I didn't think you were coming back," she said, turning to watch her sometime suitemate, Jillian Wexler, approach.

Jillian had on a black tank top, skinny jeans, and high-heeled sandals. Her blonde hair was arranged in an artfully mussy shag, and she was wearing enough makeup to almost hide the fatigue lines around her sky-blue eyes and an angry bruise on her right cheek.

"No, you're welcome to it," Jillian said, positioning herself to Nora's left at the far end of the couch. "The stuff tastes terrible."

"Yeah, I know."

Getting up, Nora adjusted her robe and carried her cereal bowl to the sink. Unlike Jillian, whose disarranged hair was a style choice, Nora came by hers naturally. Other than going to class, she wasn't getting out much, and she could use a shower. Since her immersion in the fountain, she hadn't taken many.

"Are you back or just visiting?" she asked, putting her bowl in the sink and turning toward Jillian. "Because if you're back, the cupboard is now officially bare."

"I'm back. I hope you don't mind, but my folks are paying half the rent." With a tight smile, Jillian raised her hand and lightly fingered her bruise.

"Mind? No, of course not. Why should I mind?" It wasn't as though they'd been on bad terms when Jillian left. They hadn't been on any terms at all. Mostly they'd tiptoed around each other with a walking-on-eggshells awkwardness neither of them could get past.

"Good. I'm going to take a nap. If you're around this afternoon, let's go somewhere and figure this thing out. I have the impression you don't like me."

"You're projecting," Nora said with wisdom gleaned from her psych major. "Sorry," she immediately repented. "That was uncalled for. Yes, let's. I'd like that."

She could use a friend. Since their tattoo dispute, Anita had changed study groups and was defying alphabetical order by sitting in the back of the lecture hall. A thought occurred to Nora, and she added, "I should probably warn you; I'm broke." Her credit card was maxed out from her trip to the tattoo parlor, and she wouldn't be getting her insurance check for another week.

"That's okay. My treat. My father and his new wife keep threatening to cut me off. In the meantime, we might as well spend it."

"Thanks," Nora murmured, trying to look noncommittal. Other people's families were none of her business.

"No big deal. It's only money." Jillian started toward her bedroom. "If I'm not up by four, wake me."

Taking Jillian at her word, Nora rapped briefly and softly, didn't get a response, and let it slide. Motivated by the prospect of going out, she'd cleaned herself up, done a load of wash, and donned fresh-from-the-dryer jeans and a pale-green blouse.

It was an old standby, distinctive enough to look as if she might have gone to some effort, but not so out of the ordinary it would be painfully obvious if Jillian had forgotten or had decided to blow her off.

By the time they set out, it was almost seven. To Nora's surprise, they ended up in a small, dark cellar, listening to a bunch of local bands. Jillian hadn't changed clothes. Most of what she owned was at her ex-boyfriend's, but at least she'd toned down her makeup, and her eyes were now hazel, not sky blue. It was a definite improvement. It made her look like someone Nora could talk to, just not at the moment. The music was too loud, and the din in the cellar was unrelenting.

The current band, Bad Penny, made up of four women named Penny, appeared to be still learning to play their instruments. To Nora, whose interest in music was casual, it looked more like they were fighting them. Songs ended when the last person playing quit. With nothing better to do, she passed the time munching stale popcorn and sipping wine.

By the time they left, she was buzzed and her ears were ringing. Meandering, they made it back to Jillian's car, a white Mazda Miata convertible with a parking ticket under the windshield wiper.

Jillian yanked the ticket free and handed it to Nora, and they spilled into the car. Both women were struggling, Nora with her seatbelt, Jillian with retracting the convertible's canvas top. Finally, they lurched into traffic and headed out of town. The rumbling of their tires and the air whooshing around them made conversation next to impossible.

Nora settled back. She was still holding the parking ticket. Raising her hand, she let the wind tear at it, then let go. The ticket shot backwards out of sight. With a whoop, Jillian raised her hands from the steering wheel and punched down on the gas. The car surged forward.

Nora closed her eyes. Wine and popcorn on an empty stomach were turning out to be a bad combination. When she reopened them, they'd slowed down and were pulling into a roadside rest stop.

Illuminated by harsh halogens, wooden picnic tables sat under an aluminum canopy surrounded on three sides by a hilly swath of grass. Alongside the canopy, a small building was divided into restrooms with a space in between where vending machines were locked up for the night behind a metal grate. The restrooms were also locked, as Nora discovered when she tried to use them, throwing up instead on the grass.

"Feeling any better?" Jillian asked when Nora returned.

"Yes," she lied. "I guess I'm a lightweight."

With a sympathetic smile, Jillian reached across to the glove box for a baggie containing some rolled joints. Extracting one, she placed it between her lips, took a lighter from her purse and sparked it, inhaling deeply.

"This'll help." Wisps of smoke leaked from her lips as she extended the joint to Nora. Gray-green and feeling doomed, Nora accepted the joint, puffed carefully to keep from coughing, coughed anyway, and, still hacking, handed it back to Jillian.

After a couple more hits, the churning in her stomach subsided, and the acid taste in her mouth was overlaid with another taste, pungent, potent, and distinctly herbal. Immediate crisis over, Nora angled her seat back, cradled her hands behind her head. Overhead a crescent moon glowed amid a thin scattering of stars. After a while, Jillian started talking.

As Nora suspected, they didn't have a lot in common. Jillian was a poor little rich girl whose father discarded wives like other people tossed empties.

In the third grade, she had borrowed a stepmother's diamond ring without telling her, wore it to class, and lost it. When she was fourteen, she went to camp with six large trunks and wore a different outfit every day, throwing each one out after wearing it once. At the end of the summer, she came home with six empty trunks.

It went on. When she was sixteen, her father had given her a white Corvette. Within a month, she'd wrapped it around a tree. Currently, she earned her allowance by staying away from home and her father's latest wife.

"They keep getting younger and younger. At some point, we'll cross, and I'll be older than my stepmother. Now won't that be a pretty picture?" Jillian said. The joint was a dying ember, and she flicked it away.

"Sounds tough," Nora replied. Jillian's escapades and her dad's descending marital staircase were interesting in a dishing-the-dirt way, but Nora wasn't sure how literally to take her stories. "Did you really take a whole summer's worth of underwear to camp?" she asked.

"Almost. I miscounted and ran out a couple days early."

"And all that dirty laundry, what happened to it?"

Jillian shrugged. Some mysteries were best left unexplored.

For a while, neither spoke. Holding up her hand, Nora focused on her outspread fingers, mesmerized by the way the moon glowed through them. Eventually she caught a whiff of smoke and realized Jillian had fired up another joint.

"What about you? What's your story?" Jillian asked, passing the joint to Nora.

The question waited while Nora took a hit. "It's nothing special. I'm not even sure I have one," she stalled. Secrecy was a hard habit to break.

"Of course you do. Everyone has one," Jillian replied, leaning toward Nora, smiling shrewdly. "Or are you hiding something?"

"No," Nora said.

"Then give. I swear I won't tell a soul."

"It's not that. You and I are very different. You have stepmothers. My dad never remarried."

"Point for you," Jillian said. "If you want a stepmother, just say so. Do you have any particular age range in mind?"

"Thanks, but I think I'll pass."

"Good decision. What about your mother?" Jillian asked after a moment. "Mine's a self-absorbed hypochondriac. She goes from one miracle cure to the next."

"Mine died when I was six." Nora laughed hollowly. "Cancer,

but at least she didn't suffer much, or that's what I've been told. I don't know."

The joint had burned down. Pinching it with her fingernails, she took a last hit and handed it back.

"Bummer," Jillian murmured, flicking it away. "And your dad?"

Nora grimaced. "Also gone," she said, rushing to get through it, the words honed down over time to the bare minimum. "An accident. About a year ago. He was coming home. It was late. The weather was bad. He didn't make it."

"I'm sorry," Jillian said.

"No, it's okay, but thanks."

Relieved—that hadn't been so bad, and it was over—Nora settled back, sneaking a peek at Jillian, thinking they could be friends or at least friendly. It was possible. "I just got a tattoo," she said, surprised to hear herself say it. The pot was lowering her inhibitions.

"Did you? Let's see." Jillian's enthusiasm was instantaneous.

Nora extended her right arm, indicating a spot covered by her shirt sleeve.

"On your wrist. Great. Show me."

Nora hesitated. Suddenly she wasn't so sure. First she had to tell the story, featuring a creepy tattoo artist and uptight Anita, followed by the plunge into the fountain and the arrival of the campus police. In the retelling, they were simply "good cop" and "bad cop," and the golf cart ride home wasn't embarrassing.

But that still left the statue. She was tempted to leave it out. What could she say? That what she was presenting as a lark had been ecstatic and disturbing? That despite the disappointment of her last visit to the courtyard, she still yearned for the statue with a passion bordering on idolatry?

"In the center of the fountain, there was a statue," Nora began haltingly. "It was huge. I swear it almost felt alive. I sensed something." She turned toward Jillian, concerned with what she might think.

"Great," Jillian said. "So let's see this mysterious tattoo already."

Unsure, but it was too late to change her mind, Nora unbuttoned her sleeve, rolled up the cuff, and extended her hand, palm up.

Jillian reached for it, cradling Nora's hand in hers. Bending forward, her head slowly descended, and her lips touched Nora's tattoo. Startled, Nora jerked her hand free.

"Sorry, I don't know what came over me," Jillian said on her side of the car again, swiping her hand across her face. "Did you feel it?" she asked in a shuddery voice.

"Yes," Nora said. A sudden surge, as though something was stirring. With shaky fingers, she unrolled her sleeve and rebuttoned the cuff.

Jillian started the car and pulled onto the highway. They were heading back. With the roof up, it was quiet.

"Let's not …" Nora began.

"Agreed," Jillian said.

"I don't …"

"Me neither."

"Good."

CHAPTER 26

Nora stepped off the campus shuttle and strode down the town's main drag, still troubled by the previous night's events. They'd been high, but she had gotten stoned before, and nothing like that had ever happened.

Old-fashioned lust? There's always a first time. No, that's not it either. She wasn't into women, and it had come on too fast, from out of nowhere, then died away just as fast. Was there a connection between the statue and her tattoo? It seemed unlikely.

Well, something's wrong, Nora thought, glancing at her tattoo peeking out from under her shirt sleeve. She had considered going back to see the tattoo artist—when she passed, his shop was still dark—and saying what? Accuse him of what exactly? Of giving her what she wanted? Her tattoo, with its intricate whorls and shadings, was perfect. It was everything she'd envisioned. So why this sense of foreboding?

Nora's destination was in the next block. She'd visited the shop once before, impelled by curiosity. As she entered, a magpie profusion of stuff greeted her: hash pipes and rolling papers; band T-shirts and sex aids; posters, black light and otherwise; aerosol cans clearly marked *Toxic—Do Not Inhale*; and, the real point of her visit—she'd remembered correctly—a couple display cases full of jewelry.

It took a while, but Nora eventually found what she was looking for—a plain silver bracelet, wide enough to cover her tattoo. And at $39.99, it was within her price range. Mission accomplished, her tattoo shielded beneath her new bracelet, Nora caught the shuttle and headed back to the dorm.

Last night after the incident, she and Jillian had hardly spoken and had immediately retreated to their separate bedrooms. Jillian hadn't been awake when Nora left, so there hadn't been any follow-up, but their next meeting was bound to be uncomfortable.

With a sense of trepidation, Nora turned the key and entered their suite. Jillian was seated in a chair, facing the door, paging through a magazine. As Nora approached, she closed it and looked up.

"Hey," Nora said, stopping in front of her with her hands at her side, her bracelet exposed, not quite gleaming in the dimly lit room.

"Hey," Jillian replied, taking in the bracelet with a flicker of a smile. For a moment, neither spoke. "I like it," she said. Leaning forward, she placed the magazine on the coffee table.

Not sure how to respond, Nora waited, acutely aware of the extra weight hanging from her wrist.

"You hungry? I know a great lunch place. It's about thirty miles from here. They've got a jukebox, decent chili, and the beer's cold. What do you say?"

Nora hesitated, surreptitiously regarding Jillian's lips, remembering that kiss. They were nice lips, but they were only lips, nothing more. "Yes, but—"

"My treat" Jillian interrupted. Her purse was beside her on the floor. She reached for it and stood up. "You ready? I want to get the hell out of here."

CHAPTER 27

A week later, money from her insurance check in the bank, Nora was finally getting a haircut. She'd imagined a glass-and-chrome emporium, exotically lit with electronica pulsing over the sound system while stylists dressed in black with fashion-forward haircuts and dismissive attitudes glided by.

To her relief and disappointment, the place they pulled up to was just a beauty salon in a nice neighborhood with what appeared to be a primarily middle-aged clientele.

That they were here was mostly Jillian's doing. Nora had mentioned that a haircut was on her wish list and had been almost embarrassed by Jillian's enthusiasm. She even offered to lend Nora the money. "You can pay me back later," she'd said. "Whenever it's convenient. No rush."

"That's okay. I've got it," Nora had replied. It felt good to pay her own way.

Nora's hairdresser was thirtyish and pudgy with gelled canary-yellow hair. He called himself Andre, but Nora was willing to bet he'd started out as Andy.

With Jillian alongside her, Nora followed him back. Andre pointed to a chair, and Nora sat down and waited while he examined her hair, stroking and lifting, testing the texture between thumb and forefinger with a clinical dispassion that suggested it was a separate growth that happened to reside on Nora's head.

Examination concluded, he picked up a spray bottle and

thoroughly dowsed her. To Nora, peeking in the mirror, his manner suggested an exterminator dealing with a particularly bad infestation. "I look like a drenched poodle," she said, water rolling down her face, watching as Andre stepped away to dry his hands.

His reflection smiled but didn't speak. Picking up a comb, he started on Nora's tangles, separating her hair into individual strands. He was standing so close she could hear his labored breathing.

Finished, he stepped back. "I'm thinking a pixie cut," he said in a reedy voice, looking at Jillian, not Nora. "It would be fresh and cute, and it works well with her features."

Aroused, Nora vehemently shook her head. Droplets flew from her hair. Jillian, seated nearby, immediately rose and approached them. "Andre, behave yourself," she said. "She doesn't want to look like a boy."

"Well, she'd make a very pretty one," he countered, defensive and defiant all at once.

"No, absolutely not," Nora and Jillian answered, nearly in unison.

Hands raised in surrender, Andre refocused, further contemplating the possibilities. The haircut took over two hours, and in the end Nora was pleased. Shaped to her features, her shoulder-length hair flowed and flattered. No punkish vestiges remained. Andre had stripped out the purple and tinted her hair to match its original chestnut-brown color—a neat solution, but not cheap.

Astonished, Nora examined the bill and added a decent tip. So much for her insurance check, and what difference did it make if he thought she and Jillian were lovers? That they were friends was amazing enough. And it was a great haircut. "Thanks for setting it up," Nora said as they drove away.

"Glad to help," Jillian replied, taking her eyes off the road for a moment to look at Nora. "You know, with a little effort, you could be a real heartbreaker."

"Not my thing," Nora said, choosing not to be offended. It had been a good day. She hadn't thought about the statue or her tattoo all afternoon. Why spoil it now?

CHAPTER 28

Several days later, Nora gave in and went back to the courtyard. It was possible she'd missed something, but the hashed-up ground on the other side of the fence looked as dead and desolate as ever.

From the corner of her eye, she spotted a golf cart heading her way. Moving from the fence, she strode toward the nearest building. The first door she tried was unlocked and led to the chemistry department, where she wandered long enough to determine there wasn't a back exit.

Eventually, a class let out, and Nora left with them. Glancing back, she saw that the golf cart was gone and a construction company sign had been added to the trio of Keep Out notices on the fence.

As Nora started toward the dorms, an idea interrupted her, and she changed direction. In the student union, three old-fashioned phone booths stood in a hallway leading to the restrooms. Two of the phones had been vandalized, but one still worked and could be used to place an anonymous call.

"I'm sorry, run that past me again," the woman at the construction company said in a professionally courteous voice. "What project are you referencing?"

"The one in the university courtyard," Nora replied, taking it slower this time. There was a statue. Could you tell me what happened to it?"

"And who are you with?" the woman asked, beginning to sound a little annoyed.

"I'm not with anyone; I'm just curious," Nora responded—the first answer that popped into her head, probably not a very good one.

"Okay, hold, please," the woman said, and suddenly a symphony orchestra was playing in Nora's ear. She moved the receiver away, waited, then waited some more. It was taking too long, and standing in a glass booth with people streaming past was making her feel conspicuous.

The music cut out, and the voice on the other end was saying, "Sorry, but we're not currently at liberty to divulge that information. If you give me your name, I can pass your request along to the university. Is this a good contact number?"

Rattled, Nora hung up and retreated to a nearby couch. *Am I being paranoid?* she asked herself with a glance at her wrist, covered by the bracelet and quiet since that night at the highway rest stop.

Well, something's going on. Something important. I know it. I can feel it. My destiny calling? But in that case shouldn't it be obvious? How do you answer the summons when you don't know who it is or where it leads? Maybe it's nothing at all. Just your imagination. But no, Jillian felt it too.

A copy of the *Camicus State University Beacon* lay abandoned on the couch. To distract herself, Nora picked it up. As she rustled the pages, a thought occurred to her. Small and faint at first, it kept growing.

With rising excitement, Nora went back to the front page and read the entire issue: the story about the football team's ho-hum season; an editorial about underage drinking—the writer was against it; and a gushy to-say-I-was-enchanted-would-be-an-understatement review of a touring opera company's on-campus performance.

What if you pretended to be a reporter for the school newspaper? Nora asked herself, folding the paper in her lap. *You could sleuth and pry to your heart's content. People might not like it. They might refuse to answer your questions, but if you're on assignment, they won't question your reasons for asking. It's the perfect cover.*

Best to let the idea simmer for a while, she told herself, at last ready to head back to the dorm. She would have liked to use Jillian as a sounding board, but her roommate was home in Evansville, dealing with an evil stepmother crisis.

"My allowance is at stake. They're threatening to cut me off," Jillian had said, looking grim. Her suitcase, with its handle extended, sat by the door.

"Well, that sucks," Nora had replied, genuinely indignant on her roommate's behalf.

Yesterday, Nora had sent a quick text: "Thinking about you. Hope things are going well. When are you coming back?" She hadn't gotten a response. *How much patching up could Jillian be doing?*

Turning the key, Nora entered their suite. To her surprise, Jillian was sprawled on the couch, reading a book of all things.

"Hey, you're back," Nora said, smiling as she approached. "Good news, I hope."

"No, a temporary reprieve, but that's it," Jillian replied. Sitting up, she shut the book and set it on the coffee table. "The axe is coming. They're going to cut me off."

Nora winced.

"Yeah, I know. But something will turn up. It always does. In the meantime, you go with the flow."

"Right," Nora loyally agreed. Except if there was a flow, it led straight down. Jillian wasn't going to class. If her wealthy father didn't keep bailing her out, she was most likely screwed. This probably wasn't a good time to get her opinion on the school reporter business.

"Can I get you something to drink?" she asked instead. "There are a couple juice boxes left."

"Sure, let's drink to the future," Jillian replied, glancing at her watch.

Nora fetched the juice boxes and handed one to Jillian, who promptly set it down on her book. "What a crazy day," Nora began, sitting across from her. "There's something I wanted to ask you about, an idea I'm kicking around." She was going there after all. *You're obsessed*, she told herself.

"Can it wait? I need to get ready." Jillian stood. Forcing a smile, she added, "Tomorrow for sure. I promise."

"Of course." Nora stabbed her straw into the juice box. "It's probably a stupid idea anyway."

"I didn't say that. I want to hear it, just not now."

Nora watched as Jillian headed toward her bedroom. A half hour later, she reappeared, dressed in body-hugging white jeans with a matching top and purse. She'd refreshed her makeup and combed out her hair so it tumbled onto her shoulders. "Hot date?" Nora asked.

"Hot enough," Jillian said. "Looks like you're heading to the gym."

"Gonna try." Nora had changed into black nylon shorts and a red T-shirt with the university's name across the front, and she'd pulled her hair into a no-fuss pony tail. It would be her first workout since she'd gotten the tattoo. She couldn't afford a gym membership, but the work-study students staffing the front desk would generally cut her some slack if the gym wasn't crowded and no bosses were around.

"Tomorrow. We'll chat tomorrow, as much as you want," Jillian reiterated. "How about lunch? There's a sushi place I'm dying to try."

"Okay," Nora said without enthusiasm.

"No problem, my treat," Jillian replied, misconstruing Nora's response.

"No, I'm good for it." Eating out was a luxury, but one Nora could occasionally afford. Her hesitation stemmed from the fish part. She'd mentioned it before, and she was kind of irked Jillian didn't remember. "I'm not a big fan of seafood, raw or otherwise," she reminded her.

For a moment, Jillian looked blank. "Well, something else then," she said breezily. "See you later. Gotta run."

Nora's timing was good. She had no problem getting into the gym, and it felt good to get some exercise. Afterward, she had dinner in the school cafeteria, then headed to the student union for the free movie, a mildly diverting romantic comedy, which she watched with occasional glances at her phone and the awareness that she was killing time.

It was after ten when she returned to the apartment. Nora switched on the lights and saw Jillian's unopened juice box still parked on top of her book. She retrieved it and put it in the mini fridge.

Curious what Jillian had been reading, she went back and picked up the book, fanning it open. It was a collection of true-crime stories with lurid titles and photos. Nora was about to put it down when she noticed a ripped-off strip of paper tucked inside, printed from the web. She picked it up and read it:

Females wanted for photo/video shoots. 18+ Pays same day. $$$$$.

Nora held the strip in the palm of her hand and stared at it. *Nude modeling or something worse*, she decided. There was a phone number with a 463 area code: *Indianapolis. Is that where Jillian had been, not home in Evansville? She'd said the axe was coming. What if it had already fallen?* Nora could see where $$$$$ would have a strong appeal to someone who had been cut off.

With a troubled expression, she replaced the strip of paper and closed the book, careful to place it on the coffee table where she'd found it. Sometime the next day, the book disappeared, which made it that much easier for Nora to pretend she hadn't seen it.

CHAPTER 29

Getting ready for her newspaper interview, Nora stood at the kitchen counter and reviewed her notes. The sound of a key scraping the lock caught her attention, and she looked up. A moment later, Jillian entered. "Nervous?" Jillian asked as she approached, removing a pair of oversize sunglasses and positioning them on top of her head.

"A little." Nora was still waffling, not sure she would go through with it.

"Don't worry; you've got it," Jillian said from across the counter. "Have you decided what you're going to wear?"

"What I have on," Nora snapped. They'd already had this conversation, and as far as Nora was concerned, the matter was settled. She'd gone with her second-best blouse, which unlike her first-best was clean, a pair of jeans, also clean, and she'd brushed her hair.

"You're missing the point," Jillian replied. "You're pretending to be something you're not. All I'm saying is you should look like someone you're not. A costume—nothing too radical, just enough to throw people off. Trust me, I know. With the right look, you can get away with anything. Beauty may be skin deep, but it's as far as most people can see."

"Maybe," Nora conceded. She didn't like what Jillian was saying, but it made sense.

"I've got an outfit," Jillian continued. "At least look at it. And while we're at it, we could touch up your makeup." That last remark was disingenuous; Nora wasn't wearing any.

Still deciding, Nora looked down at her notes and up again.

"It can't hurt," Jillian pressed. "If you don't like the results, wash your face and change back. It's your call. I won't be offended."

Nora took a deep breath. She had an hour and a half, so there was time. And what else was she going to do? She was tired of going over her notes and too on edge to focus on anything else. "Okay," she said, wondering if she'd regret it. "Let's see."

Jillian's room looked like a clothing store dressing room at the end of a hellaciously busy day. Clothes were strewn everywhere: crammed into the closet, piled on the bed, and crumpled on the floor. Along one wall, a row of shoes led to a corner where four suitcases were stacked.

Getting ready for another trip? Nora wondered, not lingering on the suitcases. Since she'd blundered onto the nude modeling ad, her feelings about her roommate had become more complicated. They were still friends, but Jillian wasn't leveling with her. What else might she be lying about?

Well, it's her life. Jillian didn't have to confide in her, and she didn't need Nora's permission. But Nora's unwillingness to speak up was making her feel like an inverse Anita. Instead of being sanctimonious and holier-than-thou, she'd become so permissive she felt like an accomplice. Other people's behavior—her own, for that matter—was proving to be far more complicated than anything Nora had encountered in a psych textbook.

The built-in desk in Jillian's room had been converted into a vanity. A profusion of tubes and jars were lined up on it, along with a lighted makeup mirror. Jillian pulled out the desk chair and rotated it for Nora to sit down, then busied herself, picking up and putting down containers, concentrating on the task before her.

A makeup brush approached Nora's face, and she closed her eyes, caught off guard by its feathery, light tickling touch. Time passed. Nora lost track and was surprised by a hand on her shoulder.

"Done. Wake up, Sleeping Beauty," Jillian said.

Nora roused herself, slowly opened her eyes, and turned. The face in Jillian's makeup mirror was Nora's, but it was an oddly fawn-like and rosy Nora, and slightly blank looking.

"Well, what do you think?" Jillian asked.

"It's interesting," Nora managed to say.

Jillian went over to her closet and brought back a blue dress, extending it to Nora, who was standing now. "The perfect finishing touch. Try it on," she said

Almost as though she were sleepwalking, Nora sluggishly reached for it. "Turn around," she said, uncomfortable disrobing in front of Jillian. Slowly, Nora shed her jeans and blouse, leaving them on the floor, and donned the dress. Jillian zipped up the back and, with her hands on Nora's shoulders, turned her around to face her.

"Almost perfect. One final finishing touch," Jillian said, to Nora's relief, stepping back. A red enamel bracelet trimmed in gold was lying on top of the bureau, and she handed it to Nora. Accepting it, Nora made the substitution. The new bracelet fit much better than the clunky silver one she'd been wearing.

"Now you're ready." Jillian opened the bedroom door. "Go get him. I almost feel sorry for the poor bastard. He doesn't stand a chance."

Yeah, right, if only it were that easy. You can still chicken out, Nora told herself as she headed to the bathroom. *You don't have to keep the appointment.*

Standing at the sink, she glopped cleanser into her hands and scrubbed her face until the water ran clear. And now it really was time to go. To Nora's relief, Jillian was still in her room. She retrieved her notepad from the kitchen counter, stuffed it into her briefcase, and before she could change her mind, hurried out the door.

CHAPTER 30

"I'm sorry, but you're not on his calendar," Professor Littlefield's assistant said. She was fiftyish and full-figured underneath a helmet of blonde hair. Her gardenia-scented perfume filled the space around them and tickled Nora's nose.

"Could you please check again?" Nora asked, trying not to let her distress show.

The assistant hesitated, appeared to think about it, and finally picked up the phone.

On the other side of the door, seated behind a large oak desk, Professor Littlefield twirled his fountain pen, enjoying the way light glimmered across its platinum surface. Reluctantly, he put the pen down and picked up the phone on the third ring.

"Sorry to interrupt you, Carl," his assistant said. "I know you're swamped. There's a reporter from the *Beacon* here to see you. It's not on your calendar."

"Ask him what he wants," Professor Littlefield replied. He'd just returned from a highly agreeable lunch with a nice bottle of wine, and the idea of talking to a reporter from the school newspaper held zero appeal.

"It's not a he; it's a she. Hold on. I'll check," the assistant said.

In the ensuing silence, Professor Littlefield glanced at the leather binder on his desk and the notes he was halfheartedly reviewing for the department faculty meeting, scheduled for about an hour from now in his office.

The professor's specialty was the Italian Renaissance, but as department chair, he spent far too much time doing a job most of his colleagues wanted no part of even if it came with a nice bump in pay. Fortunately, it didn't require much preparation. Professor Littlefield already knew what he thought about almost every conceivable subject.

The assistant's voice came back on the line. "It's for a story on CODPRC. She says you agreed to be interviewed."

Professor Littlefield made a glum face. Pronounced "cod-perk," it stood for Courtyard Development Project Committee and was one of the professor's bigger headaches. Thinking back, he vaguely recalled a conversation. His assistant had gone down the hall for a moment, and he'd impulsively picked up the phone.

The young woman on the other end had identified herself as a reporter for the campus newspaper. Obviously a novice, she'd sounded nervous and unsure of herself. Taking pity on her, he'd agreed to be interviewed, then promptly forgot about it when he hung up. "Okay, send her in," Professor Littlefield said with the martyred resignation of an educator prepared to do his duty.

As Nora entered, he stood and gestured to a chair on the other side of his desk, self-consciously holding the pose while he waited for her to sit down. Still dapper at forty-seven, the professor had dark-brown hair that flowed luxuriantly over his collar. His shirt was black and formfitting. He had a small gold stud in his right ear, and a pair of red–framed glasses sat low on his nose.

"Thank you for agreeing to see me," Nora said once they were both seated. Not entirely comfortable in her borrowed dress, she shifted her weight forward, acutely aware of the nervous pounding of her heart. So far no one had asked to see her credentials—which was a good thing, since she didn't have any.

"Not at all, glad to help. I understand you're interested in CODPRC." The professor's voice lacked any discernable enthusiasm.

"The project's attracted a lot of interest, and we were hoping you could give us an idea of what to expect," Nora began with a glance down at her notes, where the phrase was written out Her plan was to start slow and work her way to the subject she wanted to talk about.. "As far as I can tell, there hasn't been an official announcement," she added.

Professor Littlefield smiled joylessly. Shaking his head, he said, "There are a few details to work out, but it's basically settled."

Nora waited. Please enlighten me, her expression said.

"What I proposed was a sculpture garden featuring tasteful reproductions of classic Greek and Roman art," Professor Littlefield continued. "The educational value is obvious, and it would have been aesthetically pleasing as well.

"The administration, in its infinite wisdom, has a different, more commercial vision. What they're about to impose on us—and I'm quoting now, 'is a low-overhead, high-profit retail space serving a variety of coffee-based beverages, premade sandwiches, and snacks.'

"An *eatery* in other words. I believe that's what they're calling it. Tell me, is that something you'd like? Do you find the prospect appealing?"

"No," Nora replied, sensing an opening. "To tell the truth, I liked the old courtyard."

"Did you now? And why is that?" the professor asked, looking at her from over the top of his glasses.

Shifting uncomfortably under his gaze, Nora hesitated, not sure what to say. Certainly not the truth—that she didn't care about the courtyard, just the statue, and was intent on finding it with a single-mindedness other people might consider obsessive.

"Come now," the professor coaxed. "Something about the old courtyard spoke to you. I'm curious to know what it was."

"The general ambiance. The statue in the fountain. I thought it seemed impressive," Nora said, aware of how lame she sounded.

"I see," the professor replied. "I, for one, am glad the old courtyard's gone, even if it means accepting bad coffee and sandwiches wrapped in cellophane."

"Why?" Nora blurted out, forgetting to be deferential.

With deliberation, Professor Littlefield removed his glasses, snapped the stems shut and laid them on the desk next to his pen. "Your statue is a knockoff, pure and simple. Its creator, whoever he was, took characteristic elements from neoclassical art and cobbled them together to make something big and bombastic. Truthfully, I've seen better imitations in theme parks and on municipal boardwalks."

"So it's no one in particular?" Nora's heart sank.

Professor Littlefield held up his pen. "Think of it this way. It's an object." He waggled the pen. "It's meant to look impressive, but it's a sham. What's interesting ... what might be interesting," he corrected himself, "is the bronze that was used to cast the statue. It appears to be quite old and may have come from something of genuine historic significance.

"Unfortunately, there's no way of knowing. The answer's lost in the metal." He put the pen back down beside his glasses and openly glanced at his watch.

"But why would someone take an antique and turn it into something else?" Nora asked, ignoring the hint.

"I never said it was an antique. I said it was old. You find something that's the right age but not valuable, and with enough audacity and skill you can turn it into something people care about. An old canvas covered in amateur dabblings can be repainted and passed off as an old master. A parchment scroll of someone's household accounts can become a prophet's sacred scribblings. You might be surprised how frequently it happens."

Cocking her head, Nora waited for him to continue.

"It's quite possible your statue started out as a stack of cannonballs, or it used to be a fence. Who's to say?" He shrugged in a way that suggested he didn't much care.

"I see. Just some old metal from an ancient scrapyard," Nora said, wondering: *Is it possible the magic isn't in the figure? That it's in the metal? Some sort of alchemy?*

Professor Littlefield pursed his lips. Signaling the end of their interview, he put his glasses back on and picked up his pen—still a prop, but this time one to write with.

"But how did the statue end up here?" Nora persisted.

"That's before my time, but it's my understanding it came to us as part of an anonymous bequest. To get what you want, you sometimes have to accept more than you'd like: The good with the bad, the sublime, and the ridiculous. There are always trade-offs."

Nora was still mulling over that last comment when he stood up and started toward the door. Reluctantly, she followed him. "And where is the statue now?" she asked quickly.

His hand on the doorknob, Professor Littlefield turned toward her. "Somewhere on campus, I presume. Under the terms of the bequest, we're obliged to preserve and maintain it. If you're interested, you might check with CBRES." It sounded as though he was saying "sea breeze." "Thankfully it's their problem, not mine."

"Sea breeze? I'm sorry, what's that?" Nora asked.

"C-B-R-E-S," he spelled it out. "Campus Buildings and Real Estate Services.

Professor Littlefield frowned. "I hope my commitment to the spirited exchange of ideas hasn't given you the wrong impression. To be clear, I wholeheartedly endorse the new courtyard concept, whatever its aesthetic limitations. I trust your story will reflect that. Anything else would be a serious misunderstanding of my position."

"Yes, of course," Nora murmured. The point was academic. There was no story. She wasn't going to write one.

"And my comments about the statue—let's keep them off the record as well. No need to stir up controversy," the professor continued.

"Agreed." Nora smiled uncomfortably, eyeing the door. He was still blocking it.

"In fact, it might be a good idea to let me review your story before you submit it. Not that I question your abilities in the least or have any interest in influencing what you write. There are possible pitfalls I can help you avoid. You might be surprised how petty the university world can be—all the factions and politics."

"I see," Nora said, almost whispering, thinking, *Like now, for instance.*

"Good, then it's settled, I'm sure your story will be excellent." He held open the door and followed Nora into the gardenia-scented reception area.

"Mary," he said to his assistant, attentively seated at her desk. "This young woman is helping us publicize the courtyard project. Let's plan on staying in close touch with her. I'll let the committee know there's a story in the works and that we'll have the opportunity to review it before it's published."

"Certainly, Professor," the assistant said.

The matter settled, Professor Littlefield retreated into his office. His assistant picked up a notecard and pen and handed them to Nora. "For your contact information," she said.

Her hand shaking slightly, Nora took them. Leaning forward, she placed the card on the desk and hastily filled it out. "Here, you go," she said with feigned nonchalance, handing the card back. An alias, of course. She'd worked it out ahead of time. The phone number was bogus too. It wasn't a working number.

"Thank you, Rachel," the assistant said, reading off the card. "How soon before we can expect to see something?"

"About a week," Nora replied. "I still have some people to interview. I'll be in touch."

All this deception was making her queasy. The sooner she got back to the dorm and out of her borrowed clothes, the better. She was hopeful that Jillian wouldn't be around. She needed time to decompress and process the experience; nor did she want Jillian to know she'd scrubbed off her makeup.

"Okay, I'll let the professor know," his assistant said, jotting something on the card.

"Great," Nora replied, and made her escape.

CHAPTER 31

A knockoff. And a bad one at that. Haunted by the thought, Nora scrolled through another classical-image database, searching for her statue. So far she hadn't seen anything that even remotely resembled it. Bleary-eyed after another long session, she leaned back on the couch and thought about calling it a night.

Once again, she had the suite to herself. Jillian hadn't been around when she'd returned from her meeting with Littlefield and remained unaccounted for. Nora was about to return to her computer when she heard someone at the door. Rising, she turned and saw her roommate enter.

"Well, hey, stranger, welcome back," she said with a relieved smile. "I've been thinking about you."

"Sweet thoughts, I hope," Jillian replied as she closed the door and came toward her, rolling her suitcase. She was wearing a tailored white shirt, gray slacks, and low-heeled pumps. A dark pink purse slung over her shoulder had a Gucci logo.

Whatever role she's playing, it's not a college student, Nora thought, noticing Jillian's tired gait and the fatigue lines her makeup didn't entirely conceal. Abandoning the suitcase, Jillian sank into the chair across from the couch, kicked off her pumps, and propped her feet on the coffee table.

"Another trip home?" Nora asked, trying to keep her tone neutral.

"Yeah, family." Jillian grimaced, raising her arms to stretch out the kinks. "Sometimes I wish I was an orphan. It must be nice."

Nora, an actual orphan, managed a wry smile. "I'm not sure 'nice' describes it," she said.

Jillian caught herself. "Oh, right. Sorry, I wasn't thinking. I'm tired, I'm hungry, and my hair"—she touched the top of her head—"is a total disaster. Would you mind ordering us a pizza? I'm going to take a shower and work on feeling human again. There's money in my purse."

She reached for the purse and underhanded it to Nora. Nora caught it and set it down, looking askance at this pink thing in her lap.

"It's not real if that helps." Jillian chuckled. "Some guy was selling them out of his truck. He swore it was authentic, but come on, it's got to be a knockoff."

Nora nodded sourly. *That word again. I'm still not buying it. I know what I experienced in the courtyard, and it wasn't bad art.* Out loud, she said, "Well, it looks real. One pizza coming up. And there's wine. I'll get it."

Jillian reappeared about forty-five minutes later. Her hair was damp, and she was wearing a long, fluffy white robe, loosely belted. The pizza had come a few minutes ago and was on the coffee table along with the wine and two water glasses.

"Much better," Jillian announced. She unscrewed the cap and poured, half filling both their glasses, then settled back into her chair. "Out with it. I'm dying to know. How'd your meeting with the professor go? Did you have him eating out of your hand?"

"Not exactly," Nora said.

"The dress didn't work?" Jillian asked.

"To be honest, I don't think he even noticed."

"He must be gay."

"Could be."

"Maybe we can fix him."

"You fix him. I'm doing my best to avoid him."

"Was it that bad?"

"No, not bad. Nerve-racking. And now he wants to see my story, which is kind of awkward."

"Since you're not writing one," Jillian said, finishing the thought. Opening the pizza box, she reached for a slice. "You remembered. Anchovies." Smiling, she took a bite. Following Jillian's lead, Nora took a slice too, from the side without the fishy stuff.

"Don't worry. He probably won't recognize you without makeup," Jillian said in between bites.

"Oh, he might."

Nora's notes were on the coffee table. Giving into temptation, she reached for them, scanned down the page, caught herself, and self-consciously looked at Jillian. "I guess I really am obsessed," she said.

"That's obvious. Go ahead." Jillian helped herself to another slice of pizza and more wine. "Something's bothering you. What is it?"

Nora hesitated, not because she didn't want to tell her. She wasn't sure where to start or how much to include. Ultimately, she winged it—not a blow-by-blow account, but not the condensed version either. It included the business about the statue being a knockoff, possibly constructed from a repurposed stack of cannonballs—a fake, in other words, impressive only if you didn't know better—and a couple other choice details.

"If you ask me, your professor's full of shit," Jillian said when the recitation ended. She'd polished off the rest of the wine and was holding the empty glass in her lap. "That alias you came up with, the name you gave them—Rachel Solomon. I'm curious. Does it have some special significance?"

Jillian placed her glass on the coffee table. Her robe parted, exposing her thighs.

"Kind of," Nora said, following Jillian's hand as she readjusted the robe. "It's my mother's name. I wanted something that would be easy to remember and hard to trace."

"You must miss her," Jillian responded with the air of someone who knows better but is going there anyway. Her throat and upper chest were flushed from the wine.

"It's hard to miss someone you don't remember," Nora replied, keeping her voice even. What I mostly feel is her absence. There's a void." Restless, looking for an excuse to move, she picked up her laptop and notes and carried them into the bedroom.

"What about you?" she asked on her return, an edge in her voice. "Are you and your mother close? She's got to be better than all those wicked stepmothers."

"Mother, stepmothers, they're pretty much the same. You've got one you can't remember. I've got several I'm trying to forget." Jillian stumbled to her feet and stretched out her arms. "My bedtime. Good night, Rachel Solomon's daughter. I'm going to crash."

"Good night, Jillian," Nora replied, put off by her flippant tone. *I should cut Jillian some slack,* she reproached herself. *With her family situation, she probably can't help herself. But where was she really, and what was she doing?*

In Jillian's purse when Nora paid for the pizza, she'd found a wad of cash. She hadn't counted it, but it had to be seven or eight hundred dollars.

With a sigh, Nora headed to her bedroom to retrieve her laptop.

CHAPTER 32

Nora paused for a moment to banish second thoughts, then heaved open the administration building's heavy wooden door, and started across the lobby. Overhead, fluorescent lights imparted a yellowish tinge to everything beneath. Even the security guard stationed by the elevator seemed out of sorts. He barely glanced up as a half-dozen stony-faced riders, Nora among them, slowly filed past. She was wearing the blue dress again but no makeup.

"Hello, can I help you?" the work-study student at the CBRES reception desk asked. Caught painting her nails, she inserted the applicator into the bottle and sat up straighter. Her blonde hair was fastened into a ponytail, and her face had a light dusting of freckles. On her teal T-shirt, a cartoon unicorn pranced along with the words "Live the Fantasy" and some Greek letters.

"I'm with the school newspaper. Mr. Cushman asked me to stop by," Nora said, trying to sound casual, relieved that the person she needed to get past was almost certainly younger than her. Cushman was CBRES's Outdoor Property Maintenance manager, which made Fountains and Statues part of his domain.

What he had said was, "No, absolutely not. Now if you'll excuse me, I have work to do." If she could get in front of him, talk to him face-to-face, he might relent. It was worth a try.

"I don't mind waiting," Nora continued with a smile that was meant to be reassuring.

The receptionist looked doubtful. She checked the clock on the wall behind her—it was ten forty-five—glanced at her right hand with its three purple fingernails, and turned back to Nora. "The staff meeting's over at eleven. That's when I leave," she replied hesitantly.

Suddenly Nora got it. She wanted to finish painting her nails but didn't feel comfortable doing it with Nora hovering.

Nora glanced to her left and saw a row of doors. The one nearest to her had Cushman's name on it. "Why don't I wait in his office?" she replied, thinking, *Even better. That way he can't avoid me.*

"It's okay. He won't mind," she added. "No need to get up. I know the way."

Nora started walking. As she entered Cushman's office, the ceiling lights blinked on.

The office was small and cluttered. A computer in a docking station dominated his desk, hemmed in by towering stacks of paper that Cushman hadn't gotten around to filing, or that was his filing system.

To her right, a bureau stood crowded with mementos. Interested in knowing more about the ogre she was about to confront, Nora examined the evidence. She saw a Boy Scout leader, an avid outdoorsman and a "World's Best Dad" with the coffee mug to prove it.

A family portrait in the center of the display caught her attention. Cushman towered over a wife and two young children, a son and daughter, everyone in their dress-up clothes, everyone smiling for the camera. It was sweet and hard to square with the jerk she'd talked to over the phone.

From the corridor, barely registering at first, Nora heard voices and footsteps. She was still holding the family photo. She put it down and turned to face the doorway.

"So you're the reporter," Cushman said in a gruff voice as he entered. He was even larger than Nora had expected. His reddish-blond hair, what he had left of it, was combed straight back, calling attention to a large, dome-shaped forehead and a weather-beaten complexion. His dark-red polo shirt tented around his midsection, and he was wearing khaki pants with too many pleats.

"You should have told me you're working for Littlefield," he said reproachfully as he made his way to his desk and lowered himself into his chair.

Shifting forward, he rested his hands on the desk and glanced at a large chrome-plated watch. "Okay, miss reporter, have a seat." He indicated the chair across from his desk. "I have five minutes. How can I help you?"

Nora repeated what she'd said on the phone. She was writing a story about the courtyard project and thought it might be interesting to include a few facts about the old courtyard. As the person responsible for maintaining it, no doubt he had some interesting tidbits he could share.

Cushman cocked his head. He seemed genuinely baffled.

"You could start with the statue?" Nora suggested. "Anything that comes to mind. In case you're wondering, you'll have a chance to review the story before it's published, so no need to worry about that."

"The statue," Cushman said. "It's bronze, it's about seven feet tall, it weighs about eighteen hundred pounds, and it's hollow. Is that what you had in mind?"

Nora perked up. She had assumed the statue's power came from its appearance or from the metal used to cast it. But if the statue was hollow, something could be imprisoned inside like a genie in a bottle.

"Hollow?" she said.

"It's how they're made. It goes all the way back to antiquity." Cushman glanced at his watch again.

"Any idea where the statue is now?" Nora tried not to sound too interested. Littlefield had said the statue was part of a bequest, and the university was required to keep it. But where?

"Sorry, I can't help you with that. Time's up."

Cushman stood. Nora reluctantly followed him out. The acrid smell of nail polish hung in the air as they passed the vacated reception desk. Cushman glowered but continued walking, waiting with her at the elevator, probably to make sure she left. He could relax. Nora was done with her reporter ruse; all this lying was making her ill.

Fortunately, the wait for the elevator wasn't long. *Hollow.* The thought looped in her thoughts as she descended. *The statue's hollow. Something could be trapped inside. Farfetched? Maybe, but it could explain why the statue had felt so alive.*

By the time Nora reached the lobby, she had a new idea—a different approach she could take. It led her back to the student union and the information desk, where she picked up a campus map.

The couch where she'd found the school newspaper was vacant, and Nora sat down. She spread the map across her lap and counted thirty-six buildings spread across seventeen acres. *Now, if I was seven feet tall and weighed eighteen hundred pounds, where would I be hidden?* she asked herself.

The answer wasn't obvious.

CHAPTER 33

Nestled in her armchair, Nora plowed through her psych reading assignment. After three days spent searching for the statue, it felt good to focus on something as everyday as schoolwork. Her study group met tonight, and she planned to attend.

Around her, Jillian restlessly circulated, going from the couch, where she fiddled with her phone; to the mini fridge (empty again); and finally into her bedroom. She emerged a few minutes later clutching a manila envelope and heading for the door.

"Where to?" Nora called out, peeking up from her textbook.

"Out. I'll be back." Jillian slammed the door behind her.

She returned about an hour later, still holding the envelope. Whatever had agitated her, it seemed to have passed; she appeared almost calm.

"Are you hungry?" she asked, setting the envelope on the coffee table and planting her purse on top. "I'm thinking burgers, beer, and loud music—the kind that makes it impossible to think. Who knows," she added with a teasing grin, "maybe we'll meet some nice guys with more money than sense and let them fund our outing."

"No thanks." Nora lowered her textbook.

"Okay, no guys. I was kidding about the guys. Just an old-fashioned girls' night out. You need a break, and I could use some company."

"I'm torn, I really am, but I need to study."

There was a pause.

"I've been wondering." Nora began and stopped herself, not sure she wanted to continue.

"About what?" Jillian said with a trace of apprehension.

She's worried I'm going to ask her about all those trips home. What she's really doing. "It's nothing," Nora said softly. "In high school, were you one of the popular kids?"

"Popular? No," Jillian said, looking surprised and relieved. "I never stayed anywhere long enough to be popular. I was the girl who didn't go home for the holidays and never got invited to anyone's house. What about you?"

Nora made a face. "I was the class weirdo. It was my father's doing, but it was my fault. I should've known better."

Jillian cocked her head. "What happened?"

"As part of a promotion for Top Notch, he made up twenty-six new words, one for every letter of the alphabet, and sold exclusive rights to each of them. Your word came in a toy safe shaped like a pyramid along with a rubber stamp and a deed granting you exclusive ownership. I was his first sale. I traded one week's allowance for *N*. Pretty weird, right?"

"It's out there, but so what?" Jillian said with a tentative smile. At least she wasn't laughing. "What difference does it make now?"

"Wait, it gets worse." Nora grimaced. "I took the stamp to school and showed it off."

"No."

"Yeah, dumb. I was fifteen. Tenth grade. I should have known better. It took a long time to live that down. I'm not sure I ever did."

"Well, the good news is you're not in high school anymore. What brings it to mind?"

"I don't know. Just remembering, I guess." An evasion. The word with all its packaging—the pyramid and rubber stamp, the certificate of ownership—was stowed in a bottom dresser drawer with Nora's other keepsakes.

This morning, for the first time since her high-school blunder, she'd unpacked the word and spread the items on her dresser. She was hoping its time had finally come, that it could somehow help her find the statue, but it remained mute. It was her word, but she still had no idea what it meant.

"Sure you don't want to come?" Jillian picked up her purse with a wry smile, adding, "burgers and beer, no boys unless you insist."

"Thanks, not tonight. Maybe next time."

"Okay." Jillian's expression turned serious. "But the clock's ticking."

"I know," Nora said. "I can hear it."

Nora got back from her study group around ten o'clock. Having the apartment to herself suited her mood. She was feeling down, not just because of the statue or memories of her private-word fiasco, but most everything, and moping was easier with no one around.

Summoning the energy, Nora filled the electric kettle for a cup of chamomile tea and sat in the armchair while it steeped. Jillian's manila envelope caught her eye, and she noticed it wasn't sealed. *She put it down in front of me and left it open. Does she want me to look?* Nora wondered. *Is she trying to tempt me?*

With a pained smile, she got up and retrieved her tea and brought it back to the armchair.

Honestly, it's none of your business even if Jillian deliberately left it out. Nora took a sip of her tea. *And maybe it wasn't intentional. Maybe she trusts you to mind your own business. The other night when she tossed you her purse, you didn't rummage through it or count her bankroll. On the other hand, if it's nothing, it doesn't matter, and you'll never mention it anyway.*

Nora didn't need a psych textbook to know she was rationalizing. Setting down the tea, she picked up the envelope and glanced at the door. No one was coming. Carefully she lifted the flap and removed the document.

To her astonishment, it was a contract between Infernal Babe Productions and one "Jillian Wexler (herein referred to as The Talent)."

Running her eyes down the page, Nora picked out details. The contract was for twelve months, during which time "The Talent" agreed to fully comply with all laws, rules, and relevant regulations in all local, state, and federal jurisdictions. She further promised to refrain from drug and alcohol abuse and prostitution, including legal prostitution. And she was expected to take diligent care of her health, weight, and appearance.

Obey the law and take care of yourself. For a company that called itself "Infernal," it was a surprisingly wholesome agenda.

Nora turned the page. What followed was a double-columned list of sex acts and how much each paid, with Jillian's checkmark alongside some of them. Averting her eyes, Nora flipped to the end of the document and read, "In witness whereof, the parties have duly agreed to this agreement."

It was official. Jillian had signed on the line labeled "Porn Star," and it was dated today. Nora was holding the copy you keep for your records.

You're going to be an Infernal Babe. That's your solution to your evil-stepmother crisis. What should I do? How do I respond? It isn't as though Jillian confided in me. I'm snooping. If there's a moral high ground, I don't occupy it.

She took a last look at Jillian's signature and returned the document to the envelope, and placed it back on the coffee table. The next morning, the envelope was gone, making it one more thing Nora could pretend not to have seen.

CHAPTER 34

Back from town, Nora set her shopping bag on the kitchen counter next to her laptop and powered it up. She'd found the statue. *Probably found the statue,* she corrected herself. The evidence was strong but not conclusive.

She was dying to tell Jillian, but it would have to wait. Jillian's bedroom door was closed. Lately she'd been spending more time in her room and had started locking up when she went out. *Does she know I've been snooping? That Infernal Babe business is casting a pall over everything.*

Jillian emerged a few minutes later, talking on the phone; spotted Nora; and immediately retreated, closing the door behind her. Nora sighed and went back to her laptop.

"Sorry, family business. The usual crap," Jillian said when she reemerged a few minutes later, standing across the counter from Nora. "What's up? You look like you're ready to bust."

"I found it. I'm pretty sure," Nora said with a grin.

"The statue? Great," Jillian replied with genuine-sounding enthusiasm. "Where?"

Nora moved aside a mug of peppermint tea and swiveled her laptop toward Jillian. A three-story brick building filled the screen. "Olympian Hall," she said. "It's the old earth science building."

Early in her search, it had occurred to Nora that her tattoo and the statue really were connected. She didn't know how or why, but as she searched the campus, it seemed possible her unshielded tattoo could work like a Geiger counter. She had now visited all thirty-six buildings, some twice. No other place even registered.

"The university condemned the building eight years ago," she continued. "Since then, it's been sitting there, rotting away. When I checked it out, I felt something. It was faint, but I sensed a definite presence. If it's anywhere, it's there. It's got to be."

"So, Olympian Hall. Now what?" Jillian prompted her.

"I took some photos." Nora tapped a key, and the building disappeared, replaced by a cascading sequence of doors and windows. "This one." she pointed to an image in the third row, second from the right. She pressed another key, and the other photos disappeared from the screen. "It's in the back of the building. Someone slender and reasonably athletic could climb through once she broke the glass."

"She probably could," Jillian said, taking a moment to absorb the information. "It sounds risky."

"I know. I've picked up a few items." Nora reached for the shopping bag and pulled out a pair of thick cotton gloves and a long-handled metal flashlight suitable for both illumination and window smashing.

Jillian nodded. "And when is the big event?"

"Tonight, around midnight—the witching hour. No point in delaying."

Jillian shifted forward on the barstool. She looked as if she were about to say something.

"Yes?" Nora asked.

"Nothing, just wondering. What happens when you find it?"

"I don't know," Nora admitted. "I'm hoping it'll be obvious. Does that sound dumb?"

"No, not at all," Jillian loyally replied, and a few minutes later, she went back to her room and closed the door behind her.

That evening, to Nora's surprise, Jillian stayed in, hanging out with Nora while she waited for midnight to roll around. Nora was too jittery to go out for dinner, so Jillian picked up two orders of pork dumplings from the Chinese restaurant in town. They finished with fortune cookies, cracking them open and unrolling the slips of paper inside.

"You first," Jillian said, making a ritual of it.

"'Congratulations! You're on your way.'" Nora smiled. She wasn't superstitious, but it was a good omen.

"Mine too," Jillian said with a smirk. She extended the fortune to Nora. They were identical.

"Well then, both of us," Nora said, to herself thinking, *What are the odds? She's going to be an Infernal Babe, and you're breaking into a cellar.* She handed one of the fortunes back to Jillian.

Time crawled, but finally it was late enough. "I'm going," Nora announced, looking at her watch for the umpteenth time as she rose from the couch.

Seated at the other end, Jillian stood and, to Nora's surprise, hugged her. "I hope you find what you're looking for," she said, her voice soft, almost mournful.

"Thanks, you, too."

Dressed for breaking and entering in her navy-blue hoodie, jeans, and tennis shoes, Nora set out, taking her time to avoid looking suspicious. Her new gloves were heavy and somewhat too large, and she was carrying the flashlight, which was turned off.

Dark and looming, silhouetted against a slate-gray sky, Olympian Hall sat on the edge of the South Commons. A driveway curved around to the right, and Nora followed it to the back of the building. In the center, an overhead door wide enough to accommodate a pickup truck was flanked by windows.

Identifying the one she needed to smash once she worked up the nerve—until now, Nora had never deliberately broken anything—she approached it. She'd taken off her bracelet. The tingling sensation was fainter than it had been that afternoon, but maybe the gloves were muffling it.

What she saw stopped her in her tracks. The garage door was open just enough for her to crawl under. When she'd come by earlier today, it had been shut. Nora hesitated. Was it a trap or a stroke of good fortune? It almost didn't matter. She'd come too far; she wasn't going to turn back now.

On her knees, Nora ducked under the door and emerged into darkness as deep as a tomb. She was immediately assailed by the putrid stench of decay. Startled, she got to her feet, took off a glove, and held it over her nose to block the odor. She could feel the dumplings from dinner rising in her throat, and it was all she could do not to retch.

Her flashlight revealed a narrow path down the center of the basement between stacked wooden crates bearing obscure scientific-looking markings. As she followed the path, the stench grew even more overpowering, and she had to force herself to keep going.

Without warning, Nora stumbled upon the statue, not standing, as she'd imagined she'd find it, but lying face up on the floor. Crouched by its head, she shone her light over it. The leer she remembered from the fountain had become a rictus grin. With her bare hand—she was still holding the glove to her face—Nora lightly brushed her fingertips across the statue's forehead. The bronze felt cold and inert, a lifeless shell.

Nora's eyes had begun to tear from the stench, but sorrow and despair were mixed in as well. All that effort and time, the risks she'd taken, and it ended here, in the deadest of dead ends.

Her lungs had begun to ache; it was getting harder to breathe. With a shudder, she stood, stole a last mournful look at the statue, wiped her sleeve across her face, and headed back. It was a relief to reach the door.

As she scrambled out, Nora nearly bumped into a pair of black boots. Hastily, she scrambled to her feet. Officer Roach, her old nemesis, was waiting for her. "It's not how it looks," Nora blurted out—the first thing that came to mind, and not very convincing. It was exactly how it looked.

"Save it," he said, grabbing Nora's arm and marching her toward an idling Jeep with a university insignia on the side panel. "I knew you couldn't keep your nose clean." He opened the rear door.

"Am I under arrest?" Nora asked, staring anxiously into the Jeep's interior.

Officer Roach scowled. Heading to the trunk, he returned with a blanket similar to the one Nora had donned that night at the fountain and handed it to her. "Put this over you and get in," he ordered, handing it to her, not getting closer than necessary.

Nora gave him a perplexed look.

"To block the smell," he said impatiently. I don't know what you were doing in there, but you reek."

Death, it's clinging to me, Nora thought. *I smell like death. After tonight, I'm through. No more death. Enough death. I'm not going anywhere near it.* Mortified, she draped the blanket around her shoulders. "Where are you taking me?" she asked.

"To the station. Now get in."

Nora got in. Since she'd entered Olympian Hall, her tattoo had been resoundingly silent, but just in case, she slipped on the bracelet. The Jeep peeled out with its lights flashing and siren blaring, which was totally unnecessary. A minute later, they pulled up at the campus police station, located in the back of the Student Services building.

"In you go," Roach said, marching her to the building's entrance.

What a dick. Does he think I'll try to escape? She'd left her gloves and flashlight in the Jeep. No matter, she no longer needed them.

Seated at the dispatch desk, a woman with enameled hair and opalescent fingernails was reading a magazine. With a sinking feeling, Nora recognized her. It was Tameka Copeland, the officer who had been nice to her the night she wandered into the fountain. "Put her in 104," she said, giving Nora a brief reproachful glance.

Thoroughly deflated, Nora followed Officer Roach down a wood-paneled corridor with metal doors along the inner wall. When they got to 104, he stopped, turned the door handle, and snapped on the lights, then trailed Nora in. To her relief, it was a room, not a cell. There were no windows, and the only furniture was a desk by the back wall with a chair on either side. On the wall to the right of the desk, a clock ticked.

"Can I make a phone call?" Nora asked, not sure whom she had in mind or what the point would be.

"Knock yourself out," Officer Roach said. He'd remained by the door, and he shut it behind him as he left. When Nora could no longer hear his footsteps, she got up and tried the doorknob. It turned. She wasn't locked in—not that it mattered. She wasn't going anywhere.

She crossed over to the desk and sat down with her back to the wall, studying the clock: 12:30 a.m. With every tick, the second hand jumped ahead three seconds. Nora did the math.

An hour, twelve hundred ticks later, she was still waiting. The charnel-house smell had faded, and she took off the blanket and draped it over the back of her chair. With a yawn, she folded her hands in her lap and closed her eyes.

She was in a small sailboat on a featureless ocean. There was no breeze, and when she placed her hand in the water, she couldn't feel a current or detect any signs of life. Above her, the sky was thick, white, and endless, not a curtain she could part but endless sameness she couldn't get beyond.

And yet Nora didn't feel completely alone. Above her, a huge cloud hovered. Within it she saw two points of light that could be eyes. Their brightness made her uncomfortable, and she looked away.

It occurred to her she'd been here before: in this boat, on this sea, under those eyes—if that's what they were. She couldn't read them, had never been able to read them, had no idea what they might be seeing or if seeing was even something they did.

And here was the crux of it, why her heart was suddenly racing, and she felt as if she wanted to jump out of her skin. The eyes—they were definitely eyes—had found her. Fierce and focused, they were glaring down at her, moving closer.

CHAPTER 35

"Are you all right? You were shouting," a concerned voice asked from somewhere overhead. Still groggy, Nora raised her head and blinked as her eyes adjusted to the light. The person standing over her was tall and slender and mostly bald, with a wreath of dark-brown hair around the back of his head. The tuxedo he wore fit too well to be a rental.

"I'm Dr. D'Arcangelo, but everyone calls me Dr. D.," he introduced himself with a self-deprecating smile. "I'm dean of the Faculty of Arts and Sciences. That makes you one of mine."

Nora nodded. Apparently she was in even bigger trouble than she'd thought.

"Sorry I couldn't get here sooner. I was attending a banquet," Dr. D. continued. He was holding a Styrofoam cup, and he set it in front of Nora.

"Green tea. I got it from the caterer. After what you've been through, I thought you might like something bracing. Do you mind if I sit down?"

Nora nodded and reached for the tea. It was lukewarm but nice. Maybe she wasn't in that much trouble after all.

"First of all, how are you? Any complaints about the way you've been treated?" Dr. D. said, seated now. Close up, his eyes were smoke colored, so light they were almost transparent.

"No. No complaints." Nora took another sip of tea.

"Good." Dr. D. shifted forward and placed his hands on the

desk. They were large hands, and slender, with long, tapered fingers. No rings, not even a watch, and his cufflinks were plain gold disks. "I'm sorry, Nora. I wish I could make this whole business go away— let you wipe the slate clean and start over." He paused, looking at her with those impossible-to-read eyes. "But unfortunately, I can't. There are consequences." He sighed. "Real-world consequences. There always are."

Here it comes, she thought, *the axe*. Knowing didn't make it any easier.

"You're going to have to leave. I'm sure you understand why," Dr. D. said softly.

"Am I being thrown out?"

"No, of course not. You're withdrawing. The offenses you're not being charged with are trespassing on school property on at least two occasions, three if we count Cushman's office, and"—he chuckled—"impersonating a newspaper reporter. Did I overlook anything?"

"The statue. Something's going on. What is it?" Nora asked, emboldened by the realization she didn't have anything to lose

"Nothing's going on," Dr. D. answered. "It's a big white elephant, and we're stuck with it. That's all."

"That awful smell, what was that?"

Dr. D. hesitated. "Decay," he finally said. "The building's been closed up for a long time. That's probably why the door was open— to air it out. I'm surprised you could stand it even for a little while."

Nora looked at him, not sure how to respond. He wasn't leveling with her. The stench hadn't been coming from the building. It had been coming from the statue, as if something had been left to rot. Under her bracelet, her tattoo felt hot and constricted. Placing her wrist in her lap, she protectively draped her hand over it.

"It's late, and you've had a rough night." Dr. D. continued, noticing her gesture. "I admire your determination, Nora, but it's time to move on. As far as the university's concerned, you're leaving in good standing. Your grades are excellent. I checked. You shouldn't have any trouble continuing your schooling somewhere else. We'll even reimburse you for the unused portion of your tuition. That should help."

"Thanks," Nora said. At the moment, the idea of staying had zero appeal, but so did leaving.

Dr. D. turned his head and glanced at the clock. Smiling, he said, "I have to give you credit. You did something I thought was impossible."

"What's that?" she asked warily.

"At the last CODPRC meeting, you got Dr. Littlefield and Mr. Cushman to agree. Unfortunately, what they were agreeing about was you. Don't worry; I'm not planning to act on any of their suggestions."

The big flaw in her plan—Nora could see it now. It hadn't occurred to her people might talk and share information. Where she thought she was being clever, she was being clumsy and clueless. Like most revelations, it came a bit late.

"What do you say we get out of here?" Dr. D. said, getting to his feet. "I'll drop you off at the dorm."

Abandoning the tea, Nora followed him through the hallway. In the reception area, Officer Copeland remained at the desk, scrolling through her phone. She saw them and put it down.

"Hello again, Tameka. Long night," Dr. D. said with a tolerant smile. "I've been meaning to ask: How's your remarkable daughter?"

"Couldn't be better, sir." Officer Copeland smiled back, conspicuously ignoring Nora.

"Well, give her my regards. I know you're here by yourself. I'll drive Miss Stanfell home."

"Yes sir." She reached for the logbook and duly noted it.

Dr. D.'s Mercedes was parked by the door. Preceding her, he held the car door open and waited as Nora got in. The drive was short. Within moments, they pulled up to her dorm. Nora waited, not ready to leave the quietly purring car. For a moment, she considered appealing to him one last time, asking him what was really going on. But it was pointless. He wasn't going to tell her.

"I know. It's overwhelming. Transitions are hard even when they're desirable," Dr. D said. He reached inside his tuxedo, pulled out a small leather case and removed a card, holding it out. "Call if you'd like help."

"Thanks," Nora said, taking the card, not looking at it. "What kind of help?"

"The usual stuff: transcripts, letters of recommendation, grant applications. Or," he added with a shrewd smile, "you keep having bad dreams."

"Oh, that. It's nothing. I'm fine."

"Good," Dr. D. said as Nora reached for the door handle. "But keep the card anyway. You never know."

CHAPTER 36

That next morning, alone in the suite, Nora moped in her underwear, too listless to get dressed. After the previous night's debacle, she no longer had a reason to go to class, and there was nowhere else she wanted to be. It would be best to quietly slip away.

But where? Not back to Indianapolis. Since her father's death, it no longer held anything for her. Even her tattoo, that self-given mark of her uniqueness, now seemed like a bad joke. She was wearing Jillian's bracelet because she didn't want to see it.

Hoping to motivate herself, Nora went over to the counter and surveyed her box of teas. She skipped past lemon balm, useful for its ability to soothe jangled nerves, and went straight to yerba maté, which, according to the packet copy, was harvested from the leaves of the South American holly tree and contained twice the caffeine jolt of black coffee while providing the sheer euphoria-inducing satisfaction of dark chocolate.

Given her need, which was acute, Nora let it steep an extra minute and took a cautious sip of what she knew from experience would taste like charred twigs soaked in turpentine. She was sitting on the couch, working on the yerba maté, when she heard a knock at the door.

Startled, Nora jumped. Liquid sloshed and spilled, dripping on her hand, hot but not scalding. She hastily set the mug down and stood.

She was still in her underwear. Jillian's robe lay abandoned on the other end of the couch, and Nora reached for it, using it to wipe her hands, simultaneously calling out, "Who is it?"

The knocking continued, louder and more insistent.

"Hold on, I'm coming!" Nora shouted, donning the robe and belting it snugly. On the other side of the door, a middle-aged couple stood. The man was about five-ten and burly, his barrel chest and belly made more prominent by the ramrod uprightness of his posture.

The woman was tall and thin with steel-gray hair and a gaunt face. "We're looking for Jackie," she said in a stern I'm-at-the-end-of-my-patience voice. "She was supposed to meet us at the accounting office two hours ago. Where is she?"

"I'm sorry; there's no one here by that name," Nora replied, reaching for the doorknob, glad she could dismiss them.

"Typical, just typical." The woman laughed mirthlessly. "There's no mistake. She knew we were coming." Narrowing her eyes, she added, "You must be the roommate."

"See here, miss," her mate chimed in, "it's no good pretending you don't know her when you're wearing her bathrobe."

"Jillian? Are we talking about Jillian?" Nora asked, clutching the robe tight around her.

"That may be what she calls herself, but it's not her real name. Her name's Jackie," the woman answered.

Jillian's parents, Nora thought with a sudden shock of awareness. *These are her parents, her real parents. That poor little rich girl story, the six empty suitcases, the father who collects trophy wives—lies. They were all lies, and you swallowed them.*

"You're too late. She's gone," Nora said in an almost toneless voice. "She took off last night while I was out. Packed up and left, didn't tell me she was leaving. Come in and see for yourself if you don't believe me." She stepped aside.

His hand gripping his wife's forearm, Jillian's father supported her into the suite. Her movements were stiff and cautious, as though every step required careful calculation. They reached the couch, and he helped her sit down, then stationed himself to her right with his arms folded across his chest. In his light blue shirt, navy-blue slacks, and spit-polished shoes, he gave off a definite policeman vibe. Given Nora's recent history with the campus cops, it wasn't a happy association.

"So you're Jillian's parents," Nora said, seating herself in the chair across from them. She was still coming to grips with the enormity of her roommate's deception.

"Jackie," Jillian's mother replied. "As her friend—"

"I'm not her friend." Nora cut her off. "We were roommates. I didn't know her that well."

"Was it well enough for her to tell you where she was going?" Jillian's father broke in, his voice thick with insinuation.

"No, she didn't tell me," Nora said, thinking, *Los Angeles, Infernal Babe Productions. Jillian may have lied to me, but I'm not going to rat her out.*

"Don't cover for her. She'll only drag you down," Jillian's father said. "Or is it too late?"

"Easy, Jack. She's just a girl," his wife interceded, motionless but commanding from her spot in the center of the couch.

Jack, his name's Jack, Nora thought. *Jack and Jackie, father and daughter, his namesake.* Now that she was looking for it, she could see a resemblance. Something in the eyes and the shape of the face. He had probably been a good-looking guy.

"We called," Jillian's mother said softly, refocusing Nora's attention. "She agreed to come home with us. We're not rich. If she officially drops out, we'll get some of our tuition money back."

Jillian's father finished the thought. "So where is she? If she's gone, what are you doing wearing her clothes?"

The bathrobe again. She didn't like the way he was looking at her. With a quick glance down, she checked to make sure her robe was securely closed. It was.

"Would you like to see her room?" Once they saw it, they'd have no reason to stay.

Jillian's father turned toward his wife. "You go," she said. She appeared to be running down. "I'll wait here."

Nora led the way, opening Jillian's door. The room looked as if it had been ransacked. The closet was half empty, drawers had been pulled out, and clothes lay strewn on the floor. More clothes had been tossed on the bed. On the desk where Jillian's cosmetics had been arrayed, the Gucci purse sat by itself. *So it really is a knockoff,* Nora thought.

"See, gone," she said. All that secrecy, the locked bedroom door—Jillian had been packing to leave. While Nora was making a spectacle of herself, Jillian had been clearing out. Taking it in, Jillian's father shook his head, and his jaw tightened. With sudden anxiety, Nora watched him stride to the door and slowly, quietly shut it. Surely he wouldn't, not with his wife in the other room.

He turned toward Nora. She took a step back. "Are you certain there's nothing you want to tell me?" he asked with a creepy smile.

"No, nothing," Nora said, trying to sound like she wasn't intimidated. "She didn't say where she was going. She just left."

He shook his head in open disbelief. Nora didn't respond. *Let him think what he wants. I don't care.*

"Do me a favor," he continued after a moment. "Jackie's already wrecked her mother's health. She wouldn't like me saying it. She's a proud woman, but when you talk to Jackie, let her know she's finally done it. She's broken her mother's heart, and I hope she's happy."

Abruptly he strode toward the door, opened it, and walked out. By the time Nora caught up, he was standing beside his wife, helping her to her feet. She rose, steadying herself against him. "Good luck with your studies. I'm sure your parents are very proud of you," Jillian's mother said with a bleak expression.

'Thanks," Nora replied, not allowing herself to react.

"Remember what we talked about," Jackie's father said. "You tell her."

Speechless, Nora watched them depart. *Good God,* she thought. *One more thing to hold against Jillian. She sicced her parents on me.*

PART III

Spring 2018

There's no need to build a labyrinth
when the entire universe is one.

—JORGE LUIS BORGES,
IBN-HAKAM AL-BOKHARI, MURDERED IN HIS LABYRINTH

CHAPTER 37

Nora came to gazing at a night sky on which her reflection was faintly ghosted. Slowly the world filled in. Details emerged. She was lying on her side on a couch, a blanket tucked around her, facing a window. From nearby, footsteps sounded.

"Good, you're back. How do you feel?" Alexander Wyman asked in a relieved voice, his green-gray eyes peering at her.

Not ready to speak, Nora sat up and rearranged the blanket around her shoulders. She watched as Wyman strode to a small table at the foot of the couch, picked up a ceramic pitcher, and poured. "Here," he said, holding out a glass. "You must be parched."

Careful to keep her unbraceleted wrist under the blanket, Nora reached for the glass. "What is it?" she asked, her voice hoarse and whispery.

"Water," Wyman replied with a hint of amusement. "Just water."

Nora cautiously raised it to her lips and sipped. It was water, just water. She took a longer swallow and then another. "Thanks. How long was I out?" she asked, cradling the glass in her lap. The afternoon was coming into focus: the extravaganza, Hector's sudden appearance, a struggle, and after that a whole lot of nothing.

"About three hours. Hector brought you here. He left a few minutes ago. He'll be relieved to know you're all right." Wyman positioned a desk chair by the couch and sat down.

"It seems we got off on the wrong foot," he continued, leaning slightly forward. "That was mostly my fault. I had to be certain, and

I may have taken some liberties. I apologize. I hope you're ready to move on. We have a lot to discuss."

"May have taken some liberties?" Nora flared up. "You scared the hell out of me. Talk? Yes, we need to. You've got a captive audience. I'm not sure I can stand, let alone walk, and I have no idea where the door is. I assume the room has one, but from where I'm sitting, it's not obvious, so yeah, go ahead."

"You're not a prisoner, Nora," Wyman said, keeping his voice even. "Your car's parked out front. Hector has removed the tracking device. You can leave anytime you feel up to it. But I hope you'll stay. Believe me, it's in your best interest."

Sitting taller, Nora reached over and placed the glass on an end table and readjusted the blanket. "Okay, I'm listening," she said. "Please proceed."

Wyman looked down and appeared to ponder. He plucked an invisible bit of lint from his knee, and said, "The person who accosted you is Emil Ratskeller, also known as Ratdaddy."

Nora frowned. *Ratdaddy. It fits. Nasty guy, nasty name.*

"I know. It's ludicrous," Wyman continued, misinterpreting Nora's reaction. "Why he calls himself something so preposterous is anyone's guess. He's been shadowing you for a while, threatening the people around you. No doubt you've sensed his presence. He's about as subtle as a wrecking ball."

Nora nodded. Jillian's text had been her first inkling.

"Your friend Jack was easy. He was glad to take the money, but he screwed up."

"He was pushed," Nora said.

"He tried to have it both ways. You can't. You've got to choose. One side or the other, not back and forth. You only make people mad."

Nora was inclined to be more charitable. Jack had been trying to help her, grudgingly, but it counted.

"And then there's your boss."

Nora gave him a puzzled look.

"He's been a much harder nut to crack. Ratdaddy's been pressuring him to fire you. So far he's refused."

That explained Harry's behavior. He had principles. She was touched that they included her and pained to know she'd put him in danger. Who else was there? Jillian, obviously, but that was it. Her circle was miniscule, bordering on nonexistent.

"What about Paul Tsitak?" it occurred to her to ask. She hated thinking she might have put Paul in danger. Wyman looked surprised, and she added, "The guy who runs the historical society. Has Ratdaddy gone after him, too?"

"No, Paul's fine. Ratdaddy knows better than to mess with Paul. He'll be pleased you asked."

Of course, Paul's part of this, Nora thought. *He and Wyman are on the same side.* It made her like Wyman a little better and Paul not quite as much.

"After the home show, Ratdaddy will be out of commission for a while," Wyman continued, with a smile. "Your gentle slap sent him flying into a rather large bathroom display, most of which fell on him."

"So that was the crashing sound I heard. I thought the roof was collapsing."

"No, but we can't be complacent. Your victory today was a temporary reprieve, nothing more. Eventually Ratdaddy will get out of the hospital and be back on your trail, more determined than ever, and he won't be alone."

Wyman paused, looking thoughtful, as though he was weighing how to proceed. Finally, he said, "You're not defenseless, Nora. As you know, the mark on your wrist confers some protection. But it's a mixed blessing. What I felt the night we met was powerful. It drew blood." Ruefully, he held up his hand, palm forward. To Nora's relief, it looked fine.

"This afternoon, it was much stronger." He lowered his hand. "It sent Ratdaddy to the hospital and left you unconscious."

"I liked it better when it was only a tattoo," Nora said wistfully, aware she wasn't being honest. It had never been just a tattoo. Nor was the change sudden. There was her experience with Curt, but that was too mortifying to mention.

"The point is there's no time to waste. I want to help if you'll let me."

"What sort of help?" Nora asked cautiously, still trying to decide how much she trusted him.

"For starters, information. You need to know what you're up against." He grinned. "There's only one condition. Have dinner with me first."

"Why?" She blurted it out, immediately regretting her reaction.

If Wyman was annoyed, he didn't show it. "The usual reasons. Because you haven't eaten in a while, and you're hungry, but also because you want to hear what I have to say—at least I hope you do. We'll dine in. No interruptions. But it's your call. As I said, you can leave anytime you want."

"Thank you, yes. Dinner sounds fine."

Nora watched as Wyman stood and went to his desk, a sleek steel and wood pedestal with a glass top designed to appear almost invisible. On it, a vase filled with lilies seemed to float. Beside the vase, a small white box hovered. He picked it up and recrossed the room. "If you wouldn't mind," he said as he handed it to her.

Perplexed, Nora rested it in her lap and lifted the lid with her free hand. Inside a copper bracelet nestled on a bed of cotton. Polished and thin, the reddish-orange metal gleamed under the room's subdued lighting.

It was exquisite, much nicer than anything Nora had ever owned. Beneath the blanket, she slipped it on, pleased with how comfortable it felt on her wrist. "It's lovely," she said with a smile, bringing her arm out to admire it.

Just then, a knock sounded at the far end of the room. A panel slid open, and a woman entered, followed by two men in livery wheeling dinner carts.

The woman appeared to be in her early thirties and was slender, with olive skin and dark, coiled hair. She was dressed in a cream-colored jacket with a matching blouse, and her long skirt fluttered around her ankles as she moved.

She glanced at Wyman, who responded with a nod. In the far corner of the room, a round table stood. She motioned to the servers, who began setting it, putting down a tablecloth and place settings, laying out platters and a vase filled with more flowers—purple tulips.

"Will there be anything else, Alex?" she asked in a melodiously accented voice. As she approached them, her hazel eyes alighted on Nora, taking in the bracelet, looking at it approvingly. *It's her doing*, Nora thought. *She arranged it.*

"No. Thanks, Thalia. That'll be all," Wyman replied.

They watched her cross the room followed by the two servers. The panel door slid silently shut behind them. As though imprinted on the air, her presence slowly faded.

"Her accent, I couldn't place it. Where is she from?" Nora asked.

"Sicily, a very old house. She's part of the story, too, but we don't need to go into it now." Wyman stood. "If you're ready, let's see what Thalia has prepared for us."

Cautiously, Nora got up, not sure how ready she was to move, but it was okay. Everything was working.

In the center of the table, a large platter held sliced meats and cheeses and an assortment of olives. Next to it, a baguette rested in a basket surrounded by satellite ranks of relishes and condiments. Alongside the table on a cart, a bottle of mineral water sat in an ice bucket.

Nora hadn't realized how hungry she was. While Wyman looked on, she filled her plate, sneaking occasional glances at the bracelet. As much as she admired it, she couldn't keep it. The bracelet was far too grand. It didn't conceal her tattoo; it proclaimed it.

Finally, when she'd eaten her fill, Wyman reached over to the dinner cart. He picked up an earthenware pot, and poured a stream of sienna-colored liquid into two cups. He handed one to Nora who took a small, careful sip.

The liquid had a soft sage and sugar aroma and left a creamy, almost velvety, sweetness at the back of her throat. Intrigued, she took a bigger sip, and then another. "What is it?" she asked, finally setting the mug down.

"We call it Thalia's brew, but it goes much further back than that. In ancient times, it was especially valued by warriors for its healing properties. She must think you qualify."

Nora smiled, pleased despite herself.

Wyman pulled his chair back and steepled his hands.

Here it comes, Nora thought. *At last.*

"The old stories, the ancient myths—I believe you're familiar with them," he said.

"Maybe," Nora hedged. If she knew them, it was mostly through her father, but he had taken liberties. He'd made up stuff and mixed things together, had turned Hercules into an underwater adventure story, and he'd put a monkey god at the siege of Troy.

"Sophomore year I took Foundations of Western Civilization," she said, her other more reliable source of information.

"And got an A." Wyman smiled slyly, enjoying Nora's surprised expression. "Dr. D. sent me your file. He's sorry you never reached out to him. He wanted to help you."

"I know," she said. This was no time to pick a fight, but it was obvious to her and had been for a while: The basement door had been left open; Officer Roach had been waiting for her when she came out, and Dr. D. had been oh, so sympathetic, so supportive as he tossed her out.

And now they were picking up where Dr. D. had left off. She was almost tempted to mention it. *No*, Nora decided, settling back in her chair. *Forget it. Hear what he has to say.*

"Does the name Daedalus mean anything to you?" Wyman asked.

Nora searched her memory. It was one of her father's stories. "Daedalus, the master builder," she said. "He was imprisoned in a tower and built a pair of wings, so he could escape."

"Right."

Nora smiled. One for her, not that they were keeping score. As she recalled, Daedalus' son Icarus had fled with him, flown too close to the sun, plunged into the sea, and drowned. Except in her father's version, Icarus had been a daughter, and she'd ridden to shore on the back of a friendly dolphin.

"Daedalus also created the first labyrinth," Wyman continued. "Commissioned by King Minos of Crete, son of that celestial rapist Zeus and a mortal woman. Minos needed a prison from which nothing could escape—a place where you could wander forever without knowing where you were or where you were going."

"Sounds like just another day in the life," Nora said. She meant it as a joke, but it didn't come out that way.

"Yes," Wyman agreed, surprising her. "Walls don't make a labyrinth. It's the pathways: the way they wind and fork, branch, dead-end, and circle back. Confusion, anxiety, despair—without them you don't have a labyrinth."

"And what was so terrible it needed to be imprisoned in a labyrinth?"

"A monster. A minotaur, part-bull, part-man, with an insatiable craving for human flesh—which Minos was glad to satisfy.

"Finally a champion came; his name was Theseus. He entered the labyrinth, slayed the monster, and returned triumphant. Minos knew only Daedalus could have helped Theseus, and so he imprisoned Daedalus and his son in a tower. After Daedalus made his winged escape, it became a feud. Three thousand years of murder and mayhem with no end in sight."

"In other words, a labyrinth."

"Yes." Wyman paused, looking thoughtful. "You're wondering what this has to do with you," he continued after a moment. "Would it surprise you to know that Daedalus was also a sculptor, the finest the world has ever known? It's said his statues were so lifelike they looked like they might run off if they weren't properly secured." Wyman chuckled grimly. "If they only knew."

Nora gave him a searching look.

"Your statue wasn't just a statue. It was a prison. Daedalus sculpted it to imprison Minos. It worked until you answered Minos' summons and waded into his pool."

"The lights were on; the gate was unlocked," Nora said, remembering the soft, soothing, sensuous water.

"Minos saw his opening and took it. His spirit fled his body and entered through the wound on your wrist. You must have been bleeding. For that kind of quickening, you need blood."

"Oh," Nora replied, dismayed by what she was hearing. She lowered her hands into her lap and clasped them tightly.

"The problem is your tattoo. Until now, it's held him, but the ink is starting to weaken. If we don't act soon, Minos will break free—a crazed, almost invincible, demigod hell-bent on revenge. It won't be pretty."

"I liked it better when he was a bunch of repurposed cannonballs." Nora laughed bleakly.

"Professor Littlefield." Wyman smiled. "If you're hiding a dangerous artifact in plain sight, it helps to have an in-house expert whose convinced it's a fake. But Littlefield wasn't completely wrong. Before it was a statue, it was something else—a bathtub."

Nora gave him a perplexed look.

"A bronze bathtub fit for a monarch. But I'm getting ahead of myself again. The point is that your statue was never just a statue."

"Right. It was a prison tucked away in the courtyard of an obscure state university, a pretty good hiding place until I came along."

"Actually, it was a terrible hiding place even before you came along. It was much too conspicuous and show-offy. It smacked of hubris. That's why we were getting ready to move him."

Wyman paused, and Nora took the opportunity to glance down at the bracelet, reassured and still awed by its shimmering perfection.

"The courtyard's gone. It's a café now, an eatery, but you already knew that," Wyman said when she looked up, his voice soft and low.

"Olympian Hall's still falling down, and the statue's still buried in the basement with the rats and spiders, but no one cares anymore; it's a moldering shell."

Nora shuddered, remembering that moment crouched by the statue, gagging, tears streaming down her face. *God, how stupid could you be.* Thinking about it now made her want to cringe.

"Ratdaddy," she asked, moving on, "how does he fit in? Why all that scurrying around, harassing and hurting people?"

"We're intent on banishing Minos, this time for good. Ratdaddy and his friends are dead set on stopping us. They want to see him liberated. Scaring everyone off, frightening them away, makes you that much easier to pick off."

Nora grimaced. *Oh, great. Two sides locked in a centuries-old conflict, and you're caught between them. Wyman wants to enlist you; he obviously needs your help. And Ratdaddy, he wants to grab you. God knows what he has in mind.*

Nora yawned, raising her hand to cover her mouth. It had been a long day, and whatever boost she'd gotten from Thalia's tea was gone.

"Tired?" Wyman asked.

"A little."

"We're almost done. We just need to decide what we're going to do, where we go from here."

Nora hesitated, not sure about all those "we's." Maybe they could work together; it was more than likely. But not yet. She had some things to check, and she really was tired. "That's enough for one evening," she said.

"Of course," Wyman instantly relented. "I'll drive you home. We can arrange for you to pick up your car tomorrow."

"No, I'm okay. I can drive."

"Are you sure?"

"Positive. No more talk, not tonight."

"Very well." Wyman stood, waited for Nora, and started walking. Together they approached the exit. The panel parted, revealing an elevator. Silently they descended. As promised, her car was waiting for her out front.

"Good night, Nora. I hope you don't regret staying for dinner," Wyman said.

"No. Thank you. It was—" she hesitated, searching for the right word "—illuminating. "Please let Hector and Thalia know I appreciate their help."

"Of course." Wyman smiled dutifully. He opened the car door and handed Nora the keys, careful not to touch her. "We'll talk again soon. In the meantime, wear the bracelet. Don't take it off. It'll protect you for now. And let's not forget about Ratdaddy. He's coming back."

"Yes, I know." Nora got in. The door closed. She was anxious and frazzled; her tattoo was cursed—she'd suspected as much. Tomorrow. She'd figure it out tomorrow.

CHAPTER 38

Sunday morning, in front of her computer, Nora dug for information about Daedalus and Minos, checking what Wyman had told her and filling in gaps.

To her surprise, Socrates was part of the story. A big name from her Western Civ course, he had bragged about his kinship to Daedalus and had spoken approvingly of "statues that needed to be tightly bound or they would take-off like runaway slaves." Hercules was there, too. He had smashed one of Daedalus' statues because he thought it was attacking him.

Other revelations followed. Nora had gone to Camicus State University and knew the school and town had been named after someplace in Sicily. She hadn't realized that someplace was the palace of King Cocalus, where Minos finally caught up with Daedalus. More hubris. If it was folly to put the statue of Minos on public display, naming the university after the place where the two men had their final confrontation was almost as provocative.

There in the original Camicus, so the story went, Minos was killed by King Cocalus' daughters, who poured boiling water over Minos' head while he bathed. Except—she was remembering Wyman's comment about the statue starting out as a bronze bathtub—that didn't seem quite right.

I can picture it: A powerful king, a god's son, is bathing. Two young women approach, bearing fragrant lotions and ointments, vessels of steaming liquid. The king grins lustfully, unaware his enemy Daedalus lurks nearby and is about to strike. Flash forward. Not killed. Daedalus didn't kill Minos. He imprisoned him in a statue cast in Minos' likeness, a kind of living death in a repurposed bronze bathtub.

Thalia is from Sicily, an old house, present from the beginning, Wyman said. *A descendant of King Cocalus? Her family, her lineage? Very likely.*

Nora grimaced, recalling the trip to Olympian Hall where she'd found the statue, abandoned and left to rot after Minos' spirit had escaped.

Ugh, best not to dwell on it.

Nora got up and paced. Her mind was racing. That left Ratdaddy. The awfulness of his nickname continued to trouble her, made him seem even more menacing. It was better to think of him as Emil.

His last name, what was it? Wyman had used it. It finally came to her: *Ratskeller—Emil Ratskeller. Temporarily out of commission, more dangerous than ever when he returns. And he won't be alone; he'll have allies.*

I refuse to be a pawn, and I'm not some damsel in distress. A plan—I need one.

Eventually one occurred to her—a newspaper story to trap a rat. But could she get Harry to run it? She hurried back to her laptop and tapped keys, not bothering to correct typos, getting it down before she cooled off. Finished in what seemed like record time, she leaned back and scrutinized what she'd written, proofreading as she went.

It could work, but would Harry run something so deceptive? That's where it got tricky. According to Wyman, Emil had been harassing Harry, trying to bully him into firing her. So far he'd refused. Why?

Last night, Nora had chalked it up to principles. Harry had them, but could it be more than that? *Was there some Max Rage in Harry's makeup, or is the book's angry energy nothing but bluster? When someone struck Max, he took the assailant's head off. If I fight back, would Harry help me?*

Seeking reassurance, not ready to act, Nora got up and headed to the coffee table where she'd abandoned Harry's book. To her consternation, *Dead Certain* wasn't there. *Or anywhere else*, she concluded after a jittery search of her apartment. As far as she could tell, nothing else was missing.

Someone had taken it, but who? Hector didn't strike her as a book thief, and why would he bother? It probably wasn't Jack either. He was capable of it—he'd bugged her car and lied to her—but if he wanted his book back, all he had to do was ask.

That left Emil. He could've rummaged through her apartment and snatched it to mess with her, or he saw Harry's name on the cover and was curious. Too paranoid? In her current state, Nora couldn't tell. And in a way, it didn't matter. Emil was dangerous, and she needed to deal with him.

Flushed, feeling almost feverish, Nora went back to her story and scanned it one last time. Harry might run it. But if she sent it, her career at the *Sun* was over. There was no way she could stay after a stunt like this. Hand suspended above the keyboard, Nora hesitated. One stroke and there would be no going back.

She sent it.

⚭

At his desk, working on the new Max Rage, Harry listened for any sounds coming from the kitchen. As usual, he'd left the window open in case the cat came back. Refocusing his attention and flexing his leg—it had fallen asleep—Harry picked up where he'd left off:

> Poised for action, every muscle on high alert, Max stood by the door and listened intently. In his right hand, he held his .38 Special. The other hand gripped the brass doorknob. With catlike stealth, he slowly, silently rotated the knob, inching open the door. It was him. He had his back turned to Max and was pawing through the dresser drawer,

searching for the talisman safely stowed in Max's pocket. Now it was payback time.

"Hey, Rat, Max called out, his voice cold and steely. "Looks like you just crapped out."

The computer pinged, bringing Harry back to the here and now. A Sunday email to his work account wasn't unusual. Given the paper's current situation, it was likely to be bad news. Possibly the layoffs management had insisted weren't coming had finally come.

Harry could imagine a scenario where they kept him around to lay off staff and then, once the dirty work was done, cut him loose. He wouldn't play that game. Tomorrow he had a follow-up interview for the Portland job.

Anticipatory outrage turned to irritation and finally to reluctant interest as Harry opened the email and read Nora's story. So Ratdaddy had finally gotten his comeuppance. A fight. Two men and a woman. Only Ratdaddy was identified, but obviously the woman was Nora—Nora and someone else. *She has an ally. Good for her.*

Excited into motion, Harry got up. He paused in the kitchen and glanced at the two bowls on the floor, then at the window, which was open wide enough for a battered old tomcat to squeeze through. *He's not coming,* Harry thought with a resigned smile. *If that's the way he wants it, fine.* Leaving the window open, he made his way back to the study to take another look at Nora's story.

"Violence Mars Home Show Weekend," the headline said. Skimming to the last paragraph, he read, "Ratskeller, who is being treated for his injuries at Goldmont Municipal Hospital, has agreed to cooperate fully with the police in what is being characterized as an active investigation with potentially far-reaching implications."

Insidious. It puts a bull's-eye on Ratdaddy. Not only will he squeal, but watch out: he's spilling his guts; and oh, by the way, here's where to find him.

Someone would notice, but only if Harry published it. And of course, he shouldn't. For a while he sat there surprised he was even considering it. Someone less obsessed than Nora would have come to him and discussed it privately, not sprung it on him. At which point he would have undoubtedly said no and pretended the conversation had never happened.

But what if he agreed? He was tempted. A parting favor, because after something like this, Nora couldn't expect to stay.

"Okay, it runs tomorrow," Harry typed, almost adding, "Good luck, I hope you know what you're doing." But that was way too incriminating. It was enough to think it.

CHAPTER 39

Nora's high spirits didn't last. As the day progressed, her mood sunk and finally cratered. She now saw the Ratdaddy story for what it was—a stupid, career-killing stunt born out of desperation and doomed to fail like everything else she touched.

In short, not the ticking timebomb she'd envisioned but another dud in a long line of duds. She could see why Harry didn't mind running her story. It was harmless, and now he didn't have to fire her; she'd fired herself. And what would Wyman think? In all likelihood, he wouldn't even notice. No one would.

In the midst of Nora's despair, a thought broke through. She grabbed her car keys and headed out, ending up in the newspaper parking lot, which was mostly empty on a Sunday afternoon. Turning away from the building, Nora crossed the road and climbed the fence, landing in the municipal cemetery.

She was sitting on her bench when she heard footsteps clomping toward her. Startled, she stood and saw Hector. Today he had on a dark brown tailcoat with a matching vest and a broad-as-a-bib deep green tie. Something bulged from inside his top hat, and in his hand, he held a leather doctor's bag.

"Hello, how'd you know where to find me?" Nora greeted him when he was standing in front of her. Wyman's assurances to the contrary, she had no doubt her car was still bugged, but how could Hector have known she was down here?

"Have you spotted it?" he asked.

"He's moved," Nora said. The statue was at least two feet closer to them than on her previous visit: *Minos and Goldmont, two of a kind,* Nora thought *Another Daedalus statue. It took me long enough to make the connection.*

"Right, he's becoming unstuck; the bindings are breaking down," Hector said. He sat down. Nora watched as he placed the doctor's bag by his feet, and removed his top hat, resting it in his lap, brim up. The bulge was a stethoscope.

He's here to check on the statue, Nora thought, sitting beside him. *Does it count as a house call if it's in a cemetery?*

Hector didn't appear to be in the mood for conversation, so Nora bided her time, admiring her copper bracelet and listening to the drowsy late-afternoon chirping of birds and insects.

"Who was he?" she finally asked when the silence had gone on too long. It was fine being the strong, silent type, but Hector took it to extremes. "I know he called himself Tony Goldmont, and before that he was Count Anthony Montagna d'Oro, but there's got to be more to the story. What did I miss?"

Hector stirred, looking at the statue, then at Nora. 'Keep going,' his expression seemed to say.

"I think Paul brought me here because he knew I was stuck, and he was trying to give me a jolt," Nora obliged. "I must have sensed something. I'm sure I did, but I pushed it away. I wouldn't let myself see it. So what did I do instead?"

Hector waited. He looked interested.

"I turned Tony Goldmont into a second-rate murder mystery. One with no corpse, no killer, and no murder weapon, just lots of speculation."

Harry's critique, it occurred to her, except he'd put it more tactfully. *Predictably, Robin had missed the point.*

"I can show you," Hector said, "but you'll need to stare into my eyes."

Nora hesitated, finally swiveling toward him.

215

Hector's hand rose, hovered for a moment, and finally settled on her shoulder. "Okay, go ahead. I've got you," he announced.

Reassured, Nora allowed herself to look. His eyes drew her in, and she felt herself coasting downward. If it was an illusion, it was a convincing one. At first there was only darkness; then the darkness began to have dimensions, bands of variegated dimness, and she could hear voices—thin and querulous at first, louder and more strident as she continued her journey.

Striving to understand, Nora took in the clamor around her. Through it all, Hector guided her, and finally, her lifeline, he brought her up again. The next thing she knew, she was sitting on the bench beside him. Slowly, he withdrew his hand. For a moment, she felt lightheaded and wasn't sure where she was.

"Goldmont's a member of the house of Minos," she said when she could speak again, a note of astonishment in her voice. "He came here to establish a place in the wilderness where a new Minoan kingdom could rise with his ancestor's restored spirit at its center. It's why I'm here; it's what drew me to this place. Somehow, with every mistake I made, with every misstep and wrong turn, I was always headed here. I just didn't know it."

Nora laughed ruefully with a darting glance at the statue. "The other night I was doing some research, and I came across something, a story.

"After Daedalus' escape, Minos disguised himself and went searching for him. Everywhere he stopped, he would pull out a conch shell and offer a reward to anyone who could draw a thread through the shell. He knew it was a puzzle only Daedalus could solve and that he wouldn't be able to resist.

"He was correct. Presented with the shell, Daedalus drilled a hole in the closed end and dabbed it with honey. Then he found an ant, tied a thread around it, and placed the ant in the shell. Lured by the honey, the ant wound through the shell and came out the other end. The puzzle was solved; the shell was threaded."

Nora paused. "Is that me?" she asked softly. "Am I your ant?"

Hector's smile was mildly reproachful, and really Nora knew better. The ant didn't just survive; it went where no ant had gone before and triumphed. That was the real point of the story.

"Let's walk," she said, too restless to sit any longer.

Leaving his top hat and doctor's bag behind, Hector got up. They started toward the fence. "I know my starting point. It's the Empire Theater," Nora heard herself say. "But where am I going?"

"To the funeral museum. You're taking Minos to his final destination," Hector replied.

Startled, Nora stopped.

"The real funeral museum, not the one in your building," he clarified with a sympathetic smile. "I can't tell you what to expect. Everyone's funeral museum is different. All I can tell you is that it will be your adventure—whatever's in your head, real or imaginary. What do you think? Can you do it?"

"How soon?" Nora asked, not sure but determined; her voice quavered.

Hector took a pocket watch from his vest pocket and studied the dial. "Tomorrow evening, he said at last. "The weather will be atrocious—thunderstorms and lightning—but that's inevitable. If you get to the theater by nine o'clock, you should be okay."

Nora winced. "Should be okay" wasn't exactly a guarantee. Her reunion with Jillian was scheduled for Tuesday afternoon. *You'll have to cancel,* she thought with a guilty tinge of relief. *You might not get back in time. Or at all. Now isn't that a cheery thought?*

"Okay, nine o'clock," she replied, watching Hector put away his watch. "What else?"

"Wear comfortable clothes and hiking shoes, and bring a flashlight. You're going on a trek."

"What about food and water?"

"Not necessary. Where you're headed, no one gets hungry or thirsty."

"Oh," she said. It was sounding worse and worse. "There and back, right? It's a round trip." She needed to hear him say it.

"There and back. It's your adventure, but you won't face it alone. You'll have all the support you need. We're not going to leave you hanging."

"What kind of support?" Nora jumped on it, almost too eager.

"Guidance and counsel, help getting past tricks, traps, and surprises," he replied, not hesitating.

She recognized it. The mission statement from their website—he was quoting it. That was okay if he truly meant it.

Hector seemed to understand. He spread his arms. Nora stepped into them and let herself be hugged. The hug was awkward and stiff, and his wool tailcoat and vest were scratchy, but she didn't care. It was still comforting.

After a moment, Hector released her, and Nora stepped back. Their eyes met, and she managed a fleeting smile. Hector returned her smile and waited while she climbed over the fence. Then he went back into the cemetery.

CHAPTER 40

Harry revolved out of the lobby and headed down the street to his car. He was back in Portland, coming from a follow-up interview with the commercial real estate company. He' had been hoping for a job offer. Instead, he'd gotten vagueness and obfuscation. They were stalling. Was it possible his gray hair wasn't such a sterling asset after all? Harry wondered.

Unmolested, he continued past the spot where Ratdaddy had previously intercepted him This time there would be no ambush. Nora's doing. She'd inflicted Ratdaddy on him, unwittingly to be sure, and now she seemed to have sent him to the hospital.

Her article in this morning's paper was an ethical lapse—he couldn't pretend otherwise—but was it a mistake? Unrepentant, at least for now, he reached his car and settled himself for the drive back to Goldmont.

As Harry entered the newspaper lot, he spotted Nora standing beside her little hatchback, holding a cardboard box. He pulled into the first open spot and got out in time to see her get into her car. He considered hurrying after her, but he wasn't built for speed, and she was already pulling out.

Probably just as well, Harry decided. What would he have said to her anyway?

As he entered the building, his spirits sagged. A more-than-customary heaviness settled over him and seemed to permeate the lobby, making the trek to the elevator more uphill than usual. On the way to his office, he detoured past Nora's cubicle. She had indeed cleaned it out: her tablet, pen, and laptop were gone, and her job folders, previously scattered across her desk, were now neatly stacked in piles labeled "Pending," "In Progress," and "Completed."

As Harry approached his office, Joyce gophered to her feet, emerging from her cubicle to trail after him. "Yes?" he asked, stopping in front of his door and turning toward her.

"Nora Stanfell has resigned," Joyce announced. Behind her porthole-shaped glasses, her eyes glinted.

"I know. I saw her," Harry said and opened the door. "She'll be hard to replace. We'd better jump on it. Bring me any résumés we have on file. If we don't fill the position soon, we're likely to lose it."

Joyce nodded grimly. She knew the score. Dismissing her, Harry stepped into his office and closed the door behind him, thinking, *Well, here we go again. Another roll of the dice. What will we get this time?*

CHAPTER 41

Stationed outside Ratdaddy's hospital room, Officer Artie Merlino, a three-year veteran of the Goldmont PD, scowled at the accounting textbook balanced on his lap. He had thirty pages to review for his test tonight, and Artie was a little concerned about his progress.

He had recently discovered forensic accounting, and the realization that ledgers and other financial documents could be scrutinized like a crime scene had captured his imagination. But before you can run, you have to walk. As a first step, he'd signed up for the Introductory Accounting program at Goldmont Community College.

In high school, Artie had gotten decent grades, more than decent, but the bar hadn't been set that high. Mr. Karpas, who taught the high-school business curriculum, gave open-book tests and extra points for "at least trying."

Now Artie was grappling with *General Principles of Revenue Recognition* and *Economic Entity Assumptions* with an instructor who graded on a strict curve and automatically flunked the bottom 10 percent of every class. According to her, that was how capitalism worked. Artie wasn't sure he approved, but he was conscientious and hardworking. The material didn't come easily, but it came.

Footsteps sounded in the hallway. He looked up from his textbook and was pleased to see Nurse Capehart wheeling her cart in his direction. It was her second visit. She'd stopped by during morning rounds to introduce herself. "I feel so much safer having you here," she'd confided then.

"Just doing my job," Artie had replied, springing to his feet, acutely aware of Nurse Capehart's modest but alluring contours and the pleasing aroma of antibacterial soap. Glancing at her left hand, he was glad to see she wasn't wearing a wedding ring. She was probably about ten years older than Artie, but that was okay; in fact, he preferred it.

"Do you think he's dangerous?" Nurse Capehart had asked, dropping her voice to a whisper and nodding toward the prisoner's room.

"Probably not," Artie had said, also whispering. "I'm here just in case We did a background check and didn't come up with anything. He's clean, almost too clean."

Nurse Capehart had taken the news with a stoic nod and continued her rounds. Now, two hours later, she was back. Parking her cart along the wall, she greeted Artie with a tense smile. "How's it going?" She was whispering again.

"All quiet." He closed his book, marking his place with his finger. "Are you going in?"

"Yes." Nurse Capehart hesitated, took a deep breath, and said it again, more definitely. "Yes."

"Want me to cover for you?" The prisoner was handcuffed to the bedframe; he wasn't going anywhere, but if it would make her feel better, Artie was happy to oblige.

"No, but thanks," she replied, looking tempted. "It's just a feeling I can't shake. I'm sure it's nothing."

She placed her hands on the cart, which contained an impressive array of medical paraphernalia along with a rumpled, refolded copy of today's *Sun*, and wheeled into the patient's room.

"Looks like you made the morning paper," Artie heard her say, listening as she read Nora's story to the prisoner. It sounded like good news. If the prisoner was cooperating, there wasn't anything to worry about. Artie took his oath to serve and protect seriously, but he wasn't exceptionally brave. The uniform helped, and the gun holstered on his hip helped even more, but when Artie looked in the mirror, he saw an accountant, not a policeman.

"All good," Nurse Capehart reported when she came out a few minutes later. She looked relieved.

"Great," Artie replied, regretfully watching her go.

He was still plodding through his reading assignment when Ratdaddy darted past, handcuffs dangling from his left wrist. Startled, Artie sprang to his feet, letting his textbook fall to the floor. Nurse Capehart's cart was parked in the hall, and Ratdaddy collided with it. The cart toppled and crashed amid an explosion of shattered glass and spilled meds.

Cursing under his breath, Artie navigated the obstacle field. About fifteen feet in front of him, the prisoner flung open the emergency exit door, triggering the alarm, and raced down the stairs. The door to the front lobby was locked. Abruptly, he reversed course and barreled over Artie, who was coming the other way.

Falling back, Artie felt a sudden searing pain in his right ankle. He grabbed the railing to support himself and hobbled up the stairs after the prisoner. He caught up with him in the maternity ward, over by the nurse's station. Hands on his waist, favoring his injured ankle, Artie approached warily.

Cornered with nowhere to go, Ratdaddy clambered onto the desk. His hospital gown opened, flashing white cotton briefs and hairy legs.

"Get down; it's over," Artie shouted with a greater show of conviction than he felt. A crowd had gathered, hemming them in. Still on the desk, the prisoner glared. "I mean it. Get down. Now!" Artie barked, taken aback by Ratdaddy's ferocity.

Instinctively he reached for his gun, but he didn't draw it. *Too risky.* There were too many people around, some of them very pregnant. For a moment, nothing happened, then Ratdaddy pounced. Artie felt an onslaught of new agony in his ankle as Ratdaddy straddled his waist and began pummeling him. Suddenly, a loud thunk rang out followed by two more thunks in quick succession.

The pummeling abruptly stopped. Ratdaddy pitched forward, collapsing on top of Artie, making it hard for him to breathe. As he struggled to unpin his hands and extricate himself, Ratdaddy's body rolled to the right and came to rest alongside him.

Above Artie, faces peered down, and on her knees beside him, Nurse Capehart held a dented bedpan. "It's okay; you're going to be okay." She was trembling.

Woozy, with blood bubbling from his nose, Artie gazed into Nurse Capehart's large brown eyes. She set down the bedpan and clasped his hand. "Thank you," he would have liked to say, but he was too concussed to speak.

CHAPTER 42

Jack parked his pickup as far from the hillside as possible, and made his way into Junior's, careful not to let his attention drift to the spot where he'd come to grief. He was on a mission. Otherwise, there was no way in hell he'd be here.

Inside, the bar was quiet, and the broken-sewer-line smell didn't seem so bad, possibly because Jack's reconstructed nose didn't work that well anymore. It was about two o'clock in the afternoon, and the place was mostly empty. A solitary soul was shooting pool, and a couple guys sat at a table, nursing beers, talking quietly.

None of them looked familiar, including the bartender. Hunched over his phone, he was in his twenties with dark slicked-back hair and a dagger tattoo on his neck. Leaving his phone on the counter, the bartender approached Jack. "Hello, friend, what'll it be?" he asked with generic politeness.

"A beer," Jack said. His hand hovered close to his mouth, screening it from view. The swelling and bruising had mostly subsided, but he still hadn't gotten used to how his tongue felt on the roof of his mouth or what it looked like when he spoke. He was going to have to live with it. According to the doctors, his tongue wasn't growing back.

Jack bided his time while the bartender removed a bottle from the refrigerator case, popped the top, and placed it in front of Jack.

"Is Michelle on the schedule? I was in the neighborhood, and I wanted to say hello," he asked before the bartender could get away.

He didn't remember much from that night, but he did remember Michelle had been extra friendly. Boyfriend be damned. Perhaps he had a shot with her after all. It was worth a try.

The bartender hesitated. He seemed slow on the uptake, or maybe he was being cautious. Jack might be a victim, but these days he looked a lot like a perpetrator.

"She and I are old friends," Jack said, taking pains to articulate clearly. By now they had the bar to themselves. The two guys at the table had left a few minutes ago, and the pool player had followed shortly after with a desultory wave as he crossed the threshold into the open air.

"Before my time, but I think she quit," the bartender said.

"Any idea where she went?" *Just my luck*, Jack thought. *I don't even know her last name.*

"Maybe you should check with Roy."

"Check with me about what?" a voice from the doorway called out.

Jack took a swig of his beer, bathing his mouth in numbing balm. Placing the bottle on the counter, he turned slowly to face the bar's owner.

As usual, Roy was wearing work jeans, no belt, and a flannel shirt with lots of pockets. The shirt was snug. Roy had gained some weight, but there were muscles beneath the fat—the sort you get from working, not working out. With his buzzed hair, full beard, and upright bearing, the effect was part military, part mountain man.

Beside him on a short leash, Tess, his German shepherd mix, stood and took in the scene with relaxed attentiveness. Her presence in the bar was surely a health-code violation, but apparently no one had ever reported it. Tess was popular. She liked the mailman, didn't chase the feral cats that roamed the grounds, and even tolerated slobbery drunks who hugged her and tried to get her to drink with them.

"Well, well, look what the cat dragged in. I didn't expect to see you." Behind his dark green tinted aviator glasses, Roy's expression was dour and disapproving.

"Just passing time between assignments," Jack said. He was stretching the truth. The newspaper had stopped giving him work. The photography budget was always the first thing to go, and his lucrative side project had ended the night he got thrown into the creek. No more envelopes filled with cash to look forward to.

That had become abundantly clear the day Jack was discharged from the hospital. A big dude with muscles on top of muscles had been standing beside a black Chevy Tahoe, waiting for him. Jack's memories from the night of his "accident" were vague, but he recognized the Tahoe. The guy beside it he wasn't sure about until he spoke. "Got him. I'll take it from here," he said to the orderly.

I'm toast, Jack thought, limp with terror as he was helped into the Tahoe. "Please don't," he begged as Ratdaddy got in and slammed the door.

"Can it, Jack." Ratdaddy put the car in gear and pulled out. "You're in luck. We want you alive and out of the picture. Stay away from Nora. Don't help her, and you could live to a ripe old age. Am I making myself clear?"

"Yes," Jack had said, feeling oddly defeated.

They'd made the rest of the drive in silence, to Jack's relief stopping in front of his apartment building. Unsure, Jack hesitated.

"Remember: stay out of it. Don't push your luck," Ratdaddy had dismissed him. "Now scram."

Banishing the memory, Jack took another swig of his beer and said, "The last time I checked, this was still a free country, or am I missing something?" Given Roy's libertarian proclivities, the statement was provocative.

"It is so far, and you're perfectly free to do your drinking somewhere else," Roy replied. By now his dark lenses had turned clear, and his eyes blazed with don't-tread-on-me truculence.

"Hey, take it easy. No need to get upset," Jack said, raising his hands in a mollifying gesture because someone had to be the voice of reason but also because he wanted information. "I was hoping to talk to Michelle. Apparently she no longer works here."

"Correct."

"I guess she and her boyfriend finally took off," Jack said, lofting a trial balloon that he hoped Roy would shoot down. In his fantasies, there was no question who Michelle rode off with, and it wasn't on the back of a motorcycle.

"Take a break, Jason," Roy barked at the bartender, who'd grabbed a broom, migrated to a far corner of the bar, and was meticulously sweeping. Jason promptly rested the broom against the wall and headed for the door.

"Ten minutes!" Roy called after him, adding to Jack, "My sister's kid."

Jack nodded impatiently. He knew how important family was, just not now and not Roy's. "Any idea where Michelle went?" he asked.

"She quit after your accident," Roy said. The word "accident" was in quotation marks. "You're lucky to be alive. My advice is stay that way. I don't know who she's working for or what her game is, but you're not going to get any satisfaction. Move on."

On a few occasions, a chance remark had startled Jack into clarity, let him see what was staring him in the face. Those moments were always accompanied by a sinking feeling bordering on nausea; this current one was no exception.

"Do you know where I can find her?" he persisted. His mouth and his brain were out of sync.

"Idiot. Do what you want, but don't drag me into it." Roy gave Tess's leash a tug. Curled up beside him, she scrambled to her feet. "Jason, get back to work," Roy called out as they crossed the threshold.

Left in momentary possession of the field, Jack tried to feel okay with what had gone down, but it was no good. Roy's words stung. Michelle had played him, set him up so he could be knocked down. *And I came crawling back for more. God, what a chump.*

Abandoning his beer, which at least he hadn't paid for, Jack took one last look at the place where he'd spent so many hours, then started down the rutted parking lot. He felt certain Roy was watching.

In his truck, Jack's emotions surged, and he pounded the steering wheel with an angry roar that should have shattered glass and reduced Junior's to rubble. He'd fucked up, and he needed to make amends, but first he had to get the hell out of here. Putting the truck into gear, he peeled out.

Once he calmed down, Jack called his kid sister Rita, three years his junior, and wangled a dinner invitation.

"Of course, Jack, you know you're always welcome," Rita said. "The boys will be glad to see their Uncle Jack." She had three of them, ages eight, six, and four, and no husband, not even an ex. "But I have to warn you," Rita continued, sounding a little troubled, "all we're having is spaghetti casserole."

"Perfect; I'll bring dessert," Jack said, thinking he could stop at the quickie mart and get a nice assortment of donuts, a two-liter Coke, and a cold six-pack.

"It's a deal." There was an awkward pause, and she added, "Are you sure you're okay? Is everything all right, Jack?"

"Couldn't be better. Just looking forward to some family time," he said, which was at least partially true.

The kiddos had obviously been coached. It was the first time they'd seen Uncle Jack since his accident, and they gave him a big welcome, pretending not to notice all those patches of partially healed skin. Finally, after they were tucked into their bunk beds, no baths tonight, Jack and Rita settled down on the TV room couch and polished off the rest of the six pack and ate the leftover donuts.

Like her brother, Rita was large-boned. They both had round faces, although hers was capped with candy-blue hair whose flyaway tendencies she controlled with hairspray and lots of brushing. Also, she had tattoos: one for each of the boys, and a new one on the back of her left hand—a large eye done in dark blue ink. According to

229

Rita, it was meant to be decorative, but Jack found it disquieting, like a body part in the wrong place.

"So, what's going on?" Rita asked a little too casually once she'd brought him up to date on the boys and their doings.

Jack took a deep breath. "I've got a little surprise for you." He removed his wallet from his back pocket and pulled out a slip of paper folded in half. "Something for you and the kiddos."

With a puzzled expression, Rita took it. Her eyes grew wide.

"I won some money playing the lottery, and I wanted to share," he said, his cover story. In reality, it was most of his remaining Ratdaddy money, almost $5,000. The money was tainted, and he needed to get rid of it. Giving it to Rita helped solve the problem. The rest he was going to blow on one huge drunken debauch, after which he'd face the future stone cold sober.

"Are you sure?" Rita asked. She was still staring at the check.

"Yes."

"Thank you, big brother. You're the best. Love you." She reached over and gave him an awkward hug. Jack let the hug run its course, then got up and headed to the closet to get his windbreaker. "You're not leaving?" Rita exclaimed.

"I have to." He made a sad face. "I have some things I need to take care of." Another fib. Felony Foster was performing at the Temple. If he left now, he could make the late show.

"But the weather. Can't it wait? Why push your luck?" Rita went to the window and pulled back the curtain. From a purple-black sky, rain pummeled the glass.

"Oh." He hadn't noticed.

"Stay. I'll make up the couch. We'll have pancakes for breakfast. The boys will be excited to see Uncle Jack's still here."

"Sorry, sis, but I really need to go." He made another sad face and zipped up his windbreaker. "Don't worry; I'll be extra careful."

As he stood in the building entryway, Jack considered the Niagara of water between him and his truck, which he assumed was still in the parking lot though he couldn't see it.

He could go back, but even as he considered it, he knew he wouldn't. He had the umbrella Rita had forced on him. Defiant, not opening it, he stepped into the storm. By the time he reached the truck, he was drenched.

He turned the key. The engine started. Keen for adventure, Jack leaned forward, both hands on the steering wheel, and peered past the frantically oscillating wiper blades.

On to the Temple.

CHAPTER 43

The Temple, Goldmont's only Gentleman's Club, sat on a small rise, looking vaguely Grecian with four faux-marble columns in front and a crown-shaped cornice over the door.

Daydreaming down the road, Felony missed her exit and didn't even begin to brake until she was a good hundred feet past it. Annoyed with herself—the turnoff had been in plain sight if she'd been paying attention—she continued to the next exit and looped back.

She'd arrived in Goldmont that afternoon on what she was privately thinking of as her Farewell and Forgiveness Tour. It was her first week on the road with three more weeks to go, and she was already sick of touring. But the money was good—she still had fans—and she was meeting Nora tomorrow afternoon at the bench in front of the hotel. Their meeting was bound to be uncomfortable, but she didn't need to think about it yet.

She was early. After parking in the area reserved for employees, Felony headed to the back entrance and up the steps to a covered porch. She pressed the buzzer, waited, pressed two more times in rapid succession, waited some more, and was about to press it again when the door swung open.

Whoever opened it had vanished, presumably reabsorbed into the milling throng of dancers in various stages of undress—all of them, it seemed to Felony, going out of their way to ignore her.

She wasn't surprised. Dancing was a cutthroat business. She

came to town, stole their customers, vacuumed up the money that would otherwise have gone to them, then left. It was a good thing she had her own dressing room, even if it was a small trailer about twenty feet behind the building, connected to it by a concrete walkway with a canopy overhead to shelter it from the elements.

Felony's first stop was the manager's office. A large man, easily six four and close to three hundred pounds, he was talking on the phone, his bright red sneakers propped on the desk. A red silk shirt, open a couple buttons down, was tented around his torso and revealed a thick gold chain coiled on his furry chest.

He glanced up, acknowledging her presence with a flicker of a smile and motioned for her to wait. The phone conversation showed no sign of ending, and Felony suspected it was deliberate; he was putting her in her place. Perhaps he was wondering how this unimposing woman standing in his doorway, dressed in a loose blouse and baggy shorts, her feet in flip-flops, and wearing a scarf to hide her curlers, could be worth that hefty guarantee.

From experience, Felony knew how important it was to set the right tone. Flouncing into the room, she dropped into the chair across from him. She had a phone too, and she pulled it out of her purse to check for messages.

Her agent had sent some details about her next booking; Dr. Silverblatt still thought the tour was a mistake but was willing to conduct some sessions by phone "on a trial basis," and there was a new message from Nora. She looked up before opening it. The manager had his forearms on the desk and was leaning forward, glaring at her, so now they were even.

"Hello, Miss Foster. So glad you could stop by," he said with heavy sarcasm.

"My pleasure," Felony replied, tit for tat, tucking the phone back into her purse.

What followed was the speech, spelling out the pertinent legal statutes and rules: how close you could get, what things you could touch and which ones you shouldn't. It was strictly cover-your-ass.

If anything happened, the manager could shake his head and say, 'I assure you, officer, she was warned.'

"Oh, and one last thing," he threw in, trying to sound casual

"Yes?" Felony's guard, already high, rose even higher. *Here it comes*, she thought, *he's getting ready to fuck with me.*

"It's about the photos. We're gonna need ten dollars per picture for the house."

Felony was scheduled to dance twice, each time followed by a photo session. Fans could pay twenty dollars to pose with her, and she kept the money. All the money. That was the deal, what they'd negotiated. Now he was reneging.

"In that case, it's thirty dollars per photo," she said, biting out the words. "Twenty for me, ten for you. Either that or I walk."

The manager gave her a sour smile. "All right, we'll try it your way, but only for the first show. Let's see how it goes."

"If it doesn't go, there won't be a second show," Felony replied heatedly. Not waiting for a response, she huffed out.

Her next stop was the DJ's booth. "Hi, I'm Felony," she introduced herself with strategic friendliness. It was important to get off on the right foot. He could screw her if he messed up her music and she ended up performing to Madonna or, god forbid, Britney Spears.

"Yeah, I know," the DJ drawled, so laid back he seemed almost comatose. Thin and pale, he had dirty blond hair that tumbled to his shoulders, and his blue eyes radiated a louche spirituality.

"What's your name. sweetheart?" Felony asked, wondering, *What's eating him? Maybe he doesn't like girls.*

"Curt," he replied with a thin smile. "With a *C*, not a *K*."

"Nice to meet you, Curt with a *C*. Has anyone ever told you, you look like the other Kurt?"

"Yeah, I get that a lot," he said. The smile faded, leaving behind pretty much nothing.

Felony reached into her purse, pulled out a CD and handed it to him—her music. Languidly, he took it and glanced at the label. "Cool. A blast from the past," he said, and placed it in the rack.

"Play it loud. I want their ears to bleed." She reached into her purse again, this time bringing out a handful of twenties. You couldn't buy friends, but you could certainly encourage friendliness. With a wan smile, he took the money, barely glancing at it before he stuffed it into the pocket of his jeans.

This early in the evening, the bar was mostly empty, and Felony found a seat without needing to squeeze in next to anyone.

"Hey, Felony, welcome to the Temple. What's your pleasure?" the bartender greeted her with a smile that was a little too large. She was about Felony's age and pretty with dark brown shoulder-length hair. Her T-shirt and jeans were snug enough to make it obvious she had curves.

"A vodka Collins," Felony said, from force of habit, following the bartender's movements as she mixed the drink. In a place like the Temple, it wasn't enough to watch your back; you also had to pay attention to what got set in front of you. If you didn't see it being made, you probably shouldn't drink it.

"On the house," the bartender said on her return, setting the drink down in front of Felony with a just-between-us-girls smile. The drink was tall and fizzy and nicely garnished with an orange slice and a maraschino cherry.

Felony raised it to her lips and took a sip. "Perfect," she said. "What's your name, sweetheart?" She took out a twenty and set it on the bar.

"It's Michelle. Glad you like it," the bartender said with a flirty smile, pretending not to notice the twenty.

"Oh, I do. I like it very much" Felony replied with a calibrated smile. She picked up her drink and stood. "Talk to you later, Michelle. Time to make magic."

Outside, the sky was darkening. Rain was imminent. Felony quickly unloaded her costumes and makeup kit and headed to her dressing room trailer. The key was under the mat, where it was supposed to be.

The trailer was small but serviceable, with a closet large enough to hang her costumes, counter space for her cosmetics, a makeup mirror with decent lighting, and a bathroom stall you could turn around in if you were careful.

Seated at the dressing table, Felony put down her drink and removed her rollers, brushing her hair until it positively glistened. Finally satisfied, she set to work on her face, applying foundation to give her skin a perfect porcelain finish. Pausing to assess the results—left profile, right profile, head-on—she sipped her drink and reached for her makeup brush to highlight her cheekbones.

Eyes next: colored lenses to turn them periwinkle blue, eyeliner to create a perfect doe-like expression, and fake lashes to accentuate the effect.

Another pause, another sip, and she moved on to her lips, meticulously plumping and coloring them until they were a glossy valentine red. Studying her reflection in the mirror, she checked for flaws. She saw none.

There was no need to get dressed yet. She had plenty of time. For her first show, she was going to wear the sparkly gold thing with white stilettoes. It was a winning combination. Guys liked bright and shiny, and white was always good.

Her phone was lying on the dressing table. She reached for it and finally opened the message from Nora: "Sorry, something urgent has come up, and I've got to cancel," Nora had written. "Wish me luck. I'll need it. Hopefully, we can reschedule."

Something urgent. Felony shook her head. *The statue? Surely it couldn't be—not after all this time.*

CHAPTER 44

Harry was in his study, seated in his easy chair. He had a yellow legal pad in his lap and was holding a newly sharpened number-two pencil because that's how he did his best thinking. To his surprise, he'd gotten a job offer from the real-estate company after all. He'd asked for time to decide, and they'd reluctantly agreed. He suspected he wasn't their first choice.

Did he even want the job?

Harry tapped the pencil on his notepad. Could he see himself editing a trade magazine and a bunch of technical publications? Would he be any good at it? Not that he couldn't learn, of course. Unfortunately, the money was no better than what he was making now, but it had a lot of potential if he trusted their promises.

Did he? More tapping.

It was raining, he realized, a sudden downpour with thunder and lightning in the distance. From the other end of the townhouse, he heard a thump and got up to investigate. Under the open kitchen window, a puddle was growing. Paw prints tracked from it to a spot by the wall. A lumpy body with one notched ear was lapping milk. The cat had returned. Taking his measure, the cat glanced at Harry, then went back to the milk.

Harry headed toward the window and slammed it shut. *Hope you don't mind, but you're in for the evening.* Just then, a lightning bolt strobed the sky, followed by an enormous thunderclap. The townhouse shook, and the world went dark.

CHAPTER 45

The Temple was rocking. Guys crowded the tip rail and clustered on couches, dividing their attention between the dancers and the club's large-screen TVs, which were soundlessly tuned to ESPN. Moving among them, prospecting the crowd, women in spangles, straps, and strings coaxed table dances and private sessions, their images wantonly multiplied in the club's mirrored walls and ceiling.

Momentarily isolated from the frenzy, Felony waited to go on, smoking a cigarette she'd bummed from Michelle. Felony had mostly quit, but tonight she felt unsettled, and the cigarette helped to calm her nerves.

What's Michelle's game? Why is she coming on to me? Felony wondered. She didn't sense any real chemistry. They weren't going to end up in bed. So why was Michelle being so bending-over-backwards eager to please?

A puzzle. Felony took another drag from the cigarette and turned her attention to the stage, where a gothy-looking dancer in black spandex and night-of-the-living-dead makeup was fighting a losing battle with the TVs. *A newcomer,* Felony thought, *scratching an itch or here on a dare. Someone should have told her there's nothing sexy about dressing like a zombie or dancing like one.*

The music faded out. Felony tossed her cigarette onto the concrete floor, ground it out, and watched Goth Girl gather up her garments.

"Say goodbye to Darling Daphne," Curt's voice boomed, rising to the occasion. Maybe he wasn't hopeless after all.

"And now …"

Don't fuck this up, Curt, Felony silently commanded, waiting for her cue, checking to make sure her earplugs were in place.

"… put your hands together and welcome the adult-world goddess we all adore, the one, the only …"

The lights flashed.

"Felony Foster!" Curt called out, fading up her music, *The Revolting Cocks'* version of "Do Ya Think I'm Sexy?," amped to rupture blood vessels and shatter eardrums, just as she had requested.

With a burst of energy, Felony flounced out, teasing and flaunting while keeping her distance, careful not to toss her clothes anywhere near the edge of the stage, because someone would inevitably steal them. Slithering onto the floor, a move which was definitely against the rules, Felony arched and scissored, letting her hands roam while the Cocks crowed.

Back on her feet, big finish coming, Felony strutted; the music jeered:

> If you want my body and you think I'm sexy,
> Come on, sugar, let me know.
> If you really need me, just reach out and touch me.
> Come on, honey, tell me so.

And they did. They told her with fistfuls of cash, flung in her direction. One final pass to scoop up her clothes—all accounted for—and Felony exited to raucous applause.

A few minutes later, dressed again in her gold sheath, earplugs discarded, she returned for her photo session. Thirty-five guys had lined up to get their picture taken: $1,050 in cash, a cool $700 of it hers.

Between poses, a man lounging at the bar caught her eye, and she cast darting glances in his direction. He seemed out of place among the crowd's ball caps and T-shirts. Tall and muscular, he had long black hair combed straight back, and he was wearing wire-rimmed glasses that Felony was willing to bet he didn't need.

Oddly enough, none of the other women seemed to be hitting on him. The way he was dressed, his nicely rumpled linen shirt and those expensive-looking olive-gray slacks should have made him a prime target.

Finally finished, Felony tipped the security guard who'd worked her photo session and headed to the bar. Her mystery man had vanished, which was too bad. She'd have liked a closer look. As she approached the bar, a jowly, middle-aged guy in a velour warmup suit jumped up and offered her his seat. "Buy you a drink, darling?" he asked as she sat down, his lips hovering by her ear.

"Of course," Felony said, not hesitating. He seemed harmless enough, and it was a house rule. The answer was always yes. Drinks at the Temple weren't strong, but they were expensive, and if a guy thought he might get lucky, well that was even better.

She was still settling in when Michelle showed up to take their order. "Hey, girl, what'll it be?" she asked with a big smile.

I don't trust you, Felony thought, meeting Michelle's smile with one just as sincere. "Iced coffee," she decided. It was a perverse choice. Any coffee available at the Temple would be left over from the dinner buffet special and was certain to be toxic and highly corrosive, only slightly more drinkable than battery acid.

"You sure about that?" Michelle looked skeptical.

"Yes," Felony said. "On the rocks with cream and a shot of Kahlua."

"And I'll have a beer," the guy in the velour warmup suit interjected. He'd managed to snag the seat to Felony's right. Money clip in hand, he peeled off some bills and laid them on the bar.

"Okay, got it. Coffee and beer coming up," Michelle said, and scurried off. Felony tried to watch her progress, but the bar was too crowded.

"What's your name, sugar?" she asked, turning toward her new acquaintance.

"Hank," he said, almost too quickly.

Felony nodded. It was as good a name as any. It might even be his. Guys in strip clubs lied a lot, sometimes for the hell of it.

"Pleased to meet you, Hank. How's your night going?"

"Getting better," he said, flashing a smile. Felony smiled back. But then he added, "It sure beats hanging out at the motel." So not that much of a compliment after all. In Felony's experience, almost anything was better than that.

"What brings you to town, Hank?" she asked, resisting the urge to take a quick glance down the bar for Michelle.

For a moment, the question hung there. "Work. I'm a problem solver. People come to me for solutions, generally after they've completely fucked things up. I come in and save their ass."

Felony wasn't sure what to make of that. And anyway, Michelle was back. With a flourish, she placed a Tom Collins glass filled with tan fluid in front of Felony and handed Hank a bottle of Coors.

Felony's drink sat there, three sets of eyes regarding it with interest. Leaning forward, Felony reached for it. Before she could grasp the glass, a hand darted out from behind her and upset it. Liquid splashed and splattered, rolled off the counter and pooled at Felony's feet.

"God damn it!" She jumped from her stool, stepping back so she wasn't standing in a puddle.

Around her a crowd of gawkers had formed. Fuming, Felony glared at them, looking for a culprit. During the disturbance, Hank had vanished, leaving his beer behind. Meanwhile, Michelle had grabbed a roll of paper towels and was wiping down the bar.

Still fuming, Felony rushed to the club's back entrance and her trailer to change clothes. She thrust the metal door open and stepped onto the covered porch, letting the door slam behind her.

Inside the Temple, with its thick concrete walls, total lack of windows, and blaring music, it wasn't obvious, but out here a storm was raging. In a black sky, lightning and thunder crashed, and a sharp tang of ozone filled the air.

Felony retreated, tried the door, which was locked, then rang the buzzer. Nothing. She tried again. More nothing. Through the driving rain, she could glimpse her trailer at the end of the gravel path and noted what hadn't been obvious before.

The path was poorly lit, and the canopy over it leaked. There was no way she could reach the trailer without getting drenched, and she'd still need to return.

"Can I help?" a voice, calm and quiet but audible over the storm, said.

Felony startled. The man with the long black hair was standing to her left about five feet away.

"You," she called out. "It was you. You spilled my drink."

"Guilty," he said, not looking the least bit sorry. He'd taken off his glasses, and Felony couldn't help but notice how good he looked without them.

"If I'd wanted your help, I would've asked," she replied, still indignant but also intrigued. "I didn't need rescuing. I wasn't going to drink the damn thing." She reached behind her and rattled the doorknob again. As she expected, it didn't budge.

"I know. You were toying with the bartender, playing her. But the guy you were talking to, Hank—not his real name, by the way—he was playing you. When he said he was a problem solver, he was talking about you. You're the problem he was solving."

Felony grimaced. "Why? How am I a problem?" She was almost too astonished to be alarmed.

"It's your friend. She's going to need you. He was sent to stop you, to make sure you couldn't help her."

Nora, she thought, remembering her text. Lost in thought, Felony looked away. The storm wasn't letting up. Her trailer was out of reach. The door behind her—she wasn't going to try it again—was locked. And she didn't want to go back inside anyway.

She turned toward her porch companion, reassured to see he

hadn't moved from his original spot. His posture appeared relaxed but vigilant. He looked confident.

"What's your name, sugar?" she asked, stalling. "Your real name, please."

"Alexander Wyman," he answered with a sober smile. "Nora and I are colleagues. It's not the statue. We're past that."

"Good." Felony was relieved to hear it, but what then? Taking her time, surprised at herself, she said, "Okay, Alexander Wyman, tell me about it. I have a feeling it's important." She finished the thought silently: *For me, not just Nora.*

He raised his hand. He was holding a large black umbrella with an elaborately curved handle. As Felony watched, the umbrella flapped open like a large bird extending its wings.

Carefully clip-clopping toward him in her stilettoes, she took his arm. "Do I have time to change?" she asked, almost giddy.

"Of course," he said. "Your clothes, too."

CHAPTER 46

Earlier that evening, Nora sailed down Jupiter Boulevard and parked in front of the Empire, leaving her car pointed the wrong way on the empty thoroughfare. Without Hector stationed out front to welcome her, the theater seemed more desolate than ever. The tumbledown marquee still said "Girls Galore" on one side and "See how To" on the other, but it was a new sign posted on the door that caught her eye:

Stay Out
Authorized Personnel Only

Me, it's for me. I'm expected, Nora thought, remembering her Olympian Hall debacle. Back then she had also been expected and had walked into a trap. This time was different; it had better be.

She stepped from her car and strode toward the entrance. Around her, the air felt thick, and in the distance over the water, the darkness was shot with bands of green. Something big was coming ashore, just as Hector had predicted. He'd told her to dress for a trek, so she'd gone with her breaking-into-buildings outfit: the navy-blue hoodie, jeans, and tennies. In her hand, she held a flashlight like the one she'd taken to Olympian Hall, and she was wearing Thalia's bracelet.

Nora barely touched the theater door, and it swung open. Gathering her nerve, she took a deep breath, then one more, and stepped into the entryway, reassured by the pungent remembered odor of mildew and decay. Behind her, the door closed quietly. The demolished auditorium was dark and still. The stage where Wyman had danced for her was empty, a bare platform with rotting beams and posts.

"Pathetic, just pathetic," a male voice called out, echoing in the darkness.

Already on edge, Nora jumped, and her heart lurched. "Who is it? Where are you?" she shouted. Her swinging flashlight cut swaths through the darkness without finding anywhere to land.

"Try to guess. We've met," the voice teased, but at least it didn't seem to be coming closer.

"Why don't you tell me?"

"Wait a moment. I'll turn on the lights. That should help."

Footsteps sounded, and after a brief interval, the lights blinked on, the same colored spotlights as before with gaps where bulbs had burnt out. "How about now?" he asked, approaching slowly.

Spiky brown hair, dark eyes, a scruffy haven't-shaved-in-a-week beard. It took a moment, but Nora recognized him. It was her undergraduate, the one who had offered her his candle. Tonight's T-shirt was a faded blue with the image of a cannon across the chest and the words "Come and Take It" underneath. His baggy shorts sagged to his knees, and he was wearing flip-flops.

"Well?" he asked, to her relief stopping about eight feet from her.

"You're Curse the Dark," she replied with sudden awareness, working to sound calm. "Don't you have a show tonight?" she asked, remembering his End-of-the-World Concert at Hambone's.

"It's going to be canceled. Rotten weather." With a pointed glance at her flashlight, he added, "Could you please stop shining that damn thing at me? It's super annoying."

"Sorry." Humoring him, she turned it off.

"So here we are," Curse said in the ensuing silence. "No one around, just you and me in a condemned building. How charming. If I were you, I'd turn around and get out while you can. You'll get wet, you'll get very wet, but at least you'll live to talk about it. Go now, before I change my mind."

"And if I don't?" Nora asked, trying to ignore her racing heart and the unruly pounding of her pulse. She was supposed to be here; he was trespassing.

"Nora, this isn't existential loitering. I'm not playing games," Curse said, starting toward her. She took a step back. "Can't you see?' He stopped about four feet from her. "They're using you to do their dirty work. They don't care about you. Go back while there's still time. I'm not going to warn you again."

An impasse. Nora pulled back her sleeve and exposed her bracelet, reddish-orange and softly gleaming. Wyman had warned her not to take it off, but she would if she had to.

"Do you remember the night you got inked? Your tattoo artist?" Curse surprised her by asking, his eyes locked on the bracelet.

"Yes," she said, remembering: *Pale; almost emaciated; arms covered with ghosts and ghouls; 'HELL FIRE' inscribed on his fingers. I kind of liked him.*

"He's dead."

"How? When?" Shocked, Nora blurted the words out.

"A while back. An accident in his shop. He tripped and fell down the stairs. He missed the first two steps, struck the third with his shoulders, snapped his neck on the fourth and split his head open at the bottom, but by then it didn't matter."

"Why? He was harmless."

"He was a loose end. He needed to be tied off." Curse extended his hand and made a snipping motion with his fingers. "Leave now and it ends. No one else gets hurt."

"It's that simple?"

"Yes."

"And Ratdaddy? You can call him off?"

"Already taken care of. All that throwing his weight around, getting people worked up—it was bound to end badly." He shook his head. "Bludgeoned with a bedpan. Stupid, just stupid."

Oh. Nora was puzzled. Her story, had it worked? *Probably not, but something had—if Curse wasn't lying.*

"Make up your mind, Nora. My patience is almost exhausted. I don't want to hurt you, but if I have to, I will."

"I have a hunch," she said with a reassuring glance at her bracelet; it was still gleaming. Her heart was no longer hammering, and her pulse had gone from a gallop to something like a steady trot. "I think you're bluffing. I don't think you can stop me."

With a coolness she didn't feel, she turned on her flashlight, and directed the beam past Curse to the corridor on the other side of the auditorium.

"Don't," he warned.

With a deep breath, Nora took a step forward, braced herself, and kept going, listening for the sound of footsteps rushing toward her. None came, only Curse's angry echoing voice, shouting, "You're so screwed. They don't give a damn about you!"

As Nora entered the corridor, the yelling ceased, or she couldn't hear it anymore. *Home free*, she thought, and immediately corrected herself. She was a long way from home and more encumbered than ever. Just then, as if to reinforce that thought, the lights went out—a parting shot from Curse, no doubt.

CHAPTER 47

"What's past or yet to come, wouldn't it be interesting if you could see it in a mirror?" Wyman had said. Nora stood in front of the theater's dressing room mirror, and waited—for what she didn't know. In the near-total darkness, she couldn't even make out her reflection, and her flashlight beam barely registered on the mirror's warped surface.

Suddenly the mirror began to ripple and shimmer. An immense storm cloud covered its surface and rolled toward her. From the center of the cloud, two points of light glowed, and around the cloud, bands of fire arced and flashed.

Too startled to move—and where could she run anyway?—Nora stood her ground, braced and waiting as the cloud rushed toward her. When it looked as if it were about to break free from the glass and engulf her, she ducked.

When she looked again, the cloud had disappeared, replaced by a large creature with horns, leathery wings, and a long coiled tail. He was striding toward her without appearing to close the distance. Spellbound, she watched as the image faded and words began to write themselves across the mirror in a sprawling script:

Please proceed with CAUTION.

Slowly they, too, faded, and the mirror went dark. Perturbed. not sure what to make of it, Nora waited, but nothing else appeared. The show was over.

Still following the route she'd taken with Wyman, she found the red, yellow, and green doors. Not breathing too deeply—the dust and mold were getting to her—she carefully touched each doorknob. Nothing. They all felt the same. Perhaps it didn't matter which door she chose. Maybe they all went the same way, or they went different ways but ended in the same place.

Nora was about to leave it to chance when a thought occurred to her. The mirror had told her to proceed with "CAUTION," all caps duly noted. *Yellow for caution*, she thought, scrutinizing the doors again, this time lingering on the middle one.

A leap of faith. If ever she needed to take one, it was now—or in this case, not much faith, mostly a leap. Silently, Nora counted down from three, grasped the middle doorknob, and turned it. What she saw filled her with dismay. A pummeling curtain of rain too heavy for her flashlight to penetrate filled the doorframe. The route was impassable.

Just then, through the cannonading rain, Nora heard a whirring sound, faint at first, then louder and more insistent. After a moment, a hazy round glow appeared and advanced toward her. A golf cart came into view, swung around and parked sideways, filling the doorway. Nora couldn't immediately tell who it was. The driver's face was obscured by a broad-brimmed rain hat and a large yellow slicker.

"Greetings, Eleanora," he said. "Your chariot awaits."

It was Paul Tsitak.

"Oh, Paul, am I glad to see you," she replied, visibly relieved.

He smiled. Another slicker and rain hat lay on the seat beside him. Reaching across, he handed them to her. "Put these on, and we'll get started."

Nora hastily complied. Everything fit well enough, which is to say they completely covered her and then some. Fully outfitted, feeling as if she were inside a tent, Nora climbed aboard. They got off to another one of Paul's lurching starts. As they puttered along, lightning and thunder flashed and boomed, and rain pummeled the golf cart, running off the roof in torrents. Yet somehow, despite all that, they were staying dry. Inside her rain outfit, Nora felt almost cozy.

"Are we really going to the funeral museum?" she shouted over the storm.

"Yes." Hunched forward, both hands on the wheel, Paul peered ahead.

"Well at least it's indoors," Nora said, because anything you can joke about can't be that bad.

"Some of it is, not all of it," Paul replied, still not looking at her.

The storm finally showed signs of letting up, and a thick mist began to settle around them, blanketing everything in gray fog. Through it a building appeared, illuminated by spotlights around the perimeter. As Nora focused on it, the golf cart slowed and stopped in front of a flight of marble steps. At the top, a brightly illuminated bronze door called to her.

"Nervous?" Paul asked, settling back and turning toward Nora.

"Yes," she admitted.

"Unfortunately, this is as far as I can go. That's the door to the funeral museum. You're taking Minos to the Judgment Gate. It's at the back of the museum."

Surprised, Nora said, "So he can be tried for his crimes and face punishment?"

"No." Paul chuckled grimly. "So he can be installed as a judge over the dead and decide the fates of those souls waiting to move on. It's not fair, I know. But it's a terrible place, and he's going to be there for all eternity."

"This Judgment Gate, how do I find it? Is there a map?" Nora asked, more concerned with practicalities than matters of fairness.

"No map. You'll know it when you see it. Trust your instincts. They'll lead you there."

"I see," Nora replied, not sure she had instincts, let alone ones she could trust.

"Your tattoo's breaking down, Alex is right, and your bracelet won't keep him in check forever," Paul continued. "But there's still time. Be deliberate; don't rush."

Nora nodded. It was easy for him to say. She was the one who had to do it.

"Just make sure you're standing in front of the gate when you take your bracelet off. And this is very important: bring the bracelet back. Under no circumstances should you leave it behind."

"Okay, got it." Nora took a deep breath.

Almost as though he was reading her thoughts, Paul added, "And don't worry. Minos won't be able to harm you once he's free. As a judge, his dominion is only over the dead. He can threaten you, try to bully you, and no doubt he will, but he can't hurt you."

"So all I have to do is stay alive," Nora said. Looking at the marble staircase, she counted the steps—there were seventeen—and tried to picture herself ascending them.

"You'll do fine," Paul replied with a sympathetic smile. "The mirror—you must have looked into it. What did you see?"

"A storm cloud sweeping toward me, followed by a snarling creature with horns, wings, and a long tail."

"No need to worry about the storm. That's past; you made it," Paul said decisively. "Where you're going it never rains." He paused for a moment. "Or anything else. There's no weather at all. It's perfectly calm. Nothing's stirring."

Nora nodded. *No weather—how is that possible?* "And the creature?" she asked. "What about him?"

"It's not a minotaur; he's not one of ours." Paul sounded disappointed.

"No, it looked like a demon. It was some kind of devil," Nora replied, puzzled by his reaction. What difference did it make whose monster it was?

"It must be a newcomer, one of the upstarts. I hate how they're taking over the place. But it doesn't matter. Whoever he is, new crowd or old, the reality doesn't change. He still can't hurt you."

"Are you sure?" Nora didn't relish the idea of confronting that thing, no matter how harmless he was.

"Yes."

"Okay." She let it go. "What else?"

"Your father—he was quite a character. I know you remember his stories."

Startled, Nora looked at him. "Some of them. Why? How did you know my father?"

"Through Top-Notch. I was on the mailing list; I got the catalog; occasionally, I bought something. Your father never worried about being factual—he took all kinds of liberties—but he always stayed true to the spirit. It's what I admired about him. Follow his example and you'll do fine."

"Did you ever meet him?" Nora managed to ask, touched and troubled. She had a couple of his catalogs in the memory drawer of her bureau. When she got back, she would have to take a look.

"No, but I was delighted when his daughter appeared on my doorstep. He would be very proud of you."

Giving Nora time to regain her composure, Paul stepped out of the golf cart and slowly removed his hat and slicker, then stowed them in the back. Finished, he approached and offered her his hand. She hadn't noticed before, but he was wearing gloves. Carefully, she took his hand and stepped out.

"I guess this is it," she said when she'd shed her raingear, gazing again at the museum's massive bronze door.

"Ready?" Paul asked.

Yes," Nora said, and decided, to her surprise, she mostly meant it.

"Well then, no goodbyes." He smiled. "See you soon, Eleanora. I'll be waiting for you on the other side."

"Right, see you soon," she said with a smile of her own and started up the marble staircase.

Nora had gotten used to doors that readily opened when she touched them, but not this one. No matter how hard she strained, the funeral museum's heavy bronze door barely budged. It almost felt as though the door was fighting her.

With her hands on her hips, Nora glared at the door while she worked to catch her breath. She hadn't heard the golf cart's departing whirr. Most likely Paul was still there, observing her struggle and waiting in case she needed a ride back. After all the obstacles she'd overcome to get here, she couldn't give up.

Nora braced herself, took a deep breath, and tackled the door, pulling, straining, giving it everything she had. For a moment, nothing happened; but then the door gave a little—and then a little more. Encouraged, Nora reached deep, going beyond her limits, tapping reserves she didn't know she possessed.

Slowly, grudgingly, the door parted. *Who says brute strength is never the answer?* Nora saw her opening and took it. She darted through, barely clearing the door before it slammed shut behind her with a resounding metallic echo.

Stepping away from the door, hands on her hips, Nora waited for the burning sensation in her arms and lungs to subside. She was in a room crowded with dark wood furniture, potted greenery, and vases lush with flowers. Table lamps cast dim pools of light, and over the sound system, a string quartet played something melancholy.

Cautiously, Nora navigated the furniture, heading toward a doorway at the far end of the room. Hidden in shadow, a placard sat on an easel. As she approached it, a spotlight blinked on. To her astonishment, it was a picture of her father. He was standing at his workbench, pointing a toy gun, angled slightly upward. From the gun's plastic barrel, pink, purple, and green bubbles streamed, half obscuring his face—but not his grin, which was large and devil-may-care.

Below his image, there was a caption:

Mitch Stanfell
Aim for the Top. So What if You Miss?

Paul had warned her that whatever she experienced here would be uniquely personal, but this was an emotional sucker punch. Still, Nora couldn't help but linger, impressed by how young and confident her father looked. He was in his early twenties, she guessed, so before her time. Her mother, who wasn't her mother yet, must have taken the picture.

On guard, Nora stepped across the threshold and entered a room like the first, only smaller. On the back wall, lights came on, showcasing another photo, life-sized and mounted on a stand. It was a picture of her mother, Rachel. Nora's heart skipped a beat. Young and slender with brown hair and bangs, she was looking down, tenderly smiling at a baby bundled in her arms. Another image Nora didn't remember having seen. The caption read,

A Mother's Love. Nothing Tops It.

Rattled, Nora stared, struggling to bridge the distance, but it was hopeless. Where a mother's love should be, she felt only a dull ache; the distance was too great. The funeral museum was toying with her, and she forced herself to look away. More lights came on, this time illuminating a table. Draped in front, a banner said,

Top Notch™ Novelties. Help Yourself.

Displayed on the table, Nora saw games and gadgets—things her father had invented, none of which had made him rich or famous. Scanning the display, Nora looked for the bubble gun. She checked twice but didn't see it. *Odd.* Everything else seemed to be here, even her pyramid safe with her word locked inside and, front and center, a small wooden coffin.

From its base, a skeleton key shaped like a skeleton protruded. Nora yearned to give it a twist to see the lid fly open and the skeleton inside sit up, look left and then right, then slam the lid shut. Would it be wrong to take it with her?

"Help Yourself," the sign said, but would it help her? *Better not*, she reluctantly decided. Paul had told her to trust her instincts and be guided by her father's precepts. That meant being careful what she touched and not pocketing anything unless she absolutely needed to. Everything had consequences, and those consequences could be dire.

With a last look at the table display, Nora turned away. In a corner of the room, a figure sat obscured in darkness. For a moment, she thought her eyes were playing tricks on her, that it was a shadow. But then the shadow rose, hovered a moment, and slowly drifted toward her.

"Hello, Nora," it said in a mournful voice. "You, too?"

"Jack!" Nora called out with a shock of recognition. "What are you doing here?"

The shadow grimaced. "There was a storm. I was driving through it, and suddenly I wasn't. Am I ... Dumb question. Of course I am."

Dead, yes, Nora thought. It certainly looked like it. Jack appeared to have shape but no substance. If Nora were to reach out and try to touch him—something she had no intention of doing—her hand would almost certainly go right through. On the plus side, his scars had healed. He no longer looked as if he'd been flung headfirst down a hillside.

"But what are you doing here? You're still ... At least, I think you are."

"Yes," Nora said, "I am. Definitely."

"Good, I'm glad. But how is it possible?"

Nora hesitated. After all that had happened, she still liked Jack, but she didn't much trust him. On the other hand, it might not matter. The old saying about dead men and tales came to mind.

"It's a long story," she said.

Jack's expression suggested it was all right; he had plenty of time.

Nora reluctantly filled him in—not giving him all the details but enough of them. Jack listened thoughtfully. He didn't interrupt with questions or make a single wisecrack. When she finished, he said, "How about it, Nor? Can you stand some company?"

Nora looked at him, not sure how to respond. Paul had told her she'd have help, but surely he didn't mean Jack.

"Think about it," he continued. Nora could hear the desperation in his voice. "Our meeting here—it can't be an accident. I mean, what are the odds? You're going to the Judgment Gate. So am I, admittedly not for the same reason. It makes sense to travel together."

Glancing around, Nora scrutinized the room, the stops she'd made along the way, her mother's picture, the table display—all dark now.

"I know what you're thinking," he persisted. "I fucked up. I made a huge mess, and I betrayed our friendship. I'm sorry. Let me make it up to you now. One last chance, please."

Nora considered. Given Jack's status, she was inclined to cut him some slack. "Do you know how to get to the Judgment Gate?" she asked. From where she was standing, she saw three doorways, one along each wall, and no signs to guide her.

"Yes, of course." Jack smiled bleakly. "It's a homing instinct. I don't have a choice. Like it or not, it's where I'm going. What do you say, Nor?" His smile turned hopeful. "I swear you won't regret it."

"Okay," she decided. "Glad to have company. Let's get out of here." With a questioning expression, Nora pointed toward the middle door, then turned toward Jack to see if he agreed. He nodded, and they started out side by side. Jack's feet only occasionally touched the ground.

As they passed through the doorway, they were suddenly outside on a gravel path cutting across a broad expanse of lawn. Above them, a full moon lit the way, shining in a still sky flocked with stars.

Ahead, an iron fence loomed. Nora opened the gate, and they passed through. The grass became patchy and petered out, replaced by dark trees with drooping branches that canopied the trail. Up ahead, Nora glimpsed an opening, and they entered a small clearing. In the center stood a marble monument about five feet high. Nora approached it warily. Carved in the stone, she read,

Mitch Stanfell
Master Toymaker, Beloved Father
Arrived in 2014

Hector had told her that everyone's funeral museum was different, that what Nora experienced would reflect what was in her head, but this was a shock. Her father's actual marker, the one Nora could afford, was small, made of concrete, and included only his name and dates.

Jack was standing next to Nora with his head bowed and his hands folded in front of him. "Your dad must have been pretty cool," he said in the reverent voice people adopt to speak well of the dead.

"Yes, very cool," Nora agreed through an upsurge of emotion.

"Can I ask how—"

"A car crash, late at night," she interrupted as usual hurrying through the details: "He was heading home. The weather was bad. He should have waited. End of story." Except it wasn't. Not really.

"Me, too, only I wasn't going home," Jack said, filling the ensuing silence. If he had been breathing, he might have sighed.

"Well, there is one more thing, something I've never told anyone," Nora said, surprising herself, looking not at Jack but at her father's memorial, focusing on the bottom line with the date.

Jack waited. Finally, he said, "In case you're wondering, my lips really are sealed. It's not just an expression."

My father's death might not have been an accident." Nora was almost whispering. "A one-car crash on a stormy night. But it wasn't that stormy, and he was a good driver."

"Do you suspect foul play?" Jack asked in a hushed voice.

"No, I think there was an insurance policy with no cause-of-death exemption once the policy had been in effect for two years. She shook her head, twisting her lips into a grim smile. "With me as the sole beneficiary."

"And how long had it been?"

"Two years."

"Well, it could have been," Jack said. "An accident, I mean. You take your eye off the road for a moment or you push it because you're in a hurry. It doesn't take much."

"True," Nora agreed, thinking, *His business had failed; Top Notch Novelties had gone under, and he'd taken a job in outside sales, peddling industrial valves of all things. He was miserable, but he left you provided for. I'd rather have him. In a way, I still do.*

"Would you like a moment?" Jack asked, looking pleased he'd thought of it.

"Yes, thanks."

Jack glided to the other side of the clearing, and Nora gazed at her father's tombstone, hoping for what she wasn't sure, a message or something, but there was only silence.

Giving up, she joined Jack. They started walking, picking up the path on the other side of the clearing. After a few minutes, they approached a fork in the road, and Nora slowed to a stop. Their current path continued straight under a canopy of trees. A much narrower path veered off to the right, hemmed in on both sides by tall grasses.

She pointed to the trail on the right. Jack nodded, and they started down it.. Without warning, the path made a hard left and opened onto a manicured lawn bordered by neatly trimmed hedges.

Nora started into the clearing and froze. At her feet where it had been flung, Tony Goldmont's bronze head glared at her. Strewn around the rest of the clearing, Nora saw dented body parts. *Hector,* she thought with a shudder. *After I left the cemetery, he stayed behind. What did he have in that doctor's bag? A sledgehammer and a hacksaw?*

In the middle of the clearing, an obelisk rose—a granite column about twelve feet tall with a pyramid point, jabbing the sky. Nora threaded her way through the wreckage and headed toward it, followed by Jack. At its base, she saw a brass plaque.

Sacred to the Memory of
Count Anthony Montagna d'Oro
(a.k.a. Tony Goldmont)
Vengeance Is Coming
1860-2018

And below, in much smaller letters:

Erected by the Family and Friends of King Minos

Nora did the math: 158 years was a biblical lifespan even if most of it had been spent confined in a statue. Looking down, she reread the plaque. It was bad enough that every time she rounded a corner, she expected a horned demon to be waiting for her; now this: "Vengeance Is Coming," brought to you by "the Family and Friends of King Minos."

To reassure herself, she glanced at her bracelet—it was still gleaming—then turned toward Jack. The moonlight wasn't doing him any favors. He looked paler and less substantial than ever. "Ready to move on?" she asked.

"No, but I am anyway," he replied with a joyless smile.

"Sorry." Nora grimaced. "That came out wrong."

"It's okay. On to …" He let the thought trail off.

Oblivion? Is that how it ends? Please, no, Nora silently completed the thought.

Continuing on, they weaved around more body parts and picked up the path on the other side of the clearing.

And now the going became more difficult. The path turned perverse, took them up and down for no discernable reason, threw curves, and branched off with frustrating frequency. If there was a pattern, Nora couldn't see it. But they weren't lost. She knew where they were going; she just had no idea where they were.

Then disaster struck. They came around a bend and got stopped in their tracks. To Nora's dismay, a section of the trail had broken away, leaving a five-foot gap and a drop of at least fifty feet. Stunned, she approached the break, calculating whether she could leap it.

No, she decided. There was no running start long enough to power her over it. With a questioning expression, she turned to face Jack, who was standing behind her. She was stuck, but he could float across.

He shook his head, and pointed to his right at a rocky, desolate hillside pocked with scraggly bushes and stunted trees. As Nora looked, she saw a steep, meandering path going up, wide enough for them to follow if they traveled single file. She guessed it was at least eight hundred feet to the top. "Okay," she said reluctantly. Other than turning back, it was the only option.

They started out with Jack leading the way. Now that Nora had veered off course, she'd lost the thread and no longer knew whether she was going in the right direction. So much for Paul's glib assurance she couldn't get lost. He meant well, but his guidebook was out of date.

"Final stretch. Are you ready?" Jack asked.

They were standing on a broad jutting slab of rock about eighty feet from the summit while Nora caught her breath. The path had petered out, but footholds had been cut into the hillside, leading up to the top. *A good sign*, Nora hoped.

"Yes." *Please lead somewhere*, she silently prayed, and started climbing again.

The last part of their climb wasn't as bad as Nora feared. The footholds were deep and closely spaced, and there were plenty of rocks she could use as handholds. Jack floated alongside her, providing a wispy kind of moral support.

The summit was flat, devoid of vegetation, and strewn with stones. A long wooden bench had been placed in what appeared to be the exact center, and that's where Nora headed. From it in all four directions, she could see densely wooded hills and a tangle of trails snaking through them. She wasn't surprised there were no other people or creatures around, but had she come all this way just for a scenic lookout?

Jack was standing at the far edge of the hilltop from where they'd entered, beckoning to her. Wearily, she stood and trudged toward him. A trail led down and split into two at the bottom. One branch swung to the left; the other went to the right. She had no idea which one to take, but at least she had choices. It wasn't a dead end. Meanwhile, another matter pressed on her. Jack's fading was getting worse. At this rate, he would soon be transparent.

"It seems odd that a place like this would have only one Judgment Gate and no judge for it," she said, peering straight ahead, not at Jack.

"Actually, there are three gates: yours and two others," he replied, peering straight ahead, not at Nora.

"And you should be going to one of the others." There was a note of wonderment in her voice. Jack was defying his fate. That's why he was fading. With every step he took in the wrong direction, he was slowly being extinguished.

"I saw you coming, and I waited," he replied, still not looking at her. "Part of it was not wanting to accept the inevitable. But I also needed to make amends. I was a terrible friend." He laughed ruefully. "One last shot at redemption. Do you think it will count in my favor when I get there?"

If you get there, Nora thought, but of course she didn't say it.

"There's something else," he continued, looking miserable. He reached into his jacket and brought out a plastic, tubular thing.

"I took it off the table, but it's obviously meant for you," he said, extending the object toward Nora. It was her father's bubble gun, the one from the poster.

Nora hesitated. She had been curious about it, but that was all. "Does it work?" she asked.

From Jack's expression, it was apparent he didn't know.

"Try it," she suggested.

Just then there was a roar—loud, ferocious, and nearby. Alarmed, they turned and saw a dark blur of a figure thundering toward them. Not hesitating, Jack zoomed to meet it. They collided. The impact sent him flying, and he landed on his back with a thud. Through clouds of dust, Nora watched as the two figures rolled on the ground, flailing at each other.

At first she thought it might be the horned demon. To her surprise, as the dust settled, she recognized Jack's assailant. It was Ratdaddy, looking very much the way Nora remembered him from the extravaganza. But this time she could only watch. They were ghosts.

It didn't take long. Overmatched, Jack lay on his back, not moving. Straddling him, Ratdaddy raised a large scarred fist to pound Jack into oblivion. A sudden burst of pink, green, and purple bubbles streamed upward toward Ratdaddy, clinging and spreading, flowing over him and wrapping him in a shimmering, iridescent cocoon.

Nora watched, amazed, as Ratdaddy began to rise, lifted upward by the streaming bubbles. Higher and higher he floated, silhouetted against the moon until he slowly drifted out of sight.

Nora rushed toward Jack, who was sitting up now, and crouched beside him.

"Wow. Did you see that?" he exclaimed with a grin, undisputed king of the hill. "Sorry, I'm afraid it's ruined." His grin turned apologetic as he held out the gun. The barrel was now a deformed, half-melted plastic blob. It didn't matter. The gun had served its purpose, and Jack now looked more substantial.

Neither one wanted to say it, but the time had come to go their separate ways. Jack needed to reverse course and head back down the hill. Nora still didn't know what to do. The two trails on the other side of the hill were her only options, but she had no idea where either went, and Jack didn't know either.

"Well, goodbye, Nor; I guess this is it," he finally said, making no move to leave. He looked down, realized he was still holding the bubble gun, and extended it to her.

With a serious smile, Nora took it. *The gun should remain here,* she thought, *a memorial in the wilderness.* She had to find the right spot for it—not that anyone else would ever see it.

"I'm sorry it didn't work out better. I hate to abandon you," Jack continued glumly.

"You're not. I'm good," Nora replied, putting the best face on it. "You did your part," she added, wondering if she could give him a farewell hug. Extending her arms, she leaned forward to embrace him and kiss his cheek. The thought would have to do, but to her amusement, Jack blushed.

CHAPTER 48

Once Jack left, Nora got to work stacking stones to create a column about three feet high. Finally finished, the last stone placed, she centered the gun on top, then stepped back to assess the results. It felt right. She was ready to move on.

Time was no longer standing still, and there was weather. The moon, previously a fixed point in the sky, was creeping toward the horizon, and dark wind-driven clouds were gathering, an ominous portent in a place where it never rained. The hilltop afforded no shelter, but the path down would be treacherous in a storm.

The wind was beginning to howl. Nora looked up and saw a lightning bolt slash across the sky. In its wake, a ragged diagonal cut appeared, outlined in lurid green. Dismayed, she watched the cut grow.

From the ripped sky, a storm cloud emerged. Pulsing and flashing, glowing like molten metal, it bore an uncanny resemblance to the vision in the Empire Theater's mirror. But there was one crucial difference: this time when Nora looked away, the cloud kept coming. Her impulse was to flee, but there was nowhere she could run. The bench was her best bet. Crouching beside it, she'd be somewhat protected from the onrushing storm.

She hadn't noticed before, but the bench had porthole-shaped openings at both ends. A quick glance confirmed it was hollow with a channel running the entire length. It would be a tight fit, but Nora could shimmy in, using her flashlight to light the way.

Meanwhile, the cloud continued its descent. It was an even tighter fit than she expected. Wedged in, lying on her stomach with her arms stretched in front of her, she could barely raise her head. Around her, the howling wind was growing louder, and she could feel the bench shake as the gale raged.

Nora closed her eyes.

She must have fallen asleep. When she opened them again, the storm appeared to be over. For a moment, she didn't know where she was, and she panicked. She tried inching forward but couldn't. Back was no good either. She was stuck. *To come this far and fail so completely—could anything be more ignominious? Or fatal*, Nora thought, fighting to stay calm.

Time passed. How much Nora couldn't tell, but it seemed like a lot. Occasionally she tried to crawl out, and when that didn't work, she tried backing up, but it was hopeless. She wished she could at least shift her position and ease her aching muscles. Making matters worse, she was thirsty and hungry, almost ravenous—one more thing Team Daedalus had gotten wrong.

In the eerie silence, Nora heard footsteps. They seemed to be coming her way. "Hello. Help!" she called out, her voice echoing in the wooden box. She was still holding the flashlight, and she turned it on, a beacon to guide whoever was approaching. Friend or foe, she'd take her chances.

The footsteps sped up. A face peered at her through the opening, briefly spotlighted. Nora couldn't be sure, but it appeared to be feminine. The face vanished, and a few seconds later Nora heard a scrabbling key-in-lock sound overhead. The top of the bench swung open. Lying flat on her stomach, it took a moment for Nora to realize she'd been sprung. She scrambled to her knees, lurched to her feet, and stepped clear, ignoring the protest from her aching muscles.

To her astonishment, Jillian was standing across from her. "Where did you … What on earth … How did you ever …?" Nora blurted out.

"You're welcome," Jillian replied drily.

She was blonder and bustier than Nora remembered; and beneath her makeup tougher looking. Her sand-colored safari shirt with matching pants and sporty hiking shoes appeared to be brand-new, and she had a sling bag strapped across her waist.

"No, seriously, what are you doing here? I thought I was a goner."

"Alex sent me. He thought you could use some support. The old guy in the golf cart gave me a lift."

Nora nodded. It was a lot to process. "How did you ever find me?" she asked, thinking of the hours she'd spent on the trail, all that wending and winding, only to end up in a closed box. A box that was now—Nora glanced at it to reassure herself she wasn't dreaming—wide open. If an angry storm cloud couldn't find her, how could Jillian? And without raising a sweat. Her outfit looked immaculate.

"I came through the museum, stepped outside, and there you were," Jillian replied, sounding as if it had been the easiest thing in the world. Perhaps it was. Nora could see how two people might take completely different routes and end up in the same place.

"The bench—how did you open it?" she asked.

With an impish grin, Jillian extended her hand, palm up. In it, something metallic gleamed. Nora recognized it right away. It was the skeleton key, the one shaped like a skeleton that had been front and center on her father's table display.

"I forgot your dad was this genius toymaker. Take good care of it. According to Alex, we need it to get out," Jillian said, handing the key to Nora.

Nora took a moment to examine it, then tucked it into her pocket. *Well, that was close.* If she'd taken her father's toy coffin, Jillian couldn't have freed her.

Nora lowered the bench lid and sat down. She hadn't gotten over the weirdness of seeing Jillian again, here of all places, and now she was back where she started, which was stumped. She still had no idea which way to go.

"Almost ready," Nora stalled, not eager to confess she was lost.

"No rush." Jillian didn't sound concerned. "The old guy asked me to give you this." She shrugged off the sling bag and handed it to Nora, looking glad to be done with it. "I'll be right back," she added, and she headed to the bubble-gun shrine, giving Nora some privacy. Amazingly, the shrine had survived the storm with the bubble gun still on top.

Nora turned her attention to the sling bag, which contained a small square-shaped item wrapped in parchment and a wide-mouthed crystal bottle with a matching stopper. The bottle was clear, filled with a sienna-colored liquid that Nora instantly recognized as more of Thalia's brew. Taking a moment, she looked up and saw that Jillian had migrated to the hilltop's far edge and was gazing down at the two trails.

Satisfied, Nora carefully unwrapped the parchment square. She had to smile. It was so Paul. His idea of emergency provisions was something dry and crumbly and exceedingly grainy.

Nora took a small exploratory nibble, chewing cautiously. It tasted like barley with a sprinkling of seeds and nuts and a dab of honey. It wasn't half bad. She polished it off.

Next, she opened the bottle and took a swig and then another, not stopping until it was empty. Thalia's brew was every bit as good as she remembered. Her hunger and thirst faded rapidly, and for the first time in a long while she felt a flicker of hope.

By now Jillian was returning, not looking nearly as cheerful as when she'd left. "Ugh." She made a sour face and hugged her arms across her chest. "This place gives me the creeps."

"I know. It's supposed to, but it's okay. We're almost there," Nora said, hoping it was true. The sling bag was lying by her feet, and she picked it up, strapped it on, and put the re-stoppered bottle inside along with the parchment wrapper—no littering. She almost added the flashlight but thought better of it. If the bottle got jostled, it might break.

"Ready?" Jillian asked.

"Yes," Nora replied, trying to sound like she meant it. She

still had no idea which way they should go. They started walking. Overhead, the sky was bruised and sullen, and the sun was nowhere to be seen.

The path down wasn't steep, but they took their time—Nora because she wanted to delay the inevitable, Jillian because she was being extra cautious; hiking obviously wasn't her thing.

Navigating the last few feet, she approached Nora, who was standing in the crossroads, looking down the two paths as far as she could see. Both paths were wide and level, bordered by trees and tall grasses. *No footprints*, Nora thought, looking for signs of traffic. *Did it even rain down here?*

"Ready when you are," Jillian said.

A thought occurred to Nora. Maybe it wasn't about divining the correct path. Maybe it was about making choices and believing in them, doing your best with limited knowledge, learning as you went.

She looked again at both paths: the one that went to the right and the one that curved to the left. "That one," she said, choosing the leftward path.

They set out. Their pace was brisk but comfortable, with Nora looking ahead, hoping for a sign they were heading the correct way. "Sorry you came?" she asked after a longish silence.

"Not yet," Jillian replied with an enigmatic smile.

"Why did you?"

"To help you," Jillian promptly said. "Well, that's part of it anyway," she added after a moment.

Nora nodded, waiting for her to continue. It was very quiet, their footsteps the only sound. "The truth is I needed to do something," Jillian continued. "You can't swing from a stripper pole forever."

Nora hadn't followed Jillian's career, had made a point of not following it, and she saw no need to go there now. "Wyman," she probed. "Alex—he's an interesting guy."

Jillian smiled knowingly but didn't take the bait.

"He and I got off on the wrong foot, but I think he's basically okay," Nora tried again.

"Oh, Alex is much better than okay," Jillian said.

"Yeah, you're probably right. I'm sure you're right," Nora said, hoping it was true that Wyman was much better than okay and that they weren't lost.

CHAPTER 49

The trail took its time, but it eventually led them up a gentle rise to the crest of a small hill and abruptly stopped. Below, a swarming multitude of spirits were spread over a vast plain enclosed on three sides by massive stone walls. In the middle of the back wall, a great arch rose—the Judgment Gate. They'd arrived. Nora had chosen the right trail after all, or possibly both trails were right. She'd never know. In any case, it was a relief to be near the end of their journey and a new cause for anxiety.

Afraid?" Jillian asked with a weak smile. "I am."

"They're dead; they're ghosts. They can't hurt us," Nora said in a hushed, meant-to-be reassuring tone of voice. "We can walk through them."

Jillian shuddered. "Oh, good. That cheers me up."

"Sorry you came?"

"No ..." Jillian hesitated.

"Go ahead. What?"

"I know you and Alex don't get along, but we're not expendable. He wouldn't abandon us, right?"

"Of course not," Nora said, including Hector, Paul, Thalia, and even Dr. D. in her answer. Except they might. If it was absolutely necessary. If there was no other way. A three-thousand-year-old blood feud was bigger than anyone.

"Ready?" she asked, remembering Paul's instructions: "Be sure you're standing in front of the gate when you take your bracelet off.

And bring it back. Under no circumstances should you leave the bracelet behind."

Jillian took a deep breath. "I hope so."

With Nora in the lead, they started down the hillside. As they crossed the plain, listlessly drifting spirits scattered before them.

"Well, look who's here," a jeering voice called out.

Directly in front of them, the voice's owner stood, legs spread, hands on his hips, holding his ground. Surprised, Nora stopped and stared at him. It was Curse the Dark, dressed in his "Come and Take It" T-shirt and floppy cargo shorts.

"You could've gotten here a lot faster if you'd waited a few minutes," he said, glaring at her. "After you left, the theater exploded, collapsed right on top of me. Thanks."

"I'm sorry," Nora replied, regretful but not repentant. If their situations were reversed, he'd be gloating.

"How touching. I'm blown to kingdom come, and you're sorry. Nice, very nice." His eyes went to her bracelet, and he added, "Your turn's coming—not yet, but soon enough. I may be dead, but at least I have an in with the judge. Once you deliver him, of course."

He turned his attention to Jillian, who was standing as close to Nora as was humanly possible. "And you, Miss Foster, what a pleasure to finally meet you in the flesh—well, yours anyway. Apparently Nora's not planning to introduce us. I'm Curse the Dark. I'm afraid you're wasting your time. There's no sex here. We have a lot of lechers but a real shortage of functioning dicks. Sorry."

"I'm retired," Jillian said with a tight smile.

"Well then, you've come to the right place. This is one huge no-fucking retirement community." And with that, he zipped off.

"We have some history. He's kind of bitter," Nora said. They were moving again.

"I hadn't noticed," Jillian tartly replied. "His friend, the one I warned you about, didn't much like you either. He told me a storm's coming and that if I knew what was good for me, I'd stay out of it."

"Good advice."

"Yeah, I'm glad I listened."

They were close now. As they marched along, the spirits formed a semicircle around them, attentively watching. Nora stopped in front of the gate and surveyed the space before them. Time to take off the bracelet and let it rip. A thought occurred to her, and she tentatively placed her hand on the sling bag.

"What?" Jillian asked, an edge of concern in her voice, watching as Nora stood there, seemingly frozen.

"Just wondering. It's probably nothing." She unzipped the sling bag and pulled out the empty bottle. There were gasps from the watching spirits, which was gratifying, but the bottle didn't look any different. It was still empty. No genie was inside, clamoring to be released, and it didn't look like the sort of thing you shattered and something powerful happened.

Disappointed, Nora put the bottle back in the sling bag but didn't rezip it. *No more stalling.* She strode toward the archway, positioned herself in the center, and tugged off the bracelet. Her tattoo had devolved into an ugly brownish-yellow blotch. Not good, but there was nothing she could do about it now.

Balancing the bracelet in her palm, Nora held it at chest level. Detached from her wrist, no longer sustained by her pulse, the bracelet slowly faded and lost its coppery glow. As she continued holding it, the metal began to crumble and turned a powdery ash-gray. "Quick, the bottle!" Nora shouted.

Startled into action, Jillian reached for it. Under Nora's direction, Jillian positioned the bottle beneath Nora's cupped hands, holding it steady while Nora sifted the ashy powder into the bottle's wide mouth. Between them they managed to catch almost all of it, filling the bottle up to the neck. After that, it was quick work to re-stopper the bottle and secure it in the sling bag.

When Nora looked up again, Minos—the spitting image of his statue—towered over her. "You!" he roared in a voice like a thunderclap, glaring at her with blazing eyes. "We finally meet. The girl with the hideous tattoo. You must be pleased with yourself."

Nora winced and averted her eyes. To her dismay, Jillian was no longer beside her. Meanwhile, across the plain, quailing spirits were forming a long snaking line in front of the gate.

Reaching down, Minos grabbed Nora's right wrist and lifted her off her feet, so she was staring into his wrathful face. "Enjoy your triumph while you can," he snarled. "Your time will come, and then I'll have you—one more soul standing in line, awaiting judgment."

Dismayed, Nora took in his words. Paul had told her that Minos couldn't hurt her, that he only had dominion over the dead, but he'd left out one little detail. Nora wasn't going to live forever.

"In the meantime, be gone. Go," Minos continued, still dangling her. "You don't belong here yet. The exit's to your right. It's marked. You won't have trouble finding it. You'll be back soon enough."

He abruptly released her. Nora fell to her knees, breaking her fall with her hands. Finished with her for now, Minos looked out over the vast plain filled with waiting specters. "Commence," he thundered.

Scrambling to her feet, Nora stepped out of the archway, ignoring her aching shoulder and the pain in her wrist where Minos had grabbed her. *Still no Jillian. Where can she be?* She frantically glanced around.

Turning toward Minos again, she was horrified to see he'd sprouted horns, leathery wings, and a tail he was using to lasso spirits, coiling it around them and flinging them, one by one, into the darkness beyond the gate. *The figure in the mirror ... so that's who it was.*

Nora felt a tap on her arm and jumped. Jillian was back. "Where were you?" she asked, still spooked. "You had me worried."

"Hiding," Jillian said, trying not to look at Minos. "Are you okay?"

"No, but I will be. The exit's to the right," Nora replied, hoping Minos wasn't lying, but it felt correct. Her sense of direction was kicking in again now that she was back on track.

Leading the way, Nora scanned ahead, no longer concerned

about passing through the still-gathering spirits drifting toward the gate.

On the ground up ahead, she spotted a steel plate. It was shaped like a manhole cover and hinged with a handle on the side. Stamped in the metal, she read,

Goodbye
And
GOOD RIDDANCE

Jillian looked at her expectantly, waiting while Nora studied the plate. *No keyhole—no place for the skeleton key, not a good sign.* Nonetheless, she reached down, gripped the handle, and started to raise the plate. *No, something's off.* Nora stopped herself. Getting into the museum had taken every bit of strength she possessed and then some. This was too easy. She sensed a trap.

"No." She regretfully lowered the cover.

Jillian looked at her, disappointment evident in her expression, but all she said was "Okay."

As they trudged on, the landscape became increasingly bleak and barren. Nora tried not to let the pain radiating from her wrist and shoulder cloud her judgment, but any moment now she would have to turn to Jillian and confess: 'I was wrong. I have no idea where we are or what we should do.'

About fifty feet ahead, another metal plate came into view. As they approached it, Nora was startled to see that a word had been scratched on its surface. She recognized it instantly. It was her secret word—the one she'd bought from her father.

With surging emotions, she picked up her pace and hurried to the plate. He must have passed this way and left this sign for her. Suddenly, she knew what the word meant. It had just been waiting for the right moment to reveal itself.

"This is it; we're here," Nora said, excitedly turning to Jillian, who mostly looked relieved. She obviously didn't remember their conversation about Nora's not-so-secret, secret word.

In the center of the plate, there was a keyhole. Nora dug into her pocket and brought out her father's skeleton key. It fit perfectly; the lock turned effortlessly. The plate was another story. It took both of them struggling together to lift it, and then just barely.

Beneath the plate was a hole approximately three feet across. Retrieving the flashlight from the pocket of her hoodie, Nora crouched beside the hole and peered down while Jillian looked over her shoulder.

The flashlight beam revealed a shaft, about eight feet deep, leading to an earthen tunnel. If they lowered themselves into it, there would be no climbing back. It was too steep. Sitting on the edge, dangling her feet, Nora pushed off and landed on solid ground. As far as she could see, the tunnel ran straight and true.

"It's okay. Come on down!" Nora shouted. Her words echoed. We're going home."

CHAPTER 50

The tunnel was pitch black, with the only illumination coming from Nora's flashlight. *Thanks, Curse*, she thought, remembering his cranky insistence she stop shining the damn thing at him, unintentionally helping her save it for later. If this wasn't later, they were in big trouble.

"Did I hear you say you've retired?" Nora came out of her thoughts to ask. They'd been walking for about a half hour. It felt odd talking to someone right beside her that she couldn't see, but in some ways, it made their conversation easier, less personal.

"Yeah," Jillian said, sounding grim, immediately adding, "Felony Foster's got to die. It's time."

"How are you going to do it?" Nora asked, from force of habit turning her head in the direction Jillian's voice was coming from.

"I don't know. I could stuff her in a trunk: all her costumes, her merchandise, her trinkets and baubles, everything that connects me to her."

From beside her, Nora heard a sigh. After a moment, Jillian continued. "That's the easy part. I can't haul her out with the trash, and it's not stuff you give to Goodwill."

A funeral pyre, Nora thought. *Fire and smoke would make a satisfactory send-off, but it's not my call.*

"Well, I'm sure you'll come up with something," she said, thinking, *Well, that's lame.* "Let me know how I can help," she added and heard Jillian chuckle.

It's strange, Nora reflected as they continued through the tunnel. After all the distance she'd come, all she'd accomplished, she didn't feel much different than when she set out. And she might be worse off with Minos' threat hanging over her: "Your time will come," he had said, "and then I'll have you—one more soul standing in line, awaiting judgment."

She did a quick calculation. According to Jack, there were three gates. That made her odds two to one if the process was random. *Just please don't let it be anytime soon.* The pain in her shoulder had mostly gone away, but something was definitely wrong with her wrist.

Meanwhile, the tunnel relentlessly continued. After what felt like forever but was about an hour, they took a break. To conserve the flashlight, they sat in the dark with their backs against the tunnel wall. Nora was hungry and thirsty again—Jillian probably was, too—but all Nora had was a bottle filled with ashes.

"I've been wanting to tell you I'm sorry about the way things worked out. I lied about everything and left you to deal with my parents. It was shitty, and I regret it," Jillian said, getting it out in one long breath.

"It's okay," Nora answered. "I was angry for a while, but I got over it." No need to say it was two days ago. "I knew something was up," she continued, obliquely referring to the Infernal Babe business. "You dropped a bunch of clues. It was almost like you wanted me to know?"

Beside her, Jillian chuckled. Confirmation enough.

"I should have asked you about it," Nora went on. "I don't know that it would have changed anything. It would have been a difficult conversation, but we should have had it."

"Yeah," Jillian drawled. "I wonder how that would have worked out,"

"It doesn't matter. You're here now. I couldn't have gotten this far without you. Are you ready?" Nora stood up. She turned on her flashlight and pointed it ahead, revealing more tunnel with no end in sight. Invisible beside her in the dark, Jillian rose, and they started walking. No more talking; they needed to save their energy.

Their walk eventually became a footsore trudge, but Nora didn't want to stop; she was afraid she'd never start again. Jillian wasn't saying anything, so perhaps she felt the same way.

After who knows how long, Nora saw what appeared to be a faint fixed light far in front of them. She halted and turned off her flashlight. The light was dim, but it was there. Her eyes weren't playing tricks on her. They picked up the pace. The light grew brighter, and the tunnel abruptly ended in an underground chamber with stone stairs leading upward.

Climbing the stairs, Nora and Jillian emerged into bright blessed sunlight. They were in the municipal cemetery, not far from where Goldmont's statue had stood. As promised, Paul was there, waiting beside his golf cart, beaming like a teacher whose prize student had aced her final exam. Nora rushed toward him. They hugged. The adventure was over.

Jillian had hung back, remaining by the steps with her arms at her side. "Hello, Jillian," Paul called out when he and Nora had separated. He motioned to her, and she joined them. "Well done. Alex was right about you after all. What do you say we get out of here?"

Nora sat in front, Jillian got in the back, and they set off on a slow, puttering journey past tombstones and monuments Nora remembered from previous visits. This time she barely glanced at them. Their ride ended at the visitor's center.

Wyman was inside waiting for them. "Welcome back," he said with a broad smile, heading toward Nora. "May I?" he asked, directing his attention to her wrist.

Memories of that first encounter flashed through Nora's thoughts, and she hesitated, then shoved up her sleeve and extended her arm. The blotch, which now appeared more like a skin disease than a tattoo, had turned a deeper brown with tendrils extending from it.

"Does it hurt much?" he asked, to Nora's relief not touching it.

"A little." She lowered her arm. The pain had intensified on the ride to the visitor's center—a throbbing sensation like tattoo fever, only worse.

"Thalia will know what to do," Wyman said. "She's expecting you."

At the mention of Thalia's name, Nora perked up. "Thanks, Alex," she said, using his first name with a conscious effort. It felt awkward, but it was time.

"Not at all," he said, no doubt noticing but not reacting. "The bracelet, did you happen to bring it back?"

With all that had taken place, Nora had forgotten about it. "Kind of, she said, unzipping the sling bag and bringing out the bottle. To her astonishment, what had been a bottle full of ashes now held a gleaming metallic powder. It certainly didn't look like it had ever been a copper bracelet.

Paul and Jillian, who had been waiting by the door, came forward to see. "It's alchemy—argyropoeia," Paul said in an awed voice. "The transmutation of copper into silver. One of the ancient quests fulfilled, just as Thalia predicted. It was first—"

"Would you mind taking it to her?" Wyman interrupted, addressing Nora. "She wants it for her work, and she'd like your help."

"As a guinea pig?" Nora blurted out, immediately regretting it.

"As her apprentice," Wyman said evenly, "and she needs to look at your wrist—the sooner, the better. Paul will take you."

He turned toward Jillian. For someone who had trekked through the funeral museum and spent hours hiking in a dank earthen tunnel, she looked surprisingly good; her outfit was still immaculate, and her makeup had somehow remained perfect.

"Hey, Alex," she greeted him without any of Nora's awkwardness.

"Hello, Jillian." He smiled. "If you're ready, I have some ideas I'd like to share with you."

"Sure." She turned toward Nora, and they embraced. "Bye for now. I have a feeling we're not done."

"I hope not," Nora responded and meant it. "Bye, Alex," she added after a pause, watching them depart. It still didn't feel natural, but she was going to work on it.

"They look good together," Nora said when Alex and Jillian were out of earshot.

"I hope. We'll see." Paul grinned. "Let's get you to Thalia."

His ancient Cadillac DeVille was parked outside the visitor's center. According to the dashboard clock, it was about two in the afternoon—what day Nora didn't know, but judging from the activity around them, it was a weekday.

As they drove, Nora began to slump. Her exhilaration at being back was ebbing, exhaustion was setting in, and the throbbing in her injured wrist was getting worse. "Are there really three judgment gates?" she asked in a voice threaded with anxiety.

"Yes," Paul said. He took his eyes off the road long enough to glance in Nora's direction, an obvious look of concern on his face.

"So the odds are two to one I won't get Minos. That's not terrible," Nora replied, repeating her previous calculation.

Paul hesitated. "His brother's also a judge. He's just as bad."

Nora took a deep breath. She was beginning to feel faint. "And the third judge, is he a relative too?"

"A half-brother."

"So bad news all around. I'm doomed."

"No more than anyone else. You can't cheat death—we've tried—but you can strategize. Minos could make things tough on you, but he can't overturn the natural order. If he said that, he's lying."

They were approaching Wyman & Associates. Paul slowed down and pulled into the driveway. "We can discuss it later," he said, coming to a stop. "Right now, let's focus on getting you well."

Nora didn't respond. She was unconscious, head listing forward and arms dangling, held upright by her seatbelt.

CHAPTER 51

Eight days later, finally well enough to venture out, Nora went to see Harry. She needed to thank him if he'd let her. A phone call wouldn't do; he might blow her off. Better to show up. Given the way she'd quit, it was bound to be awkward, but Harry wasn't likely to slam the door in her face.

The For Sale sign in front of his townhouse took Nora by surprise. Had he lost his job? Was it something she'd done? So not just a thank you, an apology too. Hesitating, tempted to abort her visit, Nora got out of the car.

She was driving Thalia's Mini Cooper. Nora's little hatchback, left at the Empire, had been struck by lightning and flooded. When she had gone to inspect it, she'd been surprised to see a sign proclaiming the site "The Future Home of The Frank and Bunny Lambert Museum of the Pacific Northwest, Paul Tsitak, Curator."

So the Lamberts were bringing the museum to Goldmont after all, and Paul was going to run it. *Good.* As for the theater itself, Curse hadn't been lying. It looked like a bomb site. Presumably, Curse's body was buried in the rubble, waiting to be unearthed. The thought of it gave Nora the creeps.

As she waited at Harry's door, Nora heard footsteps and the sound of a lock being turned. "Oh, it's you, hello," he greeted her with an awkward smile.

"Hi," Nora replied, struck by his appearance. It looked as though he hadn't shaved in a week. He had on a tattered green sweater, and he was wearing gray sweatpants and brown slippers.

"I wanted to thank you before I left town," she persevered, an edge of apprehension in her voice. "I appreciate what you did."

"Don't mention it," Harry said, making it sound like a command.

"You stood up to Ratdaddy, and you let me publish that stupid story about the extravaganza," Nora went on anyway. "I hope I didn't get you into trouble. I'm sorry if I did." She nodded toward the For Sale sign.

Harry frowned. "You'd better come in," he said and stepped aside.

Nora followed him through the hallway. In the kitchen, packing boxes lay scattered on the tile floor, and the table was stacked with plates and glassware. A pulled-out drawer occupied one entire end and was filled with a jumble of batteries and pens, old keys, a corkscrew, and several pairs of scissors—and that was only the top layer.

"Have a seat," Harry said as he placed the drawer on the floor. "There's coffee. I'm out of cream, and I don't know where the sugar is."

"Just water, please," Nora replied, sitting down and waiting while Harry filled a glass from the tap and handed it to her. His coffee mug was on the counter, and he picked it up, then sat down across from her.

"Okay, I appreciate your concern, but let's get one thing straight," he said, looking very much like the boss Nora remembered. "I've been in the newspaper business longer than you've been alive. I'm perfectly capable of losing a job without your help."

"And my story?" Nora asked reluctantly. The thought of it made her cringe.

"Elicited a call from someone with Goldmont PD. She wanted to know where we got our information. I told her we couldn't reveal our sources but we're not in the habit of publishing things we can't confirm."

"And was she satisfied?" Nora asked cautiously.

"No, of course not. But as luck would have it, we were planning a big complimentary story about the police, and that unruffled some feathers." He paused to take a drink of coffee.

"Front page below the fold," he continued with a roguish smile. "With a big picture of a cop who was injured protecting a hospital maternity ward from a rampaging lunatic. He's posing with a nurse—the cop, I mean, not the lunatic. It's a real heart tug. I'm surprised you didn't see it."

"I've been away." If the Ratdaddy story hadn't gotten him fired, what had?

"The truth is, Robin aced me out," Harry continued. "She went after my job, and she got it. Good for her." He raised his coffee mug in a sardonic salute.

Not sure what to make of their conversation, Nora lifted her glass, and they clinked. Her cuff slid back to reveal her bandage. No doubt Harry noticed, but to her relief, he didn't ask. The pain was mostly gone, and the blotch was now more yellow than brown, fading and shrinking. Thalia didn't expect it to disappear completely.

A sudden commotion from outside got Nora's attention. They both turned to look. A big tomcat with a notched ear was squeezing through the partially open window. Nora watched as he thumped onto the kitchen floor and waddled toward the bowls resting along the wall.

"An old friend. He comes by whenever he's in the neighborhood," Harry said. "I'm trying to convince him to go with me."

"Where's that?" Nora asked, deciding to chance it. Harry was private and prickly, but he was no longer her boss. If he didn't want to tell her, he wouldn't.

"Southeastern Missouri, my old stomping grounds." Harry sounded almost jovial. "A newspaper there needs someone to run it. Naturally, they asked me."

"Naturally."

"Actually, it's an old college buddy. I hadn't heard from him in years. He's got a big dental practice down there. As a goodwill gesture, he bought the local newspaper. Paid a dollar for it and promised to keep it going. I have two years to turn it around."

"Great," Nora said with some reservations—not about Harry, but about the future of local newspapers.

"Yeah, I know, but it's worth a shot. Turns out he's a Max Rage fan. He tracked me down."

"Cool."

Finished eating, the cat had found a spot by the window and was emitting a raspy purr. To Nora, it sounded like a file sawing through metal.

"You missed Jack's funeral," Harry said, turning his attention toward her again.

"I wish I could've been there. A good turnout, I hope." She wasn't too concerned. She'd seen Jack recently, and he was doing fine.

"Small but decent. Some folks from the bar where he hung out came."

Nora smiled. *Junior's—the Old Farts. Jack wouldn't have approved.*

"And one very tolerant German shepherd," Harry added. "Jack's sister and her three kids were there. The kids wouldn't leave the poor dog alone. They were hanging all over it."

"Sounds like quite a show."

"Yeah, it was something," Harry said, standing—her cue to leave. They walked to the door in silence.

"Well, I guess that's it. Good luck with your new job," Nora said, waiting until they were almost there. He hadn't asked what she was going to do, which was a bit disappointing.

"And how about you? Any plans, or don't you know yet?" Harry's hand grasped the doorknob but didn't turn it.

"I'm working for Wyman & Associates."

Harry half-suppressed a smile.

"I'll be traveling." She was going with Thalia: Sicily, Greece, and Turkey—some field trips and site visits.

"Well, good luck." Harry opened the door.

"Thanks, same to you."

The door shut, and Nora stepped into a balmy Goldmont afternoon. She took one last look at her surroundings and started toward the car. She was due at Thalia's for another treatment, and she needed to pack.

ACKNOWLEDGMENTS

Special thanks to my wife Lynn for her faith in this project, and for all the hours she spent editing and proofreading to bring it to fruition. I couldn't have done it without her. To my friend Rick St. John, a big thanks for volunteering to be an early reader. His insights and suggestions were a huge help. Thanks also to my critique partner Kelli Sullivan for her encouragement and enthusiasm.

Writing workshops with Inprint, a Houston organization committed to fostering the art of creative writing, gave me a valuable reality check and helped me see my way forward.

Edith Hamilton's *Mythology, Timeless Tales of Gods and Heroes*, was a great guide to all things Greek. *Candy Girl, A Year in the Life of an Unlikely Stripper* by Diablo Cody, provided insights into a far different world, as did *I Am Jennie*, a memoir by the ex-adult film actress Jennifer Ketcham.

Printed in the United States
by Baker & Taylor Publisher Services

Printed in the United States
by Baker & Taylor Publisher Services